About the Author

Ailbhe Donohue is a woman from Kildare, Ireland, currently in her late twenties and adores anything that surrounds creativity. She values freedom and expression, and above all, she LOVES a good story. This is how and why Ailbhe turned her eye to writing and rediscovered the love she had for it as a child. Ailbhe is blessed to have a wonderful family and group of friends around her that she values so highly. Her family is also growing at the moment as she has just welcomed her first baby!

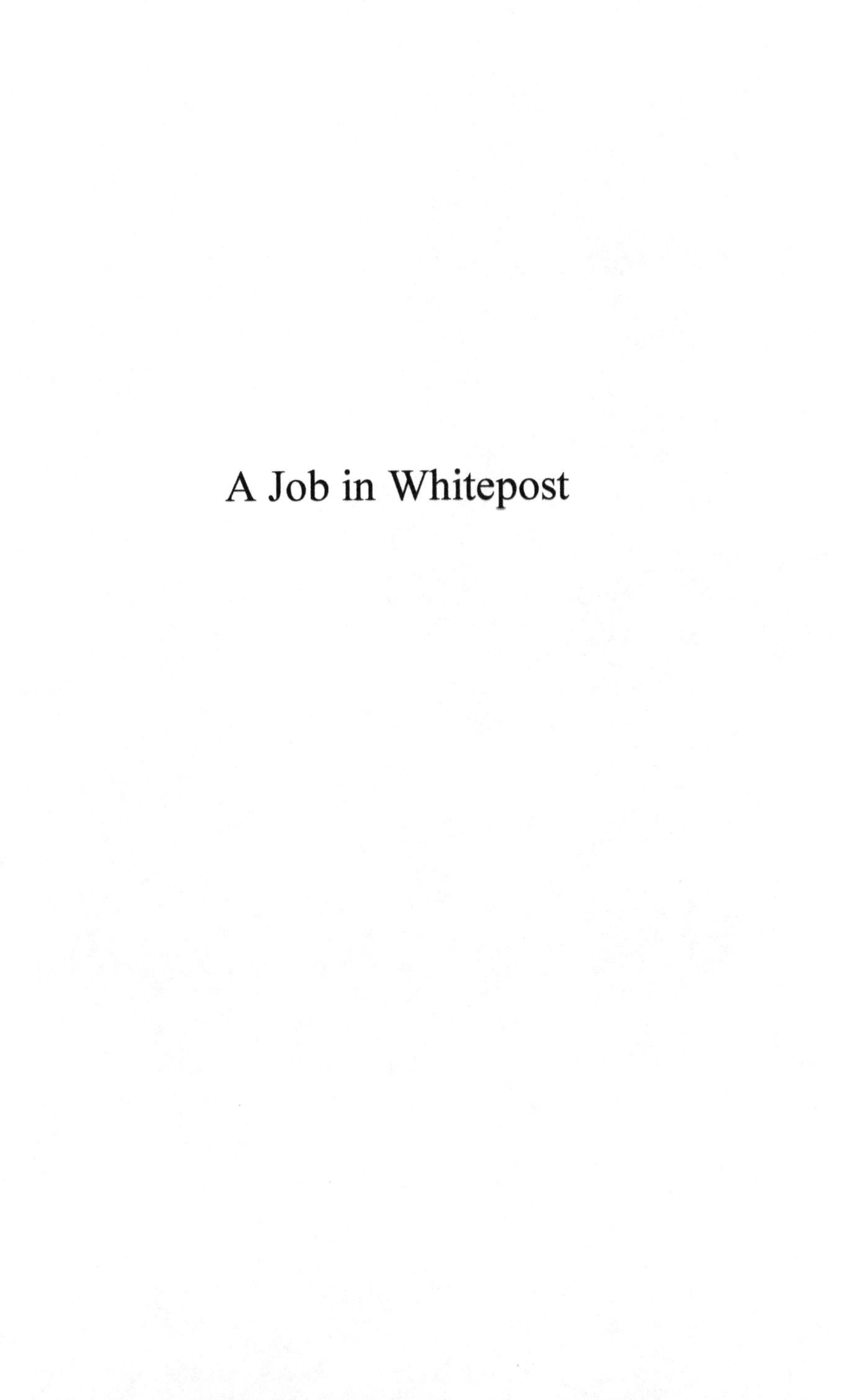

A Job in Whitepost

Ailbhe Donohue

A Job in Whitepost

Vanguard Press

VANGUARD PAPERBACK

© Copyright 2025
Ailbhe Donohue

A CIP catalogue record for this title is available from the British Library.

ISBN 978-1-83794-383-8

Vanguard Press is an imprint of
Pegasus Elliot Mackenzie Publishers Ltd.
www.pegasuspublishers.com

First Published in 2025

Vanguard Press
Sheraton House Castle Park
Cambridge England

Printed & Bound in Great Britain

Dedication

To my mam, Deirdre: Your enthusiasm, knowledge and
brilliance are what made this possible.

Acknowledgements

In writing this book, I found something I'd been looking for my whole life: a constructive and consistent avenue to articulate emotion, to express creativity, and to fuel the fire I have within my heart and mind for the arts. Doing this felt extraordinary in its own way, as I could escape my normal life and routines to the complex and wild world of the old West in America. What made the whole process the most extraordinary, however, was the people around me who gave up their own time to help see my dreams and my goals shape into existence. Even now, as an official author, I still don't know that I have the words to express what it meant… but I'll give it a try! I want to first thank my beautiful, kind sister, Rachel. From the moment I put pen to paper (or rather, fingers to keyboard, I guess?), you practically dropped everything to read through the very early drafts of each chapter whenever they were ready. You were the very first person to help me with feedback and, along with everything else you do for me, I am eternally grateful. You are truly the other half of me and I appreciate the hell out of you. Next, I would like to thank my partner, Cathal. Your constant support, your listening ears, your encouraging words, and your unwavering outlook of understanding when I constantly had the light of the laptop shining right down on your face in the middle of the night, as I wrote, means the world and more. You are the true embodiment of what a caring and encouraging partner is supposed to be. For taking the time, even when you were so tired, so worn out, to read through my work and give me your thoughts on every chapter, thank you so much, I will never forget it. Now, we move on to my beloved Grandad Jim. Your enthusiasm, advice and wisdom were invaluable and I am so grateful that you took the time to not only read through the whole story once but multiple times! Age plays no factor in your wonderful mind, and the suggestions you made were key in developing my descriptive ability further. I promise to treat you to a nice dinner as a small token of how much I appreciate your help! Next up, my dad, Seán and my brother, Connor. Thank you for cheering me on and making me feel confident and excited at each milestone of this story. You guys were so encouraging, and it didn't go unnoticed! From here, we move on to my best friends, my three paninis (they know what it means). Thank you for being the best hype women around, for showing real interest, and for uplifting and inspiring me throughout this whole journey. Each of you has been so wonderful in shining nothing but positivity on this project whenever it came up and I really love you for it. I also want to take the time to express my real and sincere thank you to the publisher, the editors and the production team – everyone involved! Through your remarkable effort and diligent work, my dream has been transformed into a physical piece to share with the world. Thank you for welcoming me and treating me with such professionalism and respect. Thank you for taking a chance on me. And now, I want to thank my miraculous mother, Deirdre. I could go on for a long time about how much your help meant to me. You went above and beyond to help me shape this fictional world. Your literary and historical knowledge helped make this story everything that it is, and that is priceless. Your passion and honesty in reviewing every single sentence of every single chapter – the corrections, the re-writes, everything – were so vital and so instrumental in making this become a reality. Spending all those evenings with you, working on my book, was honestly so much fun. I treasured every moment, and I can't wait to do it again when the next story comes to my mind! You're an inspirational, strong and brilliant woman, and I'm blessed to have you as a mam and a friend.

I want to also mention the other family members and friends who also took time to read and offer very valued feedback to me. I can't list all the names unfortunately, but you know who you are – I appreciate the hell out of you all! Finally, I want to give a shout-out to my sweet little puppy dog, Bella – what's a gal without her furry writing companion patiently waiting for me to throw the ball!

Prologue

George was meticulous in his duties within his employer's home. He had many responsibilities as the house steward in Mr Lewis' household, and Mr Lewis trusted him with such. Each day he woke, washed, dressed, made his bed, conferred with the housekeeping staff to ensure his employer's assigned dwellings were near perfection on any given day. He also attended to the management of minor administrative tasks for the benefit of Mr Lewis' office.

George took pride in his role; it wasn't easy to come by a position such as this when his background was that of severe poverty and underprivilege, but he was driven and worked hard to get where he was. Mr Lewis was a seemingly cold man, but George could see through that. From the two years he had known him, he came to feel that perhaps this wasn't a cold man after all, simply a determined one, someone resolute in achieving his goals.

You could almost say George Clarke admired him.

This impression would soon change, however, on a particularly cold evening in 1868, when George entered the private study of Mr Lewis. He had poked his head in simply to enquire whether Mr Lewis required any further assistance, only to find the room empty.

Mr Lewis must have stepped out, but there was crockery left on his desk from earlier; George decided to bring it down to the kitchen before the staff had completely retired for the night. As he stepped over to the desk and leaned across to pick up the cup, saucer and plate, his eyes became fixed on a letter the master of the house had been reading on his desk, presumably received that day. He wouldn't normally have classified himself as prying, but something about the letter seemed strangely curious, and he was drawn by some unknown feeling to read it.

He began to read. Dear Jesus… no… Oh god, what was this? George could feel his heart quicken with furious speed; his stomach sank below the foundations. No, this wasn't right. Could this man, this honourable man… Could he be capable of such things? George couldn't think; his head was in a spin. This is bad. God almighty, a man of government? To scheme in such ways and seem unburdened with guilt…

George could hear the footsteps of Mr Lewis returning through the second door; he knew instinctively that he could not let Mr Lewis realise he had any knowledge whatsoever of what he had just seen. He left with the crockery immediately and headed straight for his own room to think on what he had just read and what, if anything, he should do about it.

A name. A name from George's past, written in that letter. They are going to drag her down too. This letter is about death.

Chapter 1
Harrison James – US Marshall

Whitepost, in the newly formed Arizona Territory, in the Marshall's opinion, was certainly nothing like what he had pictured. His grandmother had a friend or pen pal of sorts she would write to, who apparently lived here when he and his brother (and deputy) Morgan were very young boys. Their grandmother had told them stories about this beautiful little town with the sweetest, god-fearing people and a large white lamp post, from which it procured its name. It was positioned outside the church in the centre of town. Although a part of the West, it was portrayed as an oasis of respectable living surrounded by a practically lawless land. The town was situated amongst the more luscious and green forests of the territory, far enough out from the dry and dusty, cactus-filled plains one normally imagines in this part of the world. His grandmother mentioned a river or creek that ran through the forest with crystal, brisk waters and tranquil sounds of babbling and rippling as the brook ran over rocks and fallen branches.

The picturesque-type town he was expecting was nowhere to be found. The smell of horse manure and piss in the air could make your eyes water. It was only the later side of the day, but many of the townsfolk appeared inebriated and stumbling about in the sludge towards the gambling house. They were staggering out of the saloon or what he believed to be a large brothel at the end of town. The once white-church looked dilapidated and possibly abandoned – was there even a minister here? Each breath in the hot, sweaty air was heavy. There were, of course, some of the usual establishments you'd expect in any town of this size – a general store, a doctor's office, a butcher peddling various meats in his stall, a stable and, surprisingly, a small gunsmith. But the majority of business seemed to be centred on the less than reputable enterprises. These wooden buildings and their protruding verandas were old, they were creaking, and they were filthy. The town looked and felt rough.

He and the deputy needed to find the sheriff first and foremost. They needed to establish what was known so far regarding the stagecoach robbery they had been sent to investigate. Upon arriving at the door of the sheriff's office, a reasonably-sized place with a glass-panelled front door, they found it to be empty. Morgan turned to enquire with a local woman passing by, "Pardon me, ma'am, my brother and I are looking to find your sheriff; would you happen to know whereabouts here we might find him?"

"The sheriff? Why he's more 'n likely reposing in his second home"

The woman could see Morgan and Harrison's visible confusion. She indicated over to the saloon and chuckled, "He's practically a part o' the furniture over there, sir – good day."

Harrison gave his brother a nod and they made their way to the bar. They were surprised to find half the town in there; the commotion was unanticipated at this time of the day. The saloon was impressive on the inside. The establishment boasted a nice, high ceiling with an interior balcony wrapping around the room on the upper floor. A grand old staircase centred the room and led up to the balcony, along with what seemed to be a hallway towards, possibly, some bedrooms. They made their way over to the bar through the crowd to speak with the barkeep, Morgan piped up immediately, "Hey there, what exactly's going on in here, crowds a little thick for early evenin'?" The barkeep leaned across the bar.

"Lenora's back in town; she don't normally perform as early, but these folks, with myself included, just love the sound of her voice - shame you just missed her last song of the evenin'! She's goddamn great for business, I'll tell you that. What can I get you boys?"

Harrison interjected before Morgan got the chance, "Two whiskeys and if you wouldn't mind pointing out which of these fine folks you have elected as your sheriff, I'd appreciate it." The barkeep pointed to the sweaty, slightly sunburned, overweight man sitting on the last stool. Harrison downed his shot and moved to walk over, dragging Morgan away before he could order another drink.

Morgan was a good deputy, but he had a predisposition towards the more enjoyable aspects of life and the job. Harrison himself was more serious, straight to the point. Just as they were about to engage the lawman, Morgan's eye appeared to catch something of interest. He turned and suggested to his brother that it might be worthwhile for him to sit in on a poker game happening on one of the tables on the other side of the room. Morgan indicated it might be an opportunity to learn about any information or gossip the townsfolk have about the crime and about the area in general. Harrison merely grunted at the idea, but his brother knew that meant a 'reluctant yes'.

Harrison tapped the shoulder of the sheriff, slumped on his barstool, clutching his warm beer and staring off into the distance – he was startled.

"I apologise; it was not my intention to disconcert you. I was told you are the sheriff? My name is Harrison James. I am a US Marshall and I have come along here with my deputy. We are here by the appointment of the Governor of New Mexico Territory to personally investigate the stagecoach robbery that happened outside of this town. I was hoping to speak somewhere quieter to…"

Harrison noticed at this point the supposed sheriff's head was drooping lower, his eyes rolled ever so slightly, and the faintest string of drool had appeared to depart from the corner of his mouth… the man was drunk.

After a moment's pause, since Harrison stopped speaking, the sheriff struggled to slur his way through a sentence: "Did you say Marshall or Marsha? I don't know no Marsha… Is Len singin' yet? She got a sweet set of pipes on her."

He stumbled off the stool and towards Harrison, who reluctantly steadied his balance. The man's breath was foul as he leaned in to mumble at Harrison.

"You married? I need t' find me a wife, I reckon... I need a whiskey." Harrison rolled his eyes and planted the drunkard back onto the stool to collapse across the bar. The place was lively, so nobody seemed to notice or really care that the town's elected official of the law was passed out. As he turned away to search for his brother, his eye suddenly caught on someone. A woman.

She was standing across the room, laughing at something one of the two men she was conversing with must have said. She was smoking a slim cigar and as she exhaled a small cloud of smoke, his view of her was blocked for a moment until it cleared, and her eyes met his.

She was striking. Not, perhaps, in a stereotypical way... but she had an intriguing look. She was quite slim around the waist but not petite overall, slightly curvaceous, and slightly tall for a woman – a strangely strong frame. Her face wasn't that of a doe-eyed young girl but of a woman grown – maybe mid-twenties or so. Dark hair, fair skin – her eyes were that which caught him most – sultry and piercing. She was looking at him with confidence beaming from her, as if she knew she could hold his gaze as long as she wanted.

As she excused herself from the company of the two gentlemen, she began walking towards him. Harrison turned back towards the bar, but not before she came close enough for him to see that those almost seductive eyes, were a chilling, wintery blue.

"Two whiskeys, please, Calvin; maybe a double for my timid new friend here." She smirked at Harrison as he calmly, but firmly, protested her statement, "I would hardly say timid, madam?"

"It's Lenora Taylor" – she downs her whiskey – "and it's Miss, by the way."

"Miss Taylor, so you're the one who performs here. Do you always distract half the town away from their work to get intoxicated during the day?"

"Do you always jump down a lady's throat before you've even introduced yourself?" Harrison paused for a moment before responding, evaluating her in a way.

"Apologies, *miss*; my name is Harrison James. I'm a…"

She cuts him off. "Wait! Don't say another word – let me take a stab at guessin'. Let me see: decent clothes, somewhat groomed, stiff as a goddamn board and… tired behind the eyes… an 1862 Colt holstered under your jacket there and… Oh! Yes, indeed, there it is – the badge of a US Marshall pinned right there on your shirt. Why am I not surprised?" She flipped the lapel of his jacket back to hide his badge once again.

Harrison quietly grunted. "You got a problem with lawmen?"

She scoffed, "Ha! No, Mr James I just got a problem with any man who don't show no manners – next time a lady buys you a drink, try starting off with a thank you.

Enjoy your evenin' *Marshall*." She sized him up once more before making her way up the stairs of the saloon.

He had never met such an audacious woman.

Harrison hadn't had too much interaction with women on a personal level, not for any reason other than choice. His profession often had him on the road, so settling down with someone was impractical at the time, in his opinion. He was handsome in a rugged sort of way, but it was Morgan who usually caught the eye of the ladies (and loved it too, to be honest), a real philanderer who could not resist womanising.

Harrison had enough for the night; they weren't going to get anything out of the practically poisoned sheriff that evening. They were better off starting fresh in the morning. He enquired with the bar staff about lodgings for him and Morgan while they stayed in town. The saloon actually did rent rooms upstairs, but they were full; he was redirected to a boarding house just a couple of paces out from the town.

Harrison approached Morgan at the card table; one of the older gents was teasing him as he pulled the pile of poker chips away from his clearly losing brother.

"Christ boy, I coulda' sworn you was old man Laudergill risen from the dead playin' like that!" He laughed.

Morgan looked determined and smiled. "Ain't nothin' but a run of bad luck, old timer; I still got all evenin' to win my money back! Evenin', Harry, you fancy joinin' us at the table here? Seeing as that lovely thing you was chatting with at the bar appears to have up and left you high and dry?" The other men at the table laughed.

"Don't call me Harry; how many goddamn times… I'm turning in for the night; I suggest you do the same before you lose more'n you have."

Harrison instructed his brother where to find his accommodation and left him to his merriment in the saloon. He was walking in the now dark street then suddenly stopped and pondered to himself: what kind of a woman would ever know the specific make and model of a handgun at one single glance?

Chapter 2
Sam Walker – Notorious Outlaw

The law across the entire West had never encountered criminals like Sam *'The Phantom'* Walker and the 'Spector' Gang. In just four years, they had racked up a significant list of offences, including train robbery, murder and horse theft (to name a few), but stagecoach robbery was never really their thing. Sam Walker knew better than to draw down the wrath of Mr Wells and Mr Fargo. Those fine gentlemen did not take kindly to disruptions to their enterprises and were well known for retribution. That is, of course, until Sam Walker met with *'the woman'*. Normally, Sam would have nothing to do with outsiders nor be inclined to trust them. But Sam had it on good authority that 'the woman' meant business, real business and that the payment for the job she was proposing would be most rewarding. And so, Sam agreed to meet with her to discuss her proposal. The woman advised she was representing an 'anonymous benefactor' who wanted them to rob the stage. A particular stagecoach, at a particular time, for a particular reason. The woman outlined they could have everything they found in the coach plus six thousand American dollars. All they had to do was find one sealed yellow letter, marked private and addressed to

New Mexico Territory, which must be delivered directly to her.

Now normally the gang must abide by certain rules, this ensured their success in the past; they rarely, if ever, hit the same town twice, each time a job was done, they'd split up and immediately ride to a camp set up before hand, always hidden, always out of sight. A different member would be tasked with burying the loot each time. They would then ride into town one by one to seek employment as weary travellers in the various local businesses. They would effectively hide in plain sight until the heat was off, then dig up the loot and make their way off to the next target.

The jobs were always scoped out in advance, no robbery was ever done on impulse and above all, there were never to be any witnesses left alive. With that being said, the woman should have been killed, but somehow Sam instinctively knew there was more to this story than met the eye. So they would need to be patient for now and bide their time.

Sam treated the gang with reasonable fairness but would remind them at times of who was '*the fucking goddamn boss*'. Through a mixture of hard-earned respect, the almost certain guarantee of a decent pay out every time and plain old fear, they would follow all orders Sam Walker made of them.

Austin was the right-hand man; he'd been with Sam since the beginning, just about four years ago. The end of the war sparked the very beginning of their legacy across the western territories. Slowly over the next couple of years, the others joined up, each an outcast in their own way: Bill, Clayton – rogues from across the country, Javier and Adelita, the Mexican twins; and finally, Michael, the Irishman. Sam admired their professionalism. They would drink, fight, whore, kill and maim with a particular dedication to the job. But Sam was the thinker; that's why Sam was the boss and that's why six blood thirsty sons o' bitches followed Sam *The Phantom* Walker.

When the day of the robbery came, they proceeded no different to any other hit in the past – the woman had already kindly provided them with all the information they needed, so it was simply a matter of knowing the stage's route and when to make their move. Sam preferred to work under the cover of darkness if at all possible, for obvious reasons, so they found a location with suitable cover that would place the coach in their sights at twilight.

The strategy was simple enough. Austin and Bill took position on the road, blocking the path of the stagecoach, who did not see them until they took a sharp turn around a cluster of trees blocking far sight. They began distracting the coach drivers with some farcical story about 'their missing horse'. Javier and Adelita stayed further down, on their horses, either side of the road to keep an eye out for the law or anyone who could blow the whistle for that matter and finally, Clayton, Michael and Sam then followed up behind the coach on foot after it came to a stop, silent, to make use of surprise in attacking.

Bill, a man with no time for stalling, fired the first shot, immediately killing one of the two men sitting atop the coach with a direct hit. The other man, instantaneously terrified, dropped from the top of the wagon in a desperate attempt for cover and landed right on top of Sam – knocking them both straight to the ground with Sam underneath.

There was a scuffle for a few moments as the man scrambled to get to his feet. He had managed to rip a pendant from Sam's neck off and land his foot right into Sam's stomach. Just as he managed to come to his feet and almost make a run for it, Sam grasped and fired the sawn-off shotgun, which had been dropped in the commotion, straight through his spine, dropping him to the ground in agony. The man's screams echoed across the night, but only for a moment before Austin put a bullet through his head to silence him.

Sam stood up and dusted off. "Christ, that stupid motherfucker was wailin' worse that a babe starved of his momma's tit. We need to move fast, get the coach doors open and let's get goin' 'fore we get those Pinkerton boys or some such on our assess." Thankfully, for the general populous, there was nobody else inside.

The gang cleaned out the stagecoach and rode off, taking different directions back to camp. It was well into the night by the time they reached the site.

Sam ordered a quick inventory of the haul before Clayton rode off to bury it – stocks, jewellery, cold hard cash… and the letter.

Michael picked it up – a yellowish envelope marked *Private* with the delivery address marked for New Mexico Territory. As he proceeded to open it, Austin protested, "The fuck are you doing? That looks like the woman's letter; drop it!"

Sam put out a cigarette and walked over before Michael could start bickering back at Austin. "Hang on a minute now, Austin; maybe it is worth seeing what all the fuss was about. Personally, I'd like to know what was so important that some rich bastard decided to send his lil' maid straight into the snake pit… Michael, seeing as you seem to have volunteered for the job, I'm assuming you can read?"

"Course I can fuckin' read!"

Sam stared Michael dead in the eye and smiled, looking almost unhinged before responding, "Snap at me like that ever again, boy, and I'll cut your fucking tongue out while you sleep, 'fore you ever have a chance to scream. Now open the god damn letter and read it out." Sam then changed to a mocking tone. "Seein' as you're *so* very proud of your literary capability."

The rest of the gang sniggered as Michael discontentedly opened the envelope. He then proceeded to read it out in full; it simply stated the following:

A,

Those fucking savages accepted our weapons. Got em' well and truly riled up.

Sam raised an eyebrow slightly, appeared deep in thought and then instructed Michael to hand over the letter for safe keeping.

Then it was time for them to get gone. Clayton needed to bury the loot and the rest needed to get some sleep. Sam, Austin, Bill and Adelita had to ride into Whitepost back to their prearranged lodgings. They rode hard and fast to Whitepost to get organised and arrange work in line with their usual strategy. The main work in town came out of what was left of the Laudergill Cattle Ranch. Javier, Clayton and Michael would stay at the campsite, posing as hunters from out of town.

They ride on different routes at different paces so as to avoid arriving in town at the same time. This gave Sam a moment's peace to think on the content of that letter and re-evaluate its worth. Sam didn't know everything, but there's one thing the leader of the Spector gang did know: giving the Indians weapons was pure gunpowder. Somebody somewhere wanted to stir up one hell of a hornet's nest. Who and why?

Chapter 3
Harrison James – US Marshall

Morgan must have arrived in bed late into the night, seeing as Harrison had to practically drag him out of bed not long after morning's first light. Morgan was surely not exactly the world's most professional deputy, granted, but Harrison needed someone he could trust when the Governor appointed him to his role.

The two brothers stepped out the front door into the bright, high, and already warm sun of a summer morning in Whitepost. With most of the town trudging around getting their day started in each of their businesses throughout town, it was about time they did the same.

They made their way through the street and arrived at the glass windowed door of the sheriff's office for the second time. Upon peering through, they could see him conscious, but leaning back in his chair, feet on the desk, with what appeared to be a damp, grimy old cloth plastered across his forehead.

Harrison still chose to maintain the courtesy of knocking on the door.

"Jesus, come in, stop your bangin', my fuckin' head's 'bout to split in two." The sheriff grunted as he moved to sit up at his desk whilst more than likely enduring one hell of a hangover.

The two men made their way in, Morgan leaned on a desk on the opposite side of the room with his arms folded, awaiting Harrison's cross examination to begin. Harrison sat in the chair opposite the sheriff, the other side of his desk.

With a deadpan expression on his face, he commenced the conversation: "Mornin', Sheriff… as far as I recall, I did not get your name last night?"

"As far as I recall, gentlemen." He glanced at Morgan, then back to Harrison. "I have never met either of you 'fore this mornin'. So why don't the two o' you just pretend like yous' ain't never met me and we'll start *fresh* now." He tensed his forehead seemingly as his headache intensified. "Just call me sheriff; there ain't nothin' more to me than that. Now what exactly is it that has brought you both into my office and my town so promptly?"

"Fine, *Sheriff*, my name is Harrison James, I am a US Marshall and I have come along with my deputy here, Morgan James. We are here by the appointment of the Governor of New Mexico Territory to personally investigate the stagecoach robbery that happened just outside of town. I am here this morning because I want any and all details you have about the crime – suspects, progress, everything."

The sheriff gave an almost sarcastic chuckle. "Suspects? You can drop them formalities, Marshall, I mean, sure, we ain't got no solid proof, but Christ, not a soul in town, don't know for near damn sure it were that Sam Walker and his pack."

Harrison was normally a difficult person to read; he didn't tend to give much away for the most part, but when he failed to agree with the previous statement, the sheriff knew immediately they must be, in this case, clueless.

"Come on now, boys, don't tell me you's livin' under a rock across the ways in New Mexico now? Sam '*The Phantom*' Walker? And the '*Spector*' Gang?"

Harrison was getting a little impatient. "Why don't you just tell us who he is and why exactly you, and apparently the whole town, are so damn sure it was him?"

The sheriff proceeded to tell the James' brothers about the infamous gang who've been ripping through the west for the last few years. They're wanted for train robberies, horse rustlin', multiple murders – once including a woman with child – and now stagecoach robbery.

"Soon as the blues came out on top, Sam and his gang went hunting capital, it seems. They ain't got no regard for folks... you ain't never gonna catch him, you know. Plenty of suckers have tried hoping to claim the bounty; can't seem to figure why they sent a Marshall down here now, though?"

Before Harrison got the chance to respond, the sheriff chimed in one final time with his garish, raspy voice. "Why in the hell you think folks call him a phantom? 'Cause the son' bitch disappears soon as the job's done... 'til next time at least."

Harrison paused a moment to make sure the uncouth and lazy sheriff wouldn't cut him off again before he stood up from his seat and assertively stared him down. "We will make it our business to catch whichever lawless creature is responsible for this crime, regardless o' who he is. Our Governor sent *us* here to catch the thief and murderer because, on this occasion, *Sheriff*, not only do we need to apprehend a criminal, something of a highly sensitive nature was stolen that needs to be retrieved. So, I will tell you this one final time – I need any and all details you have about this case."

The sheriff was taken aback a little. Perhaps used to being somewhat disregarded or partly ignored in town (albeit by his own doing), he was suddenly aware that maybe the Marshall was not someone to be dismissed so easily.

Harrison and Morgan were taken through what was known about the incident. The stagecoach was found along a fairly isolated part of the road, just a couple of miles outside of town. The sheriff indicated the rough area on a crude map he had doodled out on some paper. The coach was found along with two dead bodies – one shot directly through his face, the other with two shots – one into his back right through the spine and the second in the crown of his head. The two men have unfortunately been buried already, so Harrison and his brother couldn't make any observations or remarks on any clues that may have been present. The sheriff seemed to be lacking in detail on possible weapons used or any information really that could have been of use.

"Did you or anyone else of relevance take note of tracks in the area of the crime? Try and follow any form of trail in an attempt to identify at least where they went or how they went about attacking the postal service?" Harrison quizzed the sheriff but received a disappointing response.

"By the time we got 'round there, it was mornin' and all kinds of folks were makin' their way to and from town – traders and all kinds – muckin' up the track. Weren't much left to look at, to my eye anyway."

Harrison gave a cold retort. "I see, to *your* eye. Thank you for your assistance, Sheriff. Would you be so kind as to allow myself and my deputy make use of your office here throughout the course of our investigation? We will be sure to keep out of your way as you continue to go 'bout your daily… routine."

At this point, the sheriff seemed to just need a nap more than anything else, so he swiftly agreed to end the line of questioning as soon as possible and return to his previous position. He leaned right back and returned his feet to the desk, though this time placing his hat on his head and down over his eyes.

Morgan and Harrison stepped outside the office to have a word in private.

"Christ Harry, I know you think I'm bad, but I ain't that lazy at least. I don't think that lawman has done a real days work in his life! Those gentlemen I was playing with last night had told me a little about him, but I assumed they were exaggeratin' some," Morgan quietly jested.

"Don't call me Harry." Harrison grumbled.

"You're right, though; I do not anticipate him being of much use to us here. I want to make my way out to the scene to see if there's anythin' he missed. I want you to stay 'round here and gather up any information you can muster about this gang he remarked on. They may or may not be involved, but they sound dangerous, so I would like us to have our wits about us." No sooner had Harrison mentioned having their wits about them, he immediately noticed Morgan's attention had turned to a young, fair-haired woman across the street.

He winked and gave a smile at her before Harrison gave him a clip behind the head. "Keep it in your god damn pants. Morgan, we're here to do a job; find out about that gang while I'm gone."

Morgan rubbed his head on the point of the strike, rolled his eyes with a sigh towards his brother, gave one more glance with a cheeky smile to the young woman, then proceeded to retreat back into the sheriff's office.

Harrison moved down into the dirt from the steps of the office and walked towards the stable where his horse was currently kept.

The heat of this particular day saw every plant in sight wilt and droop, every animal seek even a slice of shade and every building along the road creak as the wood expanded. It would deter any normal man from his responsibilities, but for Harrison, duty came first.

Chapter 4
Morgan James – Deputy Marshall

Morgan was a little relieved at the thought of Harrison riding out to the crime scene for a bit. He loved his brother without question, but he took life too seriously at times. Morgan preferred a laid-back approach to the job, although, mind you, at twenty-one years old, Morgan wasn't entirely committed to this line of work all that much. He enjoyed certain aspects – there was a certain thrill in taking down federal criminals and seeing a lot of this side of the country, sure, beats being stuck in a small sleepy town, in his opinion – but at other times it just felt tedious or mundane. This felt a little like one of those times.

He was conscious that, only for the fact that his older brother had been appointed as Marshall (and subsequently selected Morgan as a deputy), he would have never cared to pursue this as a career. He sometimes fantasised about what else could be out there for him when Harrison's term was up – would he stick with his brother as he always has in the past? Would he hunt? Farm? Maybe settle in one of the towns he has favoured from their travels on the job? Open a business some day? Settling down would probably lead him to find a wife and sire children… that didn't seem all too appealing now either. Freedom, pleasure and the potential of life were Morgan's castle in the sky.

He caught himself in that same loop of romanticising in the sheriff's office after his brother had left him to find out more about this Spector gang. This 'key task' of gathering information that Harrison was so insistent on was one of those assignments that Morgan just found so wearisome, but he was going to have to get to it sooner or later, so he felt there was no point in procrastinating any further.

The sheriff was passed out at his desk, so Morgan figured he would circle back to him and catch him when he eventually wakes for food or a trip to the outhouse. He grabbed a wanted poster for Sam Walker & Co. from the office and headed out onto the stifling street. Morgan figured the best place to start was to ask around the town, see what people knew about this bad business – maybe stumble upon that gorgeous golden haired young woman he glimpsed earlier, just before Harry left. Who's to say she wouldn't be bursting with valuable information on the case or something else if his luck was in…?

Morgan made his way over to the general store to greet the shopkeeper, who was sitting on a bench out on the front porch of the establishment, fanning himself as he sat with his gut protruding out under his clothes, watching the happenings across the middle of Whitepost.

"Afternoon, sir, might I trouble you for a quick moment – I was hoping you may be able to help me gather some information of sorts."

"Why, of course – what may I assist you with, boy? Come sit down here in the shade; you'll soon start cookin' in that sun." The merchant was getting on a little in years but still had vigour about him. A wrinkled but friendly face and demeanour.

Morgan sat beside him and exhaled in reprieve. "Thank you, sir; name's Deputy Morgan and my brother is a US Marshall; we've just arrived here last night."

"I was wondering who you was, I'm assuming the tall, broodin' gentleman you had accompanying you in the saloon yesterday evenin' was the Marshall? I was feelin' a little *delicate* yesterday, so I headed home just as y'all arrived – shame too, I heard you was practically givin' money away at the poker table!" The shopkeeper snorted and tittered.

"Hey, hey now, I just needed a chance to get a read on things, nothing but a stroke of luck on their part. I'll make my money back and then some – you'll see if you venture to join in tonight?" Morgan smiled at him. "I never got your name, sir."

"Name's Abraham, Abraham Cassidy and you better believe I'll see ya' at the table tonight."

He remarked competitively back at Morgan, "Now what is it you needed my help with, son?"

"Oh right, yes, I digress. My brother and I are investigating the stagecoach robbery that happened outside o' town – I'm guessing you heard. He wants me to gather up what folks know about this 'Spirit gang'."

"*Spector* gang." Abraham corrected him with a sudden, solemn expression on his face. "Nasty bunch of god damn delinquents. I don't know much about 'em, but Old Bill out thataway – towards the riverbed – his boy was murdered by those sons o' bitches. I don't know if he'd be willin' to talk to you; been awful quiet since, tends to keep himself to himself, but might be worth a try."

Morgan's curiosity is piqued. "So they been around these parts before?"

Abraham progressed to tell him what he knew. The gang had passed through a couple of years back and broke into a home and supposedly murdered a young man and his pregnant wife. This was probably the crime that really put them on the map, so to speak. Abraham hadn't much more details than that – nothing that wasn't already listed on the wanted posters – so Morgan figured it might be pertinent to stop by this '*Bill*' fella's homestead out by the river.

He underestimated how close to town this man's home was. Morgan walked along the lengthy, dirty road for upwards of two hours or so in the blistering heat until he reached a quaint farmhouse that was falling slightly into disrepair. He could see some sickly-looking young pigs eating from a trough in a yard of sorts beside the house.

Morgan traipsed his way up to the front door and, despite the sweat stinging his eyes at this point, gathered himself to knock on the door. Before he got the chance, he heard a sharp voice from behind him.

"Who in the hell are you and what do you want?"

Morgan turned to find a tall, gaunt, and mature man standing at the side of the house near the pig yard in raggedy overalls with a pitchfork in hand.

"I won't ask you again, boy." He scowled.

"Afternoon, sir. My apologies for the abrupt and unanticipated visit. My name is Morgan and I was speaking with a mutual acquaintance from town, the gentleman from the general store and I…"

The man cut him off, "Either spit it out or get the hell off my land."

Morgan's tone became a little more stern this time round: "I am a Deputy US Marshall and I am here to ask you some questions, *sir*. I would be much obliged if you could answer them as best as you can recall. I'd also appreciate it if we could run by these questions out of this god damn heat."

"I ain't got nothin' to say to you, *lawman*." He proceeded to turn away when Morgan made a final attempt to hook him in, applying a more sympathetic approach.

"Wait! Wait, sir, please wait a minute… Bill, isn't it? I know you know good and well what it is I came here to ask you about. I know it's sure a shit the last thing you'd want to talk about, but the information you have could be the difference between those sons of bitches runnin' free and gettin' their overdue appointment with the hangman. I know you probably think that I ain't nothin' but some addle-headed young buck, but I promise you, me and the Marshall are going to catch these bastards. Won't you please just tell me even a little about your story? I swear you won't be barkin' at a knot. I know you're busy, but it won't take too long."

The man was unresponsive at first, just stared at the deputy. His face seemed withered, not so much from age itself but perhaps wilting from a lifetime of working outdoors in the sun combined with sleepless nights brought on by the grief he had surely endured. He finally responded with a defeated sigh.

"Come inside and I'll fix you a drink of somethin' strong… let's get this business over with then."

As Morgan stepped through the threshold of Bill's home, it felt eerie inside – like everything was suspended in time. Curtains half open, old crockery almost stuck to the table, a broken cup smashed on the floor but never cleaned up. The house was dark, dusty and devoid of any colour or life. There were old stains across the floor… Was it blood? Despite the intense heat of the day, when Morgan entered this place, he had a sharp chill right down the centre of his spine. With every step Morgan took, the house seemed to creak and groan forlornly at him. After the two men finally settled inside the grungy farmhouse, Bill began to tell his story. He was hesitant and withdrawn with details initially, but the more he spoke, the more the emotions of it all returned to the surface.

Morgan listened so intently, hanging on to Bill's every word in utter horror. He could feel his heart pumping through his body as Bill told him of the events that led to his son and daughter-in-law's murder. Morgan couldn't help but start to feel anger boiling up within him for what happened to this man at the hands of wretched outlaws.

Bill had an older brother who came into money after winning a very exclusive, high-stakes poker game in California. The older brother then passed on after having a bad fall from an unbroken mare and left all this money to Bill, which came as a surprise as the two had never been close.

Not too long after Bill and his wife went out to the city for a weekend trip to celebrate, they had grand plans for their little pig farm. His son and his son's pregnant wife stayed at home. Somehow the gang had found out about the money and that night broke into the house to find it, which they did, but not before cutting three people's lives short.

Bill proceeded to tell Morgan that when they returned to their house, they arrived to find the two front windows broken, the front door ajar and wild dogs gnawing on the cold, lifeless, bloody corpses of the two they held most dear.

His son had been shot in the stomach and chest, his daughter-in-law through her back. Right through the unborn grandchild.

Bill was struggling to withhold his tears by now as he continued to tell the young deputy that soon after this tragedy, his own wife passed. He believed her heart couldn't take the grief and 'God chose to relieve her of it'.

Morgan was confounded and stunned. This man had actual tears welling in his eyes, Morgan may have still been relatively young, but he had never in all his days seen a man brought to such a sheer, broken state of mind. For a man such as this to be practically brought to his knees in emotional turmoil was truly devastating. Morgan had assisted his brother in many a case in the last couple of years, but this was the first time he really, personally felt invested. This man had everything taken from him; he now lived alone in a building that served as a constant reminder of all his losses. It was time for this man to see the justice he deserved inflicted on those responsible.

"By the bye, you catch the man who murdered my son, my daughter, my grandchild *and* my wife; you make sure he hangs and when he does… I want to be there. I want to be present as Satan drags his soul to the gruesome and fiery pits of hell."

Morgan simply nodded at Bill and stood up to shake his hand before leaving, but as he crossed the threshold of the front doorframe once more, he turned to ask one last question, "Bill, sir, you mind me asking what age your son was when he died?"

"Twenty-one."

Chapter 5
Harrison James – US Marshall

The ride out to the site was refreshing, the speed of his mare galloping along the road allowed a swift breeze to cleanse him of the day's heat. He arrived at the site and at first glance, as expected, there was nothing out of the ordinary.

Harrison dismounted and began to survey the area. He was an excellent tracker, but the slightly incompetent sheriff was correct in that there wasn't really anything to go by here at this point, but he wouldn't call it a day until he was sure there had been a thorough check.

He got down on his hunkers in the long grass among the trees that lined either side of the path to try and pick up any trail from a guilty party escaping off road. His eyes scanned across the foliage meticulously when he suddenly came across something a little curious: a small wooden pendant carved to the shape of a crescent moon. The string where someone would have tied it around their neck had been snapped.

Harrison stood and evaluated the item for a moment more when he heard a horse riding towards him from the direction of town. He glanced up to observe who it may be, and he noticed a familiar face. As the horse drew in closer, Harrison spoke up.

"Afternoon, *Miss* Taylor. You in a hurry to get someplace?"

Lenora may have hidden it well, but Harrison noticed she seemed ever so slightly startled or flustered. She smiled, but her eye darted down to the pendant hanging from the Marshall's hand and then straight back up to his eyeline, almost too fast for most to notice – but Harrison rarely missed a trick. He wasted no time in quizzing her.

"I get the impression, ma'am that you seem to recognise this here pendant. Would you happen to know where it might've come from or pray tell, might it be yours?"

Lenora's demeanour immediately calmed. She scoffed and rolled her eyes. "My, my Marshall, you think that piece o' shit belongs to me? Come on now, I know you at least a little smarter than that."

Harrison stayed silent for a moment, testing Lenora in a way, seeing if she'd start to ramble at all – he had found in the past when guilty folk tend to feel under a little pressure; they'll run their mouths making excuses or idle conversation, but Lenora just stared right back at him now with that same beaming confidence from the first night he saw her.

He made another inquiry to her, "Okay, fine, would you be so kind as to advise me where you was headed in such a rush just now?"

"Now why should I be headin' anywhere, *Mr Marshall?* I just find a hard, fast ride for a spell or even longer, helps open up m' lungs and clear my mind. I didn't think there was no law against that." She was partially smirking at him by now. Harrison couldn't help return the smirk, but quickly returned to business.

"You know there isn't. Fair enough, then, Miss Taylor. Good day to you, ma'am." Harrison walked back towards his horse to stash the pendant in his saddlebags. Lenora moved to ride away, but just before she did so, she turned back to speak with Harrison again, only this time, it was like the sharp edges that normally constituted her personality, had melted away.

"Say, Marshall, listen, I… I think we got off on the wrong foot. I wanted to apologise for my behaviour towards you yesterday when we met. I've been told I can be a little fiery at times and I don't mean nothin' by it. I just gotta look out for myself, that's all. I'm sure you can appreciate that? I just really don't want there to be any hostile feelin's atwixt the two of us. Whaddya say, huh? Can we start fresh?"

Harrison appeared to nod in agreement. "Fine by me. I'll be seeing you, *Miss Taylor.*"

"Please call me Lenora; *Miss Taylor* sounds a little too formal for my likin'." She smiled sweetly at him.

"All things aside, what are you doing out here? You working on that coach robbery I heard about? Nasty business – folks 'round here been talking 'bout it near every minute."

He didn't care to engage in much conversation about it; he'd rather get back to Whitepost and see what Morgan had managed to put together (if anything) so far. "Yes, *Miss Taylor*, I am here to find out who murdered the two men on the stagecoach and stole its contents. It is a federal crime and they *will* be brought to justice."

Her interest was piqued. "They? So you reckon it's true, then? It were that gang folks keep tellin' me 'bout? Is that who you's lookin' for?"

Harrison bit his lip and lifted his eyes to meet hers directly.

"I am investigatin' this crime along with my fellow lawmen. We are gatherin' evidence that will ascertain who exactly is responsible and they *will* be brought to swift justice. That is all I have to say on the matter."

Lenora sighed at him and finally resolved to leave. "Fine, Marshall, I best let you get on with your important business… Why don't you come along to Calvin's later for a gut warmer? Or even, if you don't fancy a drink, come by and hear me sing? Enjoy a little entertainment for a change while I'm here in town, hmm?"

She smiled. A natural smile. And flashed those beautiful eyes at him. He suddenly felt very uncomfortable.

"Ehhm… em… I have a lot of work to be getting on with… Maybe some other time." He mounted his horse quickly. "Goodbye, *Miss Taylor*."

She nodded in a seemingly disappointed manner and rode away. Harrison turned in the opposite direction, back towards town. He rode hard for some time, then suddenly realised his horse was hard-pressed. He brought her to a halt, stroked her neck and told her he was sorry for pushing her like that.

Harrison found himself slightly perplexed. Why did he ride so hard under the sun at its highest? He couldn't put his finger on it, but there was something that had him uncertain and uncomfortable.

He found himself contemplating what had just passed with him and Miss Lenora Taylor. There was something about her body language that Harrison just couldn't shake. It was not something he could explain or justify to anyone, but his gut was telling him there was more to Miss Taylor than meets the eye.

Moving much slower now, Harrison thought about what had just happened with Lenora throughout the journey back. The Marshall in him analysed the conversation as logically as he could; however, despite himself, he could not help but thinking that she had one hell of a beautiful smile.

Harrison arrived back in town and, unsurprisingly, went immediately back to the sheriff's office as soon as his horse was hitched up. Morgan seemed to have just arrived back, judging by the profuse amount of sweat dripping from his brows. The greasy sheriff was nowhere to be found.

"Harry, you're back. How goes it? Did you find anything?" Morgan sat down at the desk and exhaled in relief at finally having the chance to sit down.

"Christ, why do you insist on dismissin' me when I tell you – do not call me Harry! You're not a God damn a child any more, Morgan."

"All right, all right, ain't no need to crawl his hump; I didn't mean nothin' by it. Come on now, tell me 'bout the crime site – anything to be found?"

Harrison calmed his tone. "There was just one thing that seemed a little unusual – could be nothin', just somethin' dropped by a passin' traveller, but could be somethin' belonging to the guilty party." Harrison pulled the pendant from his pocket to show Morgan.

"What, is it a moon? Whoever lost it might be missing it, looks like it were skilfully carved." Morgan gestured to Harrison to pass him the pendant for a closer look.

Harrison passed it to his brother. "There's a 'T' carved on the back of it. What about you? Did you manage to find out anything about this gang?"

Morgan told him the details of what he had learned so far. Harrison noticed a change in his brother while he was describing what happened to Bill's family. There was a distinctive sense that it had affected Morgan a little more than any investigation in the past. Not that he was an unsympathetic person, but this time round he seemed more than a little affected by the story.

After the lengthy discussion about the case, they resolved to contact other sheriffs in neighbouring towns to see about any sightings of these criminals or any suspicious happenings about town – track their movements, so to speak, try and find a pattern. Maybe there might be something not necessarily considered important, but it was worth a try. Morgan convinced his brother that contacting the sheriff's could wait until the morning, because both gentlemen had had a long day, the sun was getting low in the sky above Whitepost.

"You ain't turnin' in already, are you, brother? The night is still young! Come and have a drink o' somethin' strong at Calvin's with me, we did a good day's work today."

"Some other time, maybe."

"Come on now, that fine thing you were speaking with yesterday is singing again tonight; it'll be a hog-killin' time! One night o' merriment ain't gonna kill you, *Harrison*."

"I already told her earlier I would not be in attendance," muttered Harrison.

"Oooh, well – well, look here now, so when was you speakin' to her?"

"Morgan, I am conductin' an investigation; it is my job to question *everyone* in this town."

"Okay, okay, Marshall, I hear ya; well, what if I say, in the interests of pursuing our investigations a lil' further, we take it to the saloon?" Morgan jested playfully with him.

Harrison almost cracked a rare smile. "Fine. *One*."

Chapter 6
Morgan James – Deputy Marshall

Morgan and his brother made their way over to Calvin's. The warmth, light and sounds of merriment flooded out from the saloon onto the street outside, now under a twilight sky. The atmosphere in the bar made it impossible to enter without being affected by the air of anticipation, the excitement and expectation. Miss Taylor was about to take the stage and the tension in the audience was palpable.

The two men had arrived just as Miss Taylor was about to begin her performance. The place was pretty crowded. The crowd consisted of almost entirely men, save for the whores waiting to empty the pockets of a few drunken fools. The men varied in age and appearance, the young and rowdy made themselves known as they slammed their beer tankards down on the table and hollered in boisterous excitement. The older crowds were slightly more contained, albeit not much. They laughed and joked between themselves as they awaited the ever-more anticipated performance of Miss Taylor.

As Morgan scanned the room, his eyes fell upon a couple of amputees and war veterans for just a moment. They sat along the walls, towards the back of the room. Their behaviour was decidedly less animated; it was likely judging by just how much these men had lost of themselves; they were not here for Lenora; they were here simply to drink. He didn't think much more about them, just that he was grateful to still possess all his limbs.

Morgan followed Harrison straight through to the bar. The brothers had ordered two whiskeys just as Lenora started to sing. Lenora was, to her credit, an enchanting performer. How could she not be, of course, with an audience full of horny and lonely men, a sassy, sexy and suggestive tone in all of her songs and a dress to make a fucking nun pass out. She kept her distance from the crowd; she performed on top of a little makeshift stage with a wooden barrier around the edge. She hooked in every man she glanced at, enticing them with every move. Morgan enjoyed the entertainment, sure enough, but what caught his attention more than anything else was Harrison. No sooner had Lenora reached the bridge of her first song, Morgan turned his eye slightly to observe his older brother.

Morgan was, surprisingly, quite observant. People would tend to overlook this about him; maybe he even overlooked it in himself, but he possessed a keen eye. As Morgan turned and watched Harrison; for the first time, he saw his older brother staring intensely at a woman. It was as though he was fixated; the more superstitious type could almost say that Harrison seemed hypnotised in a way. Seeing this made Morgan feel a sense of relief.

Well, thank God, he ain't a machine after all! Morgan thought to himself and smiled lightly.

As the performance appeared to be ending, there was an almighty ruckus from the men as they called for more, demanded more. They slammed their tankards down again and again, cheering and hollering. Morgan would wager they could likely be heard in the next town over. Lenora made a savvy final remark to the crowd,

"More, gentlemen? If it's more you's lookin' for, well, I believe these remarkable young gals right on over here would be more'n happy to oblige… so long as you can afford 'em." Lenora winked and gestured towards the *ladies* from the brothel, all of them smiling and flirtatiously waving to the crowd. "Until tomorrow then… goodnight, boys!" Lenora made a swift exit down from the stage to the bar, whilst much of the crowd was distracted by the carnal gestures and indications from the whores.

Despite being somewhat of a *ladies' man*, Morgan was never bothered with the affections of whores. He saw them as nothing more than scavengers, ready to pick a weak man's financial carcass until there's nothing left. Morgan was also a man who enjoyed the excitement of courting. Whores were too easy; where's the challenge?

Lenora counted some tips at the opposite end of the bar as Morgan noticed his brother watching her with intensity.

Morgan leaned into Harrison and quietly spoke.

"Why don't you head on over?"

Harrison seemed awkward and embarrassed almost.

"To what end, Morgan? I have nothin' I need to ask of Miss Taylor right now," Harrison said, as he appeared to reset back to US Marshall mode.

Morgan laughed a little.

"Jesus, brother, just go'n talk with her! They don't bite, you know. Doesn't have to be about the case; just talk!"

Harrison looked frustrated. "I *know* Morgan… but I don't see any reason… She seems t' be engaged in conversation with some other fella now anyways."

"Who gives a shit? Why don't you go over, excuse yourself for interruptin', then tell her she got a beautiful voice. I don't know any gal who'll shy away from a kind word like that." Morgan gave Harrison a wink and a nudge.

Harrison was staring over at Lenora and the young fellow she was conversing with before necking his whiskey… and another… then *finally* mustering up the courage to make his way over.

Morgan watched with delight as his stiff and serious brother attempted to strike up a conversation with Miss Taylor. Morgan's delight and amusement came from knowing just how brutally out of his comfort zone poor Harrison was, awkwardly trying to communicate his admiration. Morgan reckoned Harrison's idea of a good conversation usually ended with a confession and an arrest; for Miss Taylor's sake, hopefully that wouldn't be the case tonight.

Please, Jesus, he might finally have a little fun for himself, Morgan thought.

No sooner had Harrison left Morgan alone at the bar when he heard his name being called through the bustling crowd. Morgan turned to find three gentlemen sitting at a table, playing cards in the corner. He recognised one of the men from playing poker here before, when the brothers had first arrived. The second, the one calling over to him, was the shopkeeper from the general store he had met earlier that day. The third, he did not know.

There was nothing like a friendly bit of gambling now and again to keep the younger James' brother in good spirits, so without hesitation he made his way over.

"Howdy there, fellers, y'all got room for one more?" The Morgan James signature cheeky smile made its appearance once more.

The shopkeeper, Abraham, responded, "So long as you brought more hard cash to hand out, you's more than welcome! Deal 'em in, Levi!" The men laughed as Morgan sat down at the table.

"*Deputy* James, I believe you met Levi already when you was playin' 'fore now, and this here's Buster." Abraham gestured to the third older, quiet man who tipped his hat.

"Just call me Morgan tonight, fellas; the law ain't got no business at the poker table, I reckon." Morgan laughed along with the men.

They played for a little while and whilst Morgan's luck wasn't the worst, it certainly wasn't the best either.

At this point, he would be happy to simply break even. The old sharks have had decades to practice their poker faces, as it would seem.

As Abraham began to shuffle the deck of cards, he looked to Levi, Buster and then back at Morgan. This time, he was much more serious.

"So… you make your way out to Old Bill's place after we spoke?"

Morgan immediately felt a little uneasy. He had intentionally put the day's events in the corner of his mind for the night. He didn't want to think about it.

"I did… yes." Morgan was avoiding eye contact as he awkwardly played with a poker chip on the table.

"Well… Did he talk to you?" Levi asked.

"Yeah, he did."

"Well, now I am impressed. I'll be honest with you; I didn't much think he'd be inclined to speak with anyone, much less a lawman. You must have been pretty damn convincin' boy." Abraham was sincere in his words, but Morgan was increasingly uncomfortable with the line of questioning. He wasn't entirely certain why it was affecting him so.

"What'd he say?" As Levi asked the question, Morgan noticed Abraham had stopped shuffling the deck, eagerly awaiting the answer.

Morgan awkwardly chuckled and went to deflect. "Come on now, this ain't the place to be talkin' 'bout such morbid things – why I reckon we outta' get the round started?"

Abraham looked down, melancholy in his words.

"He used to be here with us sometimes, you know. He'd be sat at this here table. Old Bill would have us fellas laughin' till our guts were sore."

"You remember when he found out he was gonna' have a kid? I think we was in this here saloon for two days straight of celebratin'! A true miracle o' God that was." Levi nudged Abraham with a fond remembrance.

"Why was it a miracle?" Morgan's curiosity got the better of him.

"Well, Bill's wife was told by the doctor after they was married that she couldn't have no babies. They'd long since made their peace with it when, one day, by God's good grace, they were blessed with a son. I ain't ever seen a man so happy as the day that child was born." Levi appeared forlorn as he recalled these faded memories.

That same shiver that Morgan felt down his spine when he first entered Bill's home returned. This information served now only as an added layer to the tragedy of this poor man's life. Morgan sat there in those moments, wondering what a cruelty it was for a man to be blessed with a family he must have longed for so intensely, only to have them all die within his lifetime.

Buster finally uttered his first words since Morgan sat down; he looked down at the table as he spoke.

"It wasn't right what happened to that man."

"Well, *shit*, ain't that the God damn truth of it?" Levi responded.

Buster looked up to each of the men.

"It ain't right that nobody saw justice; nobody saw the hangman after he had his life ripped away like that. A young mother with a child? Only a sick fuckin' bastard does a thing like that – an unholy deed from a retched animal."

Morgan felt ill, dizzy almost. He tuned out of the conversation and began looking around the room. He suddenly felt cold and distant as he watched all those smiling faces laughing, dancing and drinking around him. Although he had heard Bill's story earlier, he was only starting to process what was said to him now. How can one person endure all that pain? How can one person deserve all that pain? Hearing these men talk so fondly of a man they used to call a friend, there's no way to justify the hand Bill was dealt.

Buster was correct; it was not right that no one saw justice.

Just as Morgan was drifting into his own sombre thoughts, he was jolted back to reality. Abraham's hand placed right down on his shoulder had suddenly dragged him back into the conversation.

"We keep talkin' like this, we'll go and scare the young deputy away, then who'll hand us their money?" Abraham looked to Morgan with a light-hearted smile and a chuckle.

"You's right, Abe, don't you mind us old timers, young buck – ain't much for us to do now but talk 'bout the old days."

Morgan took a deep breath and smiled lightly. "Well, now that ain't true… Now you also spend your time robbin' me blind!"

The men laughed together. They continued playing into the night, in much happier spirits. Every once and in a while, Morgan would glance across the room at his brother. He was almost astounded that the lady hadn't had her fill of Harrison by now; the two of them actually seemed to be getting along famously. Morgan smiled to himself, thinking Harrison was probably going to burst if he didn't get to lecture somebody about something real soon.

It had turned into a pleasant night, Morgan was glad they came, but underneath the cheerful, carefree persona that Morgan presented to the room, he knew the deep impression from the story of Old Bill's dead family would not be leaving him anytime soon. He almost felt haunted by it and no amount of whiskey seemed to diminish his sense of sadness.

Chapter 7
Lenora Taylor – Travelling Performer

Most people who crossed paths with Lenora Taylor would think her perhaps a bit brash or cheeky, with a distinct air of unwavering self-confidence. Yes, of course, a woman performing on the stage must have a backbone to survive in the West, but most were still taken aback by her audacious behaviour. The truth of the matter is Lenora intentionally built those walls up to make sure nobody could get close.

Lenora decided early on in life that she would be the master of her own fate, the captain of her own ship. Having run away from home at just sixteen, she told herself the moment she crossed the threshold of her parent's home for the last time that she was the only person in the world she could or would rely on.

It didn't surprise her to know that her parents didn't actually care that she'd left. They were chronically neglectful and sometimes even cruel to her. The catalyst for her finally taking the leap into the unknown and fleeing her home? When her father had planned to marry her off to a man three times her age who was willing to pay handsomely for a sixteen-year-old virgin. To her parents, she was a commodity to be sold at will to the highest bidder. Her parents, her father especially, took no mind to the fact that her perspective husband a drunk and a brute.

She realised very early on that she hated her parents. She was the last of six children born to them; however, all five of her brothers that came before hadn't made it past childhood for one reason or another. All they had ever wanted was a son and the only child that survived was a daughter.

So from a very young age, she felt the resentment, as if it was her and not God who had taken their precious sons. As a young child, she had tried hard to please them, taking up chores around the house that might have been more suited to a strong boy than a weak gal. The only effect that had was to make her so strong physically that no one could knock her down. Her parents took no mind but to work her harder. As she grew, they saw a different kind of value in her. She would be sold to the highest bidder.

So, she ran. Looking back, she knew she had been running for some time.

Now, at twenty-seven, she had established herself as a travelling performer. She travelled all across the West and sang in local saloons or wherever townsfolk could congregate. Her performances lifted the spirits of those who had lost much in the war. She normally arrived at a town and placed a poster or two she had made specially to advertise the entertainment for the night. Most proprietors of these saloons were usually agreeable to negotiating some free lodgings for her in exchange for the profit they would surely make, as she encouraged more customers to come and partake in the night's festivities. Before taking to the floor, she would sometimes enquire around to see if there were any folks adept at any instruments to accompany her, but she would happily fly solo if not.

She had been to Whitepost before, so the townsfolk here were overjoyed at her return, knowing what a few nights of merriment she would bring to lift their dreary spirits. She was just finishing her routine to the delight of the gathered audience when she noticed a rather stern looking man at the bar that she later came to find out was the Marshall. For some reason, one that she didn't quite understand, she felt a little intrigued by the stranger, a voice in her head telling her she needed to know more about him, like it was almost important that she did. That is, until she actually spoke to him that night and discovered he had a poker up his ass.

After running into him again at the scene of the stagecoach robbery, she was admittedly frustrated at Harrison's rejection of her 'olive branch' and refusal to come and see her perform. This had more than a little to do with the fact that her female pride was a wounded by his rejection; however, even so, she could not help but feel curious about him.

The truth is, Lenora did know something about that pendant the Marshall found. She was startled to see it in his hand earlier. She was angry that it was there in the first place. What exactly did he know about this pendant? Her plan now was to attempt to find out. She needed to get him talking. She could not risk her connection to this investigation getting out.

The sun set over Whitepost, and Lenora made her way downstairs from her room at Calvin's to the bar. The band of townspeople playing various instruments were getting set up when she descended the stairs, and the audience was either gathering at the bar for drink or making noisy, excited commotion at their tables and around the room in anticipation of her ascending the stage. Lenora made her way across the floor, greeting and charming various people as she went.

She got herself and the band ready and just as they were about to begin, Lenora spotted just the man she was hoping for walk into the bar. Harrison and his brother had arrived, but she found herself a little irritated to see that Harrison didn't look at her at all and proceeded straight to the bar. She took a deep breath, then counted in the band. She sang all the old favourites from her wheelhouse.

The crowd loved the tones of her voice and she continued to sing, so smooth and sultry they couldn't get enough, but that didn't matter to her tonight. What did make Lenora content at this particular time was that the moment she began to sing, Harrison's eyes turned and fixated right on her.

Throughout the course of her performance, her charisma and charm grew every minute, knowing he was beholding her with a look of pleasant surprise and admiration. When the night's entertainment came to a close, Lenora bid her audience goodnight and went straight to the bar, the opposite end from Harrison and Morgan. As she waited for her whiskey and finished counting her tips from the night, she glanced up to meet his eye, and just as he might have been expecting her to walk over and speak with him, she turned to speak with a different young gentleman from town.

Lenora knew how to play a man right into her hands. She sweetly giggled at the gentleman's pitiful attempt at jokes because she knew Harrison could see. She gently touched the man's arm in a seemingly tender gesture of favour towards him. She knew this game well. But this time, however, something wasn't right. Harrison did not approach to intervene in her conversation. She was almost starting to get short with the suffocating young man, unable to contain her frustration at having to extend her pointless exchange with him, when *finally* she heard the voice she wanted come up behind her.

"Excuse me, sir, would you mind if I speak with the young woman for a moment?"

Lenora immediately excused herself from the young fellow and turned to greet Harrison.

"I didn't expect to see you here tonight; thought you were too busy for such things," she playfully quipped. "Did you enjoy the show?" She smiled.

"Well, I have to admit, Miss Taylor, I..." Harrison stopped for a split second and swerved the conversation in a different direction. "Morgan, my brother here, insisted I accompany him here for a drink and I would be remiss in my work were I to deny him that one request after doing a fine day's work." Harrison broke a faint smile, just a little one, and quick enough that she could have almost missed it, but just enough to ignite a spark between them. But no sooner did it happen; the smile faded once more and Lenora was admittedly a little disappointed.

"Oh… I thought you mighta' come t' see me."

"Well, I-I will admit I was a little curious 'bout what is involved in your trade here, I may have been swayed in my decision with that in mind."

"Well, I suppose that makes me feel a little better. Say, can I buy you a drink, Marshall?"

"I believe I owe you a drink from last night; I'll buy."

The two made their way to the bar and ordered a round of whiskeys. They engaged in a little idle chit chat to get to know each other a little better. Lenora knew Harrison was likely going for similar tactics, baiting for information. Whilst she did not know much about the man yet, she was certain he was not to be underestimated. They were both playing the same game.

"So tell me, Marshall, why were you and your brother dragged all the way out to these parts for something like a stagecoach robbery, I would have thought local law could take care o' somethin' like that?"

"Come on now, don't tell me you would put your faith in that, Sheriff; you've met him, I'm sure? Also, you needn't address me by Marshall; just call me Harrison while I'm off duty." He was deflecting. Lenora took another stab at obtaining a sliver of information.

"I've seen him '*at work*' you could say." She nodded in a gesture towards the sheriff, perched on that same stool as last night, and passed out on the bar.

Harrison cracked a little smirk. "But still though, I'm curious: if you think it's that gang, why have you both come now when they've been causin' all kinds o' trouble for years?"

Harrison was already reset to his usual controlled self. "I do not '*think it's that gang*' I am gathering evidence and information to establish in absolute certainty who carried out this crime and I will arrest those responsible when that time comes. I am curious, Miss Taylor; what makes you so interested?"

"Oh, ease on up, Harrison, I'm just intrigued by the idle gossip back 'n forth atwixt the fine folk 'round here! You can't blame a gal for lookin' to hear the juicy details straight from the source." She smiled pleasantly at him. "But besides, more seriously, as a travellin' performer with not much to protect myself but information, you can see how this affects me."

"My apologies, Lenora, I didn't mean to, um, '*jump down your throat*'," he said as he looked at her in a more serious way.

Lenora and Harrison continued to talk a while longer, the whiskey making it a little easier. They'd swayed away now from the game and were simply two people enjoying a drink or two and a laugh with one another. Lenora wouldn't admit it to herself just yet, but she genuinely enjoyed his company. She didn't usually come across a man who would match her wit toe to toe.

"Well, Harrison, I best be turnin' in for the night; it's gettin' a morsel late for me. Although I know you to be a gentleman, I think perhaps my resolve to resist your charmin' self might be compromised by whiskey." She smiled.

Harrison smiled back.

"Thank you for the company tonight… I was thinkin' maybe you could accompany me on a ride tomorrow evenin'? You know how I like to ride out and I would feel a whole lot safer if you were with me. The scenery round these parts is somethin' to behold."

"Well, I-I suppose it wouldn't hurt to get a lay of the land 'round these parts. I would very much like that. Thank you, and goodnight, Miss Taylor."

Lenora excused herself from Harrison's company and made her way up the stairs to her rented room. She didn't get the information she needed, but she couldn't deny one thing. The anticipation she was starting to feel at the prospect of seeing him again.

She entered her room and fell backwards onto her bed. She stared at the ceiling and her smile faded as reality loomed. She was telling herself the same thing over and over again: 'Do not make the mistake of getting' your heart involved. Find out what you need to know and leave him as you found him. There is no room to get tangled up with a fucking US Marshall of all people. *Len, get your damn head straight!* She kicked off her boots and rolled over to try and get some sleep. As she closed her eyes to drift away, she saw the same thing she had dreamt of for years – the same thing she sees sometimes even during her waking hours. As vivid as anything real, because it stems from a deep memory that haunted her at all times. A woman lies dead on the floor, in a pool of her own blood.

Chapter 8
Harrison James – US Marshall

Harrison and Morgan (who was nursing a bit of a hangover) spent the day in the sheriff's office drawing up letters intended for the nearby towns as they had planned. They had come to realise that this investigation was going to be slow. Even if they were absolutely sure it was that Sam Walker fella, they would still have a job and a half finding him. Nobody knew what the man looked like; his wanted poster was just a black bandana covering almost all facial features and a black hat. He apparently rode on a black stallion. Not much to go on.

Harrison knew by now they would be in town for at least a week or more, waiting to receive all the information they could in an attempt to track the gang's movements. Seeing as they had no other suspects, it seemed right to focus all their efforts on finding the Spector gang. Harrison also made a note to contact the Governor and tell him of their progress. All they could do now was wait.

"We 'bout done here, Harrison? I'm supposed to be meeting up with some o' the fellers from the bar to go fishing down by the river; I don't want those sons o' bitches gettin' first bite!" Morgan said cheerfully.

"You're supposed to be going fishing? That's funny 'cause to my recollection, you was supposed to be workin' today. Why you would arrange anythin' otherwise is beyond my fathom, sir."

Morgan stared at Harrison's serious facial expression, unsure for a moment. "You… You jest! We ain't got nothin' more to do today, right?"

"Jesus, there ain't no pullin' the wool over your eyes, eh Morgan?" He smiled at his younger brother.

Morgan rolled his eyes and stood up to put his jacket on.

"You ain't have me fooled, Harry, er, *Harrison,* I mean, I can read you better'n anyone! What has you in such a jolly kind o' mood today, huh? Bet on it, that raven-haired singer's what's got you all sweet." He playfully dug his fist into Harrison's arm. "I damn nearly lost my life at the sight of you sittin' up at that table gigglin' away with that woman!"

Harrison was immediately uncomfortable; he was feeling a little embarrassed and tried to deflect a little. "Yeah, sure, well, I mean, I just wanted to um… congratulate the woman on an entertainin' performance, then we went about our business, nothin' more'n that."

Morgan started laughing loud enough even to stir the sheriff in his sleep, which was quite a feat in itself. "Christ, brother, ain't nothin' wrong with havin' a little fun! Relax for a spell; we're gonna be here for a time. Loosen up a little! Ain't no shame *whatsoever* in admiring the beautiful creatures round here." Morgan winked at his brother. "I myself have *enjoyed* that little fair-haired, exquisite piece of splendour… last night… and again this mornin',” Morgan said with a cheeky smile and a chuckle.

“Morgan, if I end up with some furious fuckin' asshole father bangin' down my door at first light about his *disgraced* daughter again, I swear to God you will regret it.”

“Easy, *easy* now ain't no need for concern; her daddy's long dead.” Morgan flashed a mischievous smile once more before making his way to the door. “Bye, Harry. Oh, by the bye, The husband's still alive!”

“Son of a bitch,” Harrison muttered to himself as his brother was gone before he had a chance to scold him further. It was getting towards late afternoon now, so he gathered up the letters and made his way around to the mail office, sitting just a few yards from the old church. After dropping the letters in, he headed over to his rented room.

He proceeded to pull a fresh shirt, a pair of socks and pants from his travelling bag and laid them on his bed. He removed his belt and laid that down with the clothes. He left his boots at the foot of his bed, then removed the rest of his garments and folded them to carry over to the whorehouse (he heard that there were respectable women working in there that would launder your clothes for a modest fee).

Using a basin of water that had been freshly placed in his room and a small bar of soap placed on top of a dresser, he began to wash himself, rubbing a cloth across old scars on his abdomen and some on his upper left thigh –

memories of war that he had long since locked in the back of his mind. Every now and again, he could still feel a sharp twinge on these old wounds, but he chose to leave his trauma in the past, where it belonged. He diligently washed himself twice over when he started to realise he was feeling a little anxious. Why?

Harrison had been with women before, but he wasn't the settling kind. He did respect women as he had been taught to do, so he never felt he gave anyone false indications. On the one hand, the Marshall in him did have that nagging feeling or sense that Lenora was holding something back. Harrison was always on safer ground when he was the Marshall, but now he was feeling an uneasiness that felt somehow alien and unknown. He had an instinct that he was about to walk into dangerous territory.

He finished getting himself dressed and stood in front of the old, grubby mirror for a last check. He took a deep breath, placed his hat on his head and exhaled whilst saying aloud to himself, "All right."

He made his way out of his lodgings, down the stairs and out the front door, where he found Lenora leaning on the banister of the porch. She smiled at him.

"You were almost late," she teased.

"How did you know where I…"

"I have my ways and my sources." She winked, "Come on now, ol' man, let's get goin'."

The two made their way to the stables and got saddled up. They took a slow trot out of town. It was much cooler that day, but there was heavy humidity in the air with an overcast sky. The sun broke through the clouds in just a few scattered spots, but where it did, the light flooded over the terrain below.

"Hey, you see that big tree there a few miles out that away? The dead one?" Lenora indicated towards an outwardly black tree way out across the landscape.

"I see it."

"Last one there buys the drinks tonight." She winked, knocked her heels back into her stallion and was away in a flash, galloping away at full speed within seconds.

"LENORA! Aw hell…" Harrison rode out after her as fast as his mare could take him. The road was challenging for even an experienced rider, ditches and fallen trees until the vegetation cleared and it was nothing but open land.

Lenora was ahead, but the gap was closing, Harrison was determined to match her every move and drove his horse as hard as he could. Suddenly! A mighty crack of thunder… deafening in the skies… the heavens exploded and rain, such as only Noah knew, started crashing down all around them. Lenora turned back, gave a daring smile and laughed despite the deluge, and took off again like a lightning bolt. Harrison would not give up so easily, and the taunting only made him more determined.

The black tree was in sight; they were almost riding neck and neck at this point. Harrison swept up right behind her and just as he was about to take the lead, she swung a sharp right towards a separate, dead sapling. Harrison jerked his horse back to follow her, confused and soaked from the still pouring rain.

She had slowed her horse to a stop and dismounted, running to take shelter under a cluster of nearby trees.

Harrison dismounted and shouted loudly at her over the thrashing of the rain. "What was all that about, you sour that I bested you?"

"Bested me? Oh, Harry, I think you must be confused; see, I meant *that* dead tree." She grinned and pointed to the lifeless sprig. "I'll enjoy my drinks tonight," she giggled.

"Hey, woman, that's cheatin' and you damn well know it; I won fair and square."

Lenora stepped right up to Harrison, their faces less than an inch from each other. She was a little shorter than him, but could still look him dead in the eye. She sized him up once more, raised one eyebrow and quietly uttered, "Says who?"

He stared at her, deep into the magnetising blue of her eyes, as the rainwater dripped down from her long, dark hair and from her clothes. He knew in that moment he was finding her impossible to resist. He knew he didn't want to resist. He knew, as he had always known, that he wanted her. Harrison grabbed her behind her neck at the base of her head, pulled her in and kissed her.

It only took a split second before Lenora pushed him off and angrily slapped his face. "HEY!"

Harrison was suddenly panicked. Had he misread things? His stomach sank. "Len, I'm so sorry, I-I thought…" He fell silent.

She was looking back at him intensely, silently. He could almost hear wheels turning in her head. She looked distressed. And then, without warning, she grabbed the lapel of his jacket, pulled him in and kissed him with a passion and fury that took him completely by surprise. In that moment, they knew each other entirely. As Harrison moved his hand upwards on the outside of her thigh, she pulled him down to the ground by his belt buckle and climbed on top of him. The two of them were now locked into a spiralling whirlwind of intense desire. Harrison and Lenora were almost ripping through their undergarments now, just to get through to each other as fast as they could. They wanted each other. They *needed* each other. Lenora grabbed both of Harrison's hands, held them down hard, looked at him once more with the hypnotic eyes he so enjoyed, then grasped her hand around his manhood and finally placed it inside her.

In making love, their chemistry was undeniable; Harrison felt like there was pure electricity between them. It was powerful. It was animalistic. Every move between the two of them was nothing but deep, exhilarated pleasure. She was a wild female.

Yes, he had been with women before, but there was no woman like Lenora.

They were both lost in the hunger for one another. In that moment, there was no one else in the entire world but them. Right there under those trees, with the rain still pounding down around them.

Harrison now slowed his rhythm; he grabbed Lenora from on top of him and spun her down to the ground beside, with himself positioned behind her. He kissed her neck as he now began to unlace her corset. Just as he was about to slip the chemise down and witness her beautiful, bare body, she turned back suddenly, with a distinct feeling of vulnerability about her that he had never seen.

"Don't do it like that; I wanna see you. I want you to see me," she said firmly.

Harrison gently rubbed the back of his hand down the side of her face.

"I see you."

He kissed her and slipped the fabric down. He was gliding his hand over every curve of her body. Harrison tenderly massaged her breasts, adoring every corner of her form.

Afterwards, they lay there in the grass together, protected by each other's embrace. It was only for a short moment, but for that short moment, there were no words needed. Right there and then, Harrison forgot he was a Marshall. Forgot he had family to be responsible for. Forgot about all his troubles.

These two souls were intertwined by fate. They would find each other in every lifetime and in coming together like this now, it felt eternal.

Once reality started to settle back in and the fire of their encounter had been reduced to gentle embers, Lenora sat up sharply.

"I reckon we, um…" she awkwardly chuckled, "we should be gettin' on back to town, Harrison; I must be gettin' on back to Calvin's… I have a performance to prepare for and I don't know 'bout you, but uh, I'm sure to catch a chill with this weather." She smiled nervously.

She went to stand up when he pulled her back down into his arms.

"Madam, I am a US Marshall and you are hereby detained for the remainder of this evenin'." He playfully squeezed her.

She laughed a little, kissed his cheek, then suddenly slipped out of his grip and jumped up to her feet. "You'd have to catch me first," she said with a teasing tone as she went to dress herself.

Harrison was lying there watching her dress, admiring her as the sun finally broke through the clouds once more.

"You – you not comin'? she asked.

"You go on ahead, Len; I'll catch up with you later – at Calvin's."

She gave him one last smile before making her way back to her stallion. She mounted him and was away in a flash.

Harrison sat there for a time under that tree, reflecting. The magnitude of what had just happened was starting to sink in.

What had he just gotten himself tangled up in here?

Chapter 9
Morgan James – Deputy Marshall

Morgan couldn't help but take full advantage of the 'boss man's' distracted heart. Responses from other towns surrounding the Spector gang and people of interest had been very slow to return, so there wasn't a whole lot of work to be done between them. The singer, Lenora, had also finished her performances and was staying in town for a spell longer. His brother and Lenora had become practically inseparable over the last couple of weeks and Morgan, true to form, relished the opportunity to have some fun of his own.

But, in all seriousness, Morgan was glad to see Harrison like this. Being out on the path for years and after the war particularly, his brother was quite hardened and ill-humoured at times. But getting closer to Lenora, Harrison was showing a happiness that Morgan hadn't seen since they were children.

More importantly, from Morgan's perspective, he could get away with whatever merriment he so pleased without his older brother preaching at him.

On one particular day, that merriment included waking up early, after a night with a different blonde to his previous conquest, down to the riverbed to fish with some of the fellas from town, cooking up their best catch of the day, back to his room to freshen up a little, then down to Calvin's for the nightly game of poker and drinks with the boys. Truth was, he was making a particular effort to stay busy because if he spent too long sitting in one place, he couldn't stop picturing what had happened to Bill's family.

He and some of the fine gentlemen from town had been getting on famously. They would only play for coins – nothing compared to what went down in over in the gambling house across the street. There was generally a firm air of fun and a competitive spirit between them.

"Well, well, Morgan, back again to lose them nickels once more? Assuming there's any left," one of the older men joked.

"You know, boys." Morgan hitched his belt buckle up and crossed his arms. "I reckon today lady luck is flashin' that beautiful smile o' hers and I *will* be walkin' on out o' here with a full pot," Morgan chuckled with that cheeky smile.

He sat down at the table and the cards were drawn. As fate would have it, Morgan finally parted ways with his losing streak and in a twist of seemingly divine intervention, the younger James' brother started to clean the house. He was relishing his newfound success. Sometime after midnight, Morgan decided to quit while he was ahead and pack it in for the night.

"All right, fellers, I'm out and by the bye, don't be lookin' at me with them sour faces! Better luck next time!"

He flashed his charming grin at the remaining men around the table whilst scooping his winnings up.

The men grunted and continued their game while Morgan made his way to the bar for one final whiskey shot of the night. He knocked it back smooth and proceeded to head out the door into the darkness of the warm night sky.

Just as he was about to start walking away, towards his lodgings, he heard a loud scuffle coming from the whorehouse in the opposite direction. Despite his desire to not really get involved, he found himself trying to see what was happening, but the low light revealed nothing. He did, however, suddenly hear and spot a horse riding fast out of town away from the establishment. Morgan told himself, 'He ain't on duty' but the pull of curiosity was a little too much. Maybe his brother's voice was in his mind somewhere, telling him to go and check it out.

Morgan trudged over to the brothel to find most of the ladies gathered around one of the younger girls in the main doorway. The madam of the house was standing in front of her, so Morgan hadn't a clear view, but he had the instinctive feeling something bad had happened here.

"Evenin' ladies, what appears to be the probl'…"

"Oh, Deputy Morgan, right? That's you, isn't it? That son of a god damn bitch has beaten my Marybelle black and blue! He's a no-good dirty swine and I demand some kind of repercussions!" the madam snapped.

The madam had stepped aside from cleaning the wounds to reveal a sickly-framed young thing that had been beaten senseless. Her left eye was swollen so badly it was entirely shut. Her mouth bloody and missing a front tooth. Bruising was all over her tiny body, with blood all over her clothes, dripping down from her nose. Morgan was gobsmacked.

"Jesus Christ… What happened here? To whom exactly are you referring to ma'am?"

"Gabe, God dammit, Gabe Hammerton! The motherfuckin' family owns this place, so they think they can do whatever it is they so please, I'm done with it!"

"Start from the beginning here now; what did Gabe do to this gal and why?" Morgan quizzed the madam, but the young, beaten girl piped up.

"He – he came to see me like he does most times he's here. I was doin' what I do and when it came time for payment, sir, I-I asked him for such. He grumbled at me and threw me half. I mean, I never thought he'd get so angry with me, but I opposed him when he didn't give me what I was owed…"

"Opposed him? Marybelle, you was callin' him a cheap dirty bastard that's a whole barrel more'n just opposed," snarled one of the older whores.

The women of the brothel all began arguing about whether Gabe was within his rights to beat her. Morgan felt there was an air of jealousy towards this girl more than anything else. The madam was trying to stop them, but Morgan was losing patience.

"All right, ALL RIGHT, EVERYBODY SHUT THE HELL UP!"

The women fell silent.

"So let me get this straight now. This gal here was beaten 'cause she called the Hammerton boy cheap after he was payin' you half what you was owed? And I'm assuming he was the *gentleman* I seen ridin' off from here in a hurry? And he reckons he doesn't owe you nothin' 'cause the family here owns the joint? Am I right in all this?"

"Yes, Deputy Morgan, now what are y'all gonna' do about this? I won't have my girl's bein' laid into like this. He thinks he's untouchable or some such now that he's 'soon to be the *richest son of a bitch in the whole damn west*'," the madam said sarcastically.

"To what exactly are you referring, ma'am? What do you mean exactly by 'soon to be the richest'?" Morgan quizzed.

"Aw hell, I don't know. That's just what he was sayin' to Marybelle here when he was bustin' up her face. Now what are you going to do about this Morgan?"

"I'll take this to your sheriff, ma'am; the matter will be resolved. Go on now, take your ladies inside and get Marybelle to bed."

The madam was very disgruntled but reluctantly retreated inside with the other women. Morgan was left in the street alone, pondering what a rogue town this place was. He had heard of the Hammerton family, not much though – just that they had money, enough to own some businesses – about the place, but not much more was known about them on his part. Why did this seem like a bigger deal than just a man raising a fist to a whore?

He walked out towards the boarding house and thought to deal with it all in the morning. He began daydreaming of his head resting on that nice fluffy pillow, having a 'well earned' lie in after first light, and getting an ample breakfast with all the fixin's. He arrived at the steps of the boarding house porch, went inside the front door, up the inside stairs to the first floor. As he walked towards his bedroom door, he couldn't help but stare at Harrison's bedroom door down the end of the hallway.

A nagging feeling started circling his mind until he finally caved.

"Maybe I should tell Harry about this… might be somethin' in it."

Chapter 10
Harrison James – US Marshall

Lenora was none too pleased about Morgan banging his brother's door down in the middle of the night. Harrison stepped outside the room to let her get back to sleep while Morgan filled him in on all the details.

"Sorry, Harrison, I know it's damn late, but… I don't know. I just felt like I should tell you. Should I get the sheriff up?"

"I would wager the sheriff is well-oiled by now; if not entirely passed out, we'll dispatch him out to the Hammerton house in the mornin'; it's his responsibility to deal with such things, not ours. I was actually gonna' tell you at first light, but we received some information back, at long last, of past occurrences involving the gang, so I want you to read through and piece together what we have. Muster up any kind of pattern to their movements or any other information that might be of use."

Harrison could see the disappointed look on his younger brother's face.

"Come on now, Morgan, the time off wasn't gonna' last forever now; we're here to do a job, you know that."

"Well, you seem to be *enjoyin'* the job a lot more than usual this time 'round, brother," Morgan said playfully as he nodded towards the bedroom door.

Harrison couldn't help but smile with a purely smitten look across his face. "Shut up, Morgan." He light-heartedly shoved his brother. "Get to bed."

The two brothers got back to bed after that and woke up early, ready to get back to work.

Harrison set Morgan to work on the timeline of the gang. He knew the beating last night was not his concern, but he instinctively felt the need to gather a little bit more information on the Hammerton family and their pull around these parts. Lenora had gone for a ride that morning, but Harrison was hoping she'd have arrived back to engage her in a line of questioning. She did, after all, 'have her ways and her sources'.

He got himself washed up and ready for the day when he ventured out to Calvin's. To his pleasant surprise, Lenora was perched at the bar, reading a local penny paper.

"Afternoon, fine lady; wasn't sure you'd be back by now."

"But you decided to check up on me anyway, hmm?" Lenora smirked and placed the paper down on the bar.

"I wanted to ask you about somethin', if you would be obliged?"

"Ooh, my – my, it's *Marshall James* today, now is it? My Harry's gone all serious now, I see," she joked.

"No, no, nothin' like that, just some whore got her face smashed up bad by one of the Hammerton's shoutin' his mouth off 'bout somethin' and nothin'. You know anythin' about 'em? Ever heard tell from folk?"

"The Hammertons? Well, I ain't heard much, but from what I know, they's the ones that own half o' Whitepost. Think they live in that big house on the edge of town…"

"What do you mean when you say they own half the town?" Harrison's curiosity was triggered.

"They the ones that opened the Whorehouse, the Gamblin' House… shit, I even heard they run a fightin' club after dark round here. I heard tell they found silver on their land."

"Silver? Is that so? How many in the family?" asked Harrison almost immediately after Lenora finished speaking.

"I mean Christ, I don't know… I know *Old man* Hammerton is a decrepit, nasty son of a bitch who's stuck to his bed these days. Folk say he spent so much o' his time in the Devil's company that he smells o' sulfur. The mama's still livin'; she has a few sons, I think, and a couple o' daughters. They like to flaunt their supposed wealth about the place," Lenora said with a slightly bitter tone.

"I'm assuming then one of the sons is Gabe?"

"I don't know for sure; I would guess so. Why you wanna know about him?" She quizzed intently.

"Why would he claim to be coming into a lot of money to people when they already have a position of considerable wealth 'round here?" Harrison seemed to nearly pose this question to himself.

"Well, now hang on; I said *supposed* wealth… I heard tell they found silver on their land, sure, but it wasn't *that* much from what I hear. Ladies round here been gossipin' and I heard a rumour that the well's run dry, so to speak," said Lenora with a smug look on her face. "You say he's been claiming he'll be comin' into big money?"

"He said it to some folk last night. Thanks, Len, I'm heading back to the office." Harrison lowered his voice. "Will I see you later?"

Lenora leaned in closer to him and gently whispered, "If you're lucky." She winked as he went to leave the saloon.

Harrison smirked as he left Calvin's and made his way across the town towards the sheriff's office. He arrived to find Morgan rustling through the letters and scribbling down some notes on a piece of paper beside him. The sheriff was surprisingly sober and standing beside him, presumably attempting to help.

"Afternoon, fellers, what've we got so far?" Harrison asked as he removed his hat and walked over to observe the progress laid out on the desk.

Morgan and the sheriff ran Harrison through what they'd put together so far. The Spector gang had indeed made their way across many towns in the West; their crimes were sinister and their leader, Sam, ruthless. Almost unholy. But until the stage robbery, they had never hit the same area twice. Granted it was a couple of years back, but this was still the first time this had happened. On top of that, they had never set a target on a stagecoach. Why the change? Harrison pondered this for himself. Knowing that stage robbery would attract a higher level of attention from the law, they must have had a good reason for the change in tactics. If they'd gone on this long without being caught, this Sam fella must be of at least some level of intelligence, but would still take the risk of breaking their pattern.

"When exactly did you say the gang passed through these parts before and attacked Bill's family?" Harrison quizzed Morgan and the sheriff.

In unison, they both responded, "July, 1866."

Harrison suddenly had a concerning thought. He didn't want to say anything just yet, as it was only a hunch, but he had a horrible feeling that something was not right. He needed to get back to the bar.

"I'll be back in a spell; I need to run by Calvin's and ask him something – you two keep workin' on this."

Harrison grabbed his hat and dashed out the office door. He hurried over to the saloon and made his way in. The barkeep was cleaning down some glasses as Harrison approached him.

"Afternoon, Marshall, what can I get you? If you's looking for Lenora, she left not long after you."

"No, no… I need to ask *you* somethin', if you have a moment? You mentioned to me when we first met that Lenora, *er*, Miss Taylor had been in town before, right?" Harrison asked.

"Well, yes, she came here first a couple years back,"
Calvin replied.

"And she hasn't been again until now?"

"No, sir, not to my recollection."

"Tell me, Calvin, when was it exactly she came first?"

"Oh, I don't know… '66 or thereabouts, maybe."

"You sure it was 1866? In the summer?" Harrison was
starting to seem a little agitated.

"Er… yes, actually, now you mention it, was hot as
hell, maybe June or…"

"July?" Harrison cut across him with a defeated voice.

"Yes! Why you ask, Marshall?" Calvin smiled.

"Just wanted to check somethin'; thank you, Calvin."

Calvin had responded to him but Harrison suddenly
couldn't hear anything but his own heart beating as the
anxiety of this suspicion was starting to consume him.

He originally felt drawn to Lenora because his gut was
telling him she was hiding something. Over the last few
weeks, he started to believe that maybe he was actually
drawn to her because she was meant for him, they were
meant to be together, maybe, but now the cold touch of
reality was dragging him back down to earth. That gut
feeling was telling him something. It's too much of a
coincidence. His heart was sinking below the ground.

Spector was in town in July '66, so was Lenora…
Spector was in town in July '69, so was Lenora. She knows
something.

Chapter 11
Sam Walker – Notorious Outlaw

Sam and the gang had been slyly mingling right under the noses of everyone in town and the townsfolk had been none the wiser. It had been a few weeks since the robbery, but hiding in plain sight was, for now, working a charm. Sam was attending the general store, the stables, the gunsmith, hell, even drank in Calvin's saloon. It was strict policy that gang members would not converse with each other whilst laying low to ensure no connection could be made between them. With that in mind, Sam would instead natter with the townsfolk. Sam was, in fact, very charming when needs be.

It was getting near time to rendezvous with *'the woman'* to hand over the letter and collect their reward. Everything was going to plan until one faithful day, when Sam picked up on something the Marshall had been saying at the bar. Sam was sitting right there under the nose of the law and the Marshall had no idea that what he had spoken of could be used to the gang's advantage. Harrison James had been speaking of a Hammerton boy; this Hammerton boy, in particular, had caused a commotion in the brothel one night and began claiming his family would be coming into some affluence very soon. Now, that in itself was not major news… It was not until the Marshall mentioned the Hammerton boy's name in full that something clicked in Sam's mind.

Gabe Hammerton. *G.H.* from the stagecoach letter.

Gabe Hammerton was one of at least two parties potentially connected to this letter, engaged in nefarious dealings against the natives. What did the Hammerton family stand to gain by starting up that kind of bad business? It was starting to seem like the letter the gang had come across was somehow linked to this mighty windfall the Hammerton family would be coming into.

Two things Sam knew for certain: it was starting to sound like the anonymous benefactor was someone who knew the Hammerton family, *and* this letter was potentially worth a damn sight more than six thousand dollars.

Not long after this revelation came the day of the rendezvous. *The woman* was to meet them in the woods during daylight hours, some distance out of town. With the usual hustle and bustle, comings and goings of town, nobody would notice a few riders heading out.

Sam arrived first, made it a point to do so, but remained out of sight, enjoying a moment of peace with a smoke. One by one, the other gang members arrived on the scene.

Adelita began complaining to the group the moment she dismounted, "If I have to listen to one more *cabrón maloliente* mouthing at me to fuck him in that stupid god damn place, I am going to slit someone's throat I am telling you truly! Talking to me like I am some piece of shit whore!"

"Come on now, Lita, don't tell me when you got the job doin' laundry at the brothel; you's really just '*doin' laundry*'," Bill sniggered. "I bet you love them, sweaty sons o' bitches breakin' you in – one. After. Another." He smugly smiled.

Javier stepped right up to Bill, infuriated. "You want to repeat that *muchacho*? One more word like that about *mi hermana* and my blade goes in your neck! *Comprendo*!"

Sam laughed and they all turned surprised.

"Bill, shut the hell up; I do not need Javier here getting all riled up 'fore we take care of business. This woman 'be here any minute now."

"I wasn't even talkin' to him… I were talkin' to his whore sister."

THUMP! Javier punched Bill straight in the nose. The two broke into a fight, Adelita rolled her eyes, Clayton, Michael and Austin cheering them on. The two were now rolling in the dirt, beating on each other senselessly, when all of a sudden they heard the sound of two guns cocking. They looked up to see Sam standing over them with a pair of LeMat Revolvers aimed at each of their temples and a look of untethered fury behind the eyes.

"I ain't in the habit of repeatin' myself, cocksuckers. Stand up. Shut the hell up right God damn now or I swear to God, I will either blow your brains out the back of your head or burn you alive and revel in your screams."

The two men took a moment, then stood up slowly, dusted off and backed away from each other.

Sam lowered the guns. "Now listen to me, you sons o' bitches, there's a change of plans – originally, we was gonna' give this woman her letter and she would send word with the location of our payment. BUT what is actually gon' happen is this: We are gonna' hold out for more money."

Adelita piped up. "Wait, so does this mean we are staying longer in this pile of shit town?"

Austin questioned after, "How do you know we can get more'n six thousand? That's already a hell of a payout."

"Have I ever steered any o' you wrong in the past? That letter is more valuable than any o' you simple motherfuckers realise. Something big is goin' down here and this here letter is key to it all. I think this letter is gon' be used for blackmail. Somebody is likely planning on getting a hell of a lot of money from this little piece of paper, so why shouldn't we get a chunk o' that? Hell, we was the ones that found the damn thing!"

The gang had no idea what Sam was talking about; they just heard more money.

Not too long after, *the woman* made an appearance.

'The woman' made her way over to stand a foot or two away from Sam.

"Good Afternoon. My employer has dispatched me here to recover the letter as discussed and afterwards…"

Sam cut her off. "Hold up there a moment, little missy. I'm curious… What exactly does your employer want this here letter for? Seems to me they be goin' to a mighty amount of trouble for one little piece o' paper."

"I am unaware of the details myself, Ph… *Phantom*." The woman was starting to seem nervous. "I have just been advised to collect the letter, if you would be so kind and deliver it."

"Pfft *Phantom*. Haha! Jesus, that nickname always makes me smile. You know what little bird? You can call me Sam; after all, we's practically pals now, ain't we?"

The gang was sniggering a little by now.

"Well… I… ehhm, Sam, I really must be getting back so if you could please, the letter?"

"See, now here's the thing, miss. Me and my associates here, we had a little read of this here letter and I have ascertained that this little piece of paper you so desperately need to collect… is worth a whole lot more'n was originally agreed."

The woman's nerves were becoming more and more obvious. "I-I was just told to bring the letter back and that's it. I don't know nothin' about its contents… I'm just a messenger. I was told to advise six thousand, no more, no less."

Sam stepped right up to the woman now. "Well, you said it yourself now; you's a messenger, so why don't you go and deliver a message then – we want more."

"Please, Sam… I-I can't leave without this letter." The woman was trying to hold her resolve when Sam suddenly cocked a revolver to her head.

"One thing my *pals* gotta know 'bout me? I don't like havin' to repeat myself. Now me and you was just startin' to hit it off, I reckon, so I'll give you the benefit of the doubt and tell you one more goddamn time – you will leave now and tell this employer o' yours that we want more *or* I will paint the trees right here, right now, with your blood and your brains… You understand, little bird?"

The woman's face had drained of all its colour as she nodded in agreement.

"Good, that's what I thought." Sam lowered the revolver. "Now, time's a waistin', get the hell out of here. Come back in a week – same place, same time."

The woman couldn't get away fast enough. Sam looked around to the gang now.

"All right, same goes for you, sons o' bitches. Get on back to your business and we'll meet again in a week's time."

Michael suddenly piped up, "another fuckin' week, Sam? I thought we'd have seen the back o' this place with money in our pockets by now, I'm sick of here!"

"Listen to me, you little piece of shit; you won't see a damn cent of that money if you open your mouth one more time." Sam was standing off to Michael when the others started to complain as well.

"He's got a point, Sam; it's a little god damn convenient. You's havin' such merriment in this here town, minglin' with the *wrong* kind and suddenly we all have to stay longer, slavin' away like a bunch o' Pickaninnys!" Clayton moaned.

Sam immediately swung around from Michael and in a split second, grasped the back of Clayton's head in one hand and jammed the revolver right into Clayton's mouth with the other. Clayton was now dangerously alarmed at Sam's rage.

"WHAT DID I FUCKIN' SAY ABOUT USING THEM WORDS AROUND ME!" Sam shouted, pressing the gun deeper into Clayton's throat. Bill and Austin moved to try and pull Sam away.

"Either of you motherfuckers takes a step closer, I'll blow his goddamn tongue out the back of his neck." Sam threatened. The men took a moment and backed off.

Sam took a deep breath and slowly removed the revolver from Clayton's mouth as he retched. "You *know* I do not like that kind o' talk."

Sam took a look around the group; everyone quiet now, staring right back, Clayton rubbing his throat. Sam holstered the weapons.

"Listen, y'all need to keep a fuckin' lid on it for just a few more days and if I'm right, which I know I sure as shit am, we'll have the biggest payout we've seen in god damn years. Just quit your complainin' and keep your heads down. Now get the hell out of my sight... Oh, and Clayton?"

"Yeah?"

WHACK! Sam clubbed him with the back of the revolver and split his head open. Clayton fell to the ground, clutching his forehead.

"Count yourself damn fuckin' lucky. I'm inclined to be forgivin' today. Ever speak to me as you did again? I'll kill you right there and then without a second thought."

Chapter 12
Harrison James – US Marshall

Every minute that went by as Harrison waited to meet with Lenora felt longer than the last. His mind was being swallowed by the worrisome thoughts that his affection and faith in Lenora might just be entirely misplaced. Every elated feeling from the last few weeks with her may just come crashing down. Harrison originally went back to the sheriff's office in an attempt to help them and more importantly, to distract himself, but he could not focus his mind.

Harrison instead made his way back to the boarding house and sat on the edge of his bed, waiting. It was nearing twilight and Harrison knew Lenora would be along soon, but he decided he had waited long enough. He was going to see her.

Harrison paced intently over to Calvin's saloon. He barged past the townsfolk littered across the room, straight to the stairs. Just as he made his way to her door, it opened. Lenora was startled to see him.

"Harry! What are… I thought I was comin' to you? You look white as a damn ghost. What's goin' on? You all right?"

"Lenora… I need to talk to you. May I come inside?"

"Well, er… sure, of course… what's goin' on, Harrison?"

Lenora stepped aside as Harrison walked in, avoiding eye contact. Harrison walked over to the window and stared out. He took a deep breath in. Lenora closed the door.

"Lenora, I need to ask you somethin'. I-I will just come right out with it. Do you know anythin' about the Spector gang?"

"What? Where in the hell has this come from?"

Harrison had turned to face her now. Lenora looked rattled, but Harrison couldn't determine if that was from panic or shock.

"Answer the question, Lenora – what do you know about the Spector gang?"

"No, God dammit, you answer my question! What in the hell would make you say somethin' like that to me?"

"Morgan and I have put together a trail of the gang's movements, and for some reason it seems where they go you surely follow… you were right here in Whitepost the last time they attacked?"

"Me and possibly fifty or sixty other folk. What in the hell is wrong with you? Two plus two equals five, is that it?"

"It's certainly a coincidence, and you still haven't answered the question."

"NO! I do not know nothin' about that gang! I can't bear to look at you right now. Get out of my room, Harrison! Now!"

Harrison was starting to feel guilty now. Lenora was visibly distressed. Maybe he'd made a mistake? Maybe it was just a strange coincidence. What the fuck was he thinking? *She travels the West and so does the gang.* Surely they'd be bound to cross paths unknowingly in that case. What if he's ruined things with her when she's done nothing wrong? His head was in a tail spin.

"Lenora, wait, hang on a minute, let me…"

"Let you what? Interrogate me some more? Not a God damn chance. Get out of my room, Harrison. Get out!"

Harrison stepped over and grabbed both of her arms.

"Listen to me!" he said loudly at her!

"What?"

"I'm sorry, all right? I'm sorry! I don't know why I said that. I don't know why I thought that. I really am sorry."

He took his hands off her and she calmed down as well.

"Harrison, are you seein' ghosts around every corner? So I'm a suspect? Maybe the sheriff's a suspect? Maybe even Morgan?"

"Can we just forget about it? You look really beautiful, by the way, if it's any consolation." He lightly smiled at her.

She stared back at him for a moment with no response, until she leaned in finally, and kissed him.

They didn't bother making their way back to Harrison's; they spent the night together there, in Lenora's room. Harrison found sleeping difficult that night. He couldn't say why.

Harrison woke early to the sound of the birds first song. Lenora was still fast asleep beside him, the sun shining down on both of them. It was a rare moment of peace that he could have stayed in for hours. He rolled onto his side to face her. He gently brushed the back of his hand across her face and progressed down her arm. His eyes moved to the dresser beside the bed, where he noticed her poster. The poster she used to advertise her performances in the saloon was a portrait, a stunning likeness to her.

He was admiring it for just a moment when his mind suddenly burst into flames. His heart sank to the bottom of his body and the rage he suddenly felt was engulfing him more and more every second.

In the portrait, Lenora was wearing the same crescent moon pendant Harrison found at the crime scene.

He ripped himself out of the bed and immediately began to dress. Practically tearing his clothes to get them on as fast as possible. Lenora stirred and started to open her eyes and see what the commotion was all about.

"Harry, what..." She yawned. "What's goin' on? Where you goin'? It's first light; what's the rush all of a sudden?"

He ignored her.

"Harry? Harrison! What is goin' on?"

"You lied," he said with a growl in his voice.

"What are you talking ab..."

"Don't fuckin' start with the god damn excuses, Lenora; you lied to me!"

"Jesus Christ, Harrison, I don't even know what you're talkin' about! Is this the same crap from last night? I already told you I ain't involved!"

"Oh, you ain't no? You must take me for a God damn fool... I know you're involved, Lenora, so cut the shit!" Harrison grabbed the poster from the dresser and pointed straight at the pendant. "This here pendant seems mighty familiar; seems to be the very same one you denied any ownership or knowledge of, doesn't it? Now, why would an innocent person lie about such a thing? What the fuck is goin' on here?"

Lenora's face dropped. This time he knew, she wasn't startled by the accusation, almost relieved.

"You are going to get up and get dressed and then, *Miss Taylor*, I will be taking you down to the sheriff's office."

"No, Harrison, please wait a second; let me explain..."

"More lies? I don't have the time, get the hell up and get dressed right God damn now."

"Harrison! Christ, do I mean nothin' to you all of a sudden? I know you ain't so cold now; if nothin' else, will you at least hear what I have to say? You a man of the law; surely you believe that I am at least entitled to defend myself?"

Harrison didn't respond, but he didn't object either.

"Yes, I did lie to you. I am sorry I lied, but I need you to believe me that I had good reasons. I needed to protect myself because if you didn't know me, you would jump to the wrong conclusions. Along with everyone else around here. I did want to tell you the truth about me and my past, but it's very complicated."

"What in the hell are you talkin' about?" Harrison was a little calmer now, somewhat curious about what her reasons could possibly be.

"I don't know nothin' about the gang, but Samuel Walker… I know him."

Chapter 13
Lenora Taylor – Travelling Performer

As Harrison threatened to end everything and drag her down to the sheriff's office, Lenora opened her eyes to how much this man was starting to mean to her. She had been telling herself that it was a bit of fun, a distraction and that she was in complete control. The reality was that when the end became a very real possibility, she felt panicked, agitated and upset – not the emotions you'd expect from someone in total control.

In all her years, Lenora had only ever briefly spoken of her past after she ran away from her parents once. Lenora hated to speak of it. It was something she kept deeply locked away and hidden behind a thick wall of brash confidence and charm, so that nobody would ever see a flicker of her buried heartache. But when Harrison backed her into a corner, she had no choice; she was going to have to tell her story. She was Samuel Walker's ward.

Harrison looked at her in slight disbelief when she told him this.

"What in the hell are you talkin' about, Lenora? You told me 'bout your folks already?" he questioned her.

"Yes, Harrison, I told you about those pieces of shit, but I didn't tell you what happened after I ran away."

Harrison sat at the end of the bed, ready to listen but still keeping a distance from her.

Lenora started at the beginning, the first night she spent alone in the woods after leaving her parents' home, about three years before the war. Lenora had no money, no supplies, no nothing except the clothes on her back and the shoes on her feet. She was a strong girl, yes, but the wilderness of New Mexico Territory, without any means of protection or sustenance, would create fear in the most able-bodied man.

It was getting dark, and Lenora needed to find somewhere safe enough to sleep where she could hopefully light a fire and try not to freeze to death on day one of her independence. She managed to accomplish this after what felt like hours of roaming. She came across a small cave, so small it was more like a large hollowed-out boulder. This would, at least, keep her protected. She then set out to find kindling and flint to get a fire going while there was still a sliver of light breaking through the trees. Before long, however, she began hearing threatening sounds. Sounds of a nasty carnivore looking for his next meal. She tried to hide, but the noises were getting closer and closer. By now, it was almost fully dark, with only the moon's light offering a glimpse into the shadowy forest. Lenora had placed herself behind a tree, praying that she would be okay, when suddenly she stepped on a twig and the crack seemed to echo across the night. She looked across from her, no more than ten yards, and saw the massive set of vicious teeth reflecting the moon's beam, lowly growling. A fucking grizzly.

She ran. She knew now that was the worst thing she could have done, but it was pure instinct. The bear thrashed through the woods after her. She sprinted as fast as her legs could move her. By the time the bear had given up the chase, it felt like she had been running for a lifetime. Lenora was scratched, bruised and bleeding from forcing her way through the undergrowth of the woods.

She was struggling to catch her breath; she collapsed down by a tree and eventually passed out. At some point, the cold of the night woke her up and within five minutes of opening her eyes, she began to hear the howls of a grey wolf. This wolf sounded closer than she cared to hang around for, so she had to get moving again.

It seemed like every time she stopped for just a moment of respite, the woods would remind her she was not welcome. By the time morning's light came, she was frozen, hungry, exhausted, battered and bruised. Her dress ripped in twenty places. She dropped down onto an old tree stump and began to cry. Was this truly going to be any way better than her life before? How would she survive another night? She couldn't bear the thought of returning to her parents' home, but what choice did she have? She would want to die there, but she *would* die here.

Just then she heard a gentle voice call out – it was a man.

"'scuse me, miss, you all right? Would you like some help? If you don't mind me sayin' so, you look like you's been through hell."

She immediately wiped her eyes and looked up. Although she was nervous now, alone in the woods with a stranger, she could not help but notice those eyes. The kindest eyes she had or would ever see. It was Samuel Walker.

After a while of convincing her that he genuinely just wanted to help, he took her back to his small cabin. It was a ways walk before they got there, but he had a fresh rabbit in his hand, so she decided it was worth it for a hot meal and a soft bed to sleep in for a few hours.

During the walk back, they got to chatting. She was reserved in revealing any details about herself, but he didn't pry. He was kind, funny and pleasant company. Once they arrived at the cabin in the mountains out by Wolf's Pass, Samuel showed Lenora an old chest of his late mother's clothing that she could change into should she like, a basin of fresh water to freshen up with and clean her scrapes and a bed to lay down on. When she was good and ready, he said she could come outside and join him for vittles. Lenora slept for hours – the best sleep she'd had in years.

When she woke up, the aroma of the cooking rabbit was sweet heaven. It was absolutely delicious. Samuel offered to let Lenora stay as long as she liked or needed, but Lenora's first reaction was to be suspicious.

"What is it exactly you want from me, Mr Walker? I don't wanna be in nobody's debt. Now I appreciate the rest and the meal, but I reckon I should be on my way."

"I don't want nothin' from you, Lenora; you may stay for as long as you like or leave whenever you like. The choice is entirely yours."

"What's in it for you, huh? Why would you help me then if you ain't gettin' nothin' in return?"

Samuel looked at her for a moment and sighed.

"I live here alone in this here cabin. I have been alone for many years since my mother died. I am an outcast and for the most part, I accepted that my life would have to be a solitary one. But when I saw you crying in those woods and you looked back at me, I could see very clearly that, although in a different way, you are an outcast too."

"How could you possibly know that?"

"Because why else would a girl like you run from your home, spend a night in those woods and speak to a man like me as an equal… because you're different."

They continued their conversation and Lenora decided to stay another night. And another. And another.

After some time had passed, the two became thick as thieves. Sam came to love her as a daughter and she came to love him as the father she had always wished for. He loved her independent spirit; he encouraged her curiosity and intelligence; and he enjoyed her quick wit. Samuel Walker never once treated her with disrespect, nor did she. They lived off the land around their isolated little cabin, hunting, fishing and growing a few crops where they could. Just the two of them. And Lenora loved every single second of it. This was her home, and he was her family.

Seven years went by, Lenora had grown to be a woman of twenty-three years and the war was over. Lenora woke on a warm summer's morning, the 1st of June 1865. She wrote in her journal that it was going to be a special day. It was Samuel's birthday, and she was planning a real treat! She rode into a nearby town to sell some rabbits and other goods at the general store and use the money to purchase him something lovely as a gift. She had never been to town before, and she found it very exciting. She couldn't help but peek her head into each of the establishments dotted across the town. Chuckle at the different characters she could overhear as they went about their business. She eventually had a peruse in the general store and left with everything she needed to make Sam a delicious sweet potato pie.

Sam was stunned when she produced the delicious treat. He was grateful but also nervous that she might have been followed back, Sam did not want anyone to know where they lived.

"Would you stop your worryin'? It was just a one-time treat! It's a special day and I just wanted you to know how much you mean to me."

"You don't have to do all this for me to know that. I just want us to be safe."

"Hush your whinin' and eat your pie!" She smiled.

The two sat around the fire late into the night, wrapped in blankets, as Lenora told Sam all about the happenings in town she had witnessed that day, all the newest trinkets and knick-knacks they had for sale. The newest fashion for men and women. All of a sudden, they heard voices.

Sam immediately jumped up and put the fire out, but they had been found.

"Well, now it's a little late for that now, isn't it, hmm? We seen the smoke from a ways out," sneered the first man as he cleared the trees.

"We seen this little dark-haired beauty sneaking about the town and just *had* to know where she'd been hidin' – ain't never seen her around 'fore now." The second man smirked as he emerged behind the other.

Finally, a third man came through. Each of them sweatier, uglier and drunker than the last. The third man spoke up.

"What we didn't expect is that she'd be holding out up here with some uppity nigger."

Lenora and Sam were frozen still in the first moment, trying to calculate their next move. Sam was then trying to stand in front of her, but it was no good; she was never one to cower behind anyone.

"What do you want, huh? Go back home to your families, you drunk pieces o' shit, ain't a damn thing for you here!" Lenora demanded.

"Oooohwee! Looky here, fellas, looks like we got ourselves a live one!" The second man sniggered.

The first man then walked right up to her and spoke, his breath stinking of moonshine.

"Now what in the hell would make you think a nigger lovin' bitch like yourself is makin' any demands, hmm? If I was you I'd sit your ass down while I decide what to do with you."

Lenora didn't move.

"You testin' my patience now, gal. You best sit down or so help me, God, I *will* teach you a lesson." He glared at her.

Sam couldn't help himself; he was so terrified the men would hurt her, so he spoke up.

"Sir, you and your men here are free to take whatever you want from my cabin; any food, drink… any… anything of value, it's yours and then you can be on your way, and we won't be bothering you no more. Just please don't hurt the girl; she's just passing through here."

The third man cocked a pistol and pointed it right at Samuel's temple.

"Well, now it seems to me the item of value might be you yourself, nigger. I'd bet some family out there would pay for the return o' their property. I reckon we should take you with us; one of you hand me some rope!" he slurred.

Lenora shouted before she took a second to think.

"NO! You cannot do that; he ain't nobody's slave; he's a free man. God dammit, don't you touch him, motherfuckers!"

WHACK! The first man cracked the back of his hand across her face with all of his force and she fell to the ground.

She heard Sam protest immediately and the second and third man began to beat him mercilessly. Lenora tried to come to her feet and go to Sam's aid with blood gushing from her nose when the first man grabbed her aggressively by the arms.

"Albert, Nathaniel, show that son of a bitch what happens to a nigger with attitude! And as for you, *whore*…" He pulled Lenora in close. "I'll show you what we do to slave-lovin' sinners like you."

Lenora knew what he meant. She started viciously struggling to get out of his grip. She could still see Sam almost beaten to a pulp on the hard ground. Blood all over him, swollen and bruised – wheezing for breath.

She kicked and hit this man, but he beat her back. He threw her to the ground, face first. She mustered every ounce of will she had to try and scramble away, clawing her hands into the dirt as fast as she could. He dragged her back by her dress and ripped it open at the back. She screamed as hard as her lungs would carry and tried once again to kick her way away from this man.

BANG! The second man, Albert, kicked her right in the head. She was delirious, lying face down in the filth. Her vision was foggy, with blood dripping from her head. She was losing this fight.

"You can scream all you like, bitch; ain't nobody comin' t' save *you,*" sneered the third man, Nathaniel.

"Please… don't do this." She quietly sobbed. "I ain't done nothin' to nobody."

Nathaniel and Albert laughed and the first man thrust himself inside her. He was brutal, feral, and cruel. Just as Lenora felt she was living through hell itself, the man leaned in and whispered.

"Now don't you act like you ain't enjoyin' it."

The first man finished raping her, but it was not over. The second man then had his turn. Then the third man after him.

By the time, the third ugly, sweaty and foul man was almost done with her, she had become numb. She could no longer feel the banging, throbbing headache from her head injury. She could no longer feel the deep bruises around her abdomen from the beatings she received in between. She could no longer feel the sharp and intense pain from her body ripping as each man forced their way inside her. All she could feel was the deepest and most profound sadness she could ever fathom as she lay on the ground. Across from her, no more than four or five yards, the man she loved as a father was lying in a heap on the ground, looking right back at her. The last thing she saw before falling unconscious was a tear falling from his one open eye.

As Lenora recalled this story, for the first time ever, she could not help but relive the emotions of it and began to cry – an angry cry. It felt like something she had bottled and sealed up a long time ago was now flooding out of her. Harrison sat silent and stunned. He then moved in close to her and embraced her as tight as he could. He didn't say anything, but she could feel his profound sorrow for her.

After a few minutes, when Lenora had regained her composure a little, she pushed him off.

"You don't need to mollycoddle me, Harry. It was a long time ago; I'm fine," she said as she defiantly wiped tears from her eyes.

Harrison spoke.

"Did the law ever catch those animals?"

"No, but *Sam* did."

Chapter 14
Harrison James – US Marshall

Harrison was knocked for six after hearing Lenora's story, horrified at what this woman had to endure. A lady of any standing deserved respect as far as he was concerned and for Lenora to be treated as she had been was vicious. Harrison had never seen this side of Lenora… wounded, vulnerable. It made him feel so angry, but he didn't want to lose his composure.

All of his personal feelings were those of fury and rage. He was stunned by what she had just told him. He sat silent, staring at her, trying to process it. Trying to understand it. Trying not to lose his head. He took a deep breath. He didn't really know what to say, but he knew he had to say something. He swallowed, cleared his throat, and said as calmly as he could,

"Len, I am so sorry for what those sons of whores did to you. I hope they rot in hell."

She raised her eyes and looked intently at him. He stared back at her, but he knew that there was still something that she hadn't quite explained. He knew now was not the time to ask, but at that moment, he needed the truth from her. He took her hands in his and in a quiet, gentle tone of voice, he said, "Lenora, forgive me now, but what you've told me does not explain why you lied about the pendant? Or how it came to be where it was when I found it?"

"I'm gettin' to that." She sighed.

After Lenora had fallen unconscious, the men had tied her up and placed her on the back of one of their horses. Probably because they were drunk or stupid or both, they hadn't done a very good job of restraining her. When Lenora came to, she was dangling over the backside of the second man's horse, still a little hazy, but she could hear them slurring to each other, laughing, drinking out of some hipflasks. She knew these woods like the back of her hand by now having roamed them for years with Samuel, so she could tell she was about a mile or two from the cabin. The men were too drunk to notice her squirm her way out of her bonds; it was only when her body dropped to the ground they noticed the loud 'thump' and turned around.

"Well, shitfire! She got loose! Nathaniel, get after her!" the first man shouted.

Lenora had already scrambled to her feet and began to sprint away, as fast as her very first night in this mountainous forest. She didn't want to lead them back to the cabin for fear that they'd give Sam another beating, so she had a better idea; she would lead them to a known grizzly den.

Nathaniel and Albert were chasing her on their horses, but the forest was becoming too dense for them to keep up, so they dropped down on foot. Lenora was a ways in front of them. She reached the den, prayed the bear was in it, picked up a large stone and threw it right in. She heard the bear's low growl and she dragged herself up a tree right beside the bear's dwelling. High enough to be out of sight when she started calling out to the men.

"Why don't you come and finish me off, you dirty motherfuckers? I'm up here, waitin', you sons o' bitches! Come find me!" she shouted from the treetop across the night.

The men emerged from the vegetation below and almost immediately, as though it were divine intervention, the bear emerged from his den, infuriated. The two men absolutely shit themselves with fear and ran for their lives, with the big, bad grizzly giving chase.

As soon as she could, she descended the tree and ran to the cabin, desperate to make sure Samuel was all right, but when she got there, it was too late. Samuel had gone.

Lenora was trying to contain the deep emotion at recalling this tragedy.

"Once I realised he was gone, I was devastated. My entire life had been torn apart in one evenin'. My innocence, my happiness and my family had been ripped from me. Samuel had left his pendant; his mother gave it to him – the crescent moon – and I took it. I wanted something of his to carry with me always." She sniffled as she stubbornly refused to allow herself to cry again.

"Why was it by the road then?" Harrison gently asked.

"After I heard *The Phantom* Walker had been out near Whitepost and I knew what happened, I went out to the scene. I don't really know why I just wanted to see. I don't know." She took a deep breath. "I was standin' there, asking myself if Sam had any good left in him… If God could forgive a person like that someday, if he knew why they did the things they did, anyway, while I was there, I must have dropped the pendant. I hadn't realised I'd lost it until after you and Morgan arrived in town. I rode out to find it, but by the time I got there, you had already found it."

"And so you lied because you was afraid I'd accuse you?" Harrison confusedly quizzed.

"You didn't know me then; you wouldn't have taken my word for it. I panicked."

"Len, you should have just told me the truth; it would have saved a lot of trouble."

"What and tell you about the worst night of my whole life when I barely knew your first name? Nobody knows that, okay. Nobody. I'm trusting you now to keep it to yourself. Please."

"I won't tell nobody, Len."

Lenora took another deep breath. "Harrison, I-I have a complicated history. More than you know still, but I want you to know, truly, I… you really do mean somethin' to me… and I am sorry."

"What are you sorry for?" He sweetly smiled.

"I'm just sorry for who I am."

Harrison pulled her in close to hug her tightly once more, kissing her forehead. He became overwhelmed with an almost instinctual need to protect her, to comfort her… to be with her always. In this moment, he was coming to a profound realisation – something he had never felt for a woman before – and it was engulfing him faster than he could control.

"Don't be sorry… I can't believe it myself, but… I *love* you for who you are."

Lenora didn't respond. Instead, her eyes watered a little before looking down.

"I wanna' ask one more question though, if you don't mind? It's to do with those men you mentioned."

"Yeah?"

"I'm nearly sure a name or two came up in some of the letters myself and Morgan received in the days previous. You said Albert and Nathaniel, and I am sorry for imposin' on you to recall this night yet again, but did you happen to get the final piece o' shit's name?"

"Wayne. I heard one of those shitheads mention it when I were strapped to the horse." Lenora paused for a moment before asking Harrison a final question on the matter.

"Do you… do *you* know what exactly Sam did to those men?"

"I didn't look too much into it at the time; those names had no significance to me before now and Morgan has been reviewin' the letters in detail. I'll look into it, though… Is that something you would like to know? Although I gotta' tell you, Len, I don't think you wanna' hear it… From what I've heard, the Sam you knew sounds like he's long gone, this man now he's… he's twisted. Ruthless."

Lenora seemed ever so slightly agitated by his remark. A fire in her eyes.

"Well, maybe he wouldn't have to be twisted and *ruthless* if life had o' dealt him a kinder hand."

"I'm not tryin' to upset you, Lenora; I'm just givin' you a fair warnin' that I don't know that you'd benefit from hearin' about such things."

Lenora paused again before responding, looking at Harrison deeply in his eyes now.

"You're right, Harry; don't bother diggin' up old news. I don't want to hear about it and their ain't no use in you trifflin' through history either; it won't help you find him anyway, so what's the point? Let's just talk about somethin' different now. I'm tired of this kind o' talk."

Harrison wanted to cheer her up a little, so he decided to drop the topic, but in the back of his mind, all of this information was swirling around. It was almost overwhelming with the mix of emotions he was feeling. Angry that those animals had violated the woman he was in love with, saddened they had robbed her of the dreams she might have held for herself back then, but also confused… confused and conflicted about his feelings. He really realised now that he loved this woman, but she has a direct connection with one of the most notorious criminals the West has ever seen. She even seemed to hold sympathy for him, despite *all* his wrongdoing. He knew Lenora was a good person; he could see it in her eyes, but he could not silence that voice in his head. That voice that had guided him for years to being the decorated US Marshall he was. If she is this closely connected to the man he is hunting, could he really trust her?

As God was his witness, he truly hoped so.

Chapter 15
Morgan James – Deputy Marshall

Morgan didn't usually worry about his brother, but when Harry left the sheriff's office the day before, something was off about him. He wasn't himself at all and Morgan knew him well enough to know something was wrong.

Harrison hadn't shown up to the sheriff's office first thing the next morning either, knowing they had work to do. Morgan knew something was amiss. He took a stab at asking the sloppy old sheriff if he knew anything.

"Hey, Sheriff, you haven't seen the Marshall about the place, have you?"

"I ain't seen him since he was here yesterday. No. Wait, I did see him I think, last night at Calvin's." He slurred.

"I did not see him there; when was this you say you saw him?"

"Um, I'm not exactly sure. It was near midnight, I reckon, dark outside anyway. He was only there long enough for a passin' glance. Barged right through everyone and up them stairs. That was the last I seen of him"

"He didn't come down again?"

"Not to my recollection."

"Right, okay, thank you, Sheriff; I'll go see if I can find him."

"He's probably with that, *er*, Lenora," the sheriff muttered under his breath with a cheekiness to his tone.

"What was that, sir? What exactly do you mean?"

"I mean, your brother was more'n likely just *burnin' the midnight oil* with that woman. Maybe he has just forgotten his duties this mornin'."

"Forgotten his duties? You step outta' line, sir. I ask you to watch your tone when you are speakin' about the Marshall!"

"Simmer down, boy, ain't nothin' to get all twisted up over. I just mean it's easy to lose track o' time when you payin' a visit to a woman like th'…"

At that exact moment, the office door slammed open, with Harrison standing in the doorway.

"A woman like what? Sheriff?" He said it with a thread of anger in his tone.

"Nothin' Marshall… I was just sayin' to your boy here that…"

"My *boy* here is US Deputy Marshall Morgan James and you *will* address him as such. With regards to my personal connections to any folk around here? Well, that ain't yours or anyone else's God damn business, so if I were you, *Sheriff*, I would keep my mind on the work at hand."

The sheriff gave a nod and looked down at his desk, fussing about with papers in a poor attempt to seem busy. Harrison turned to Morgan, and lowered his voice.

"Morgan, I need a word in the back room here."

"Harrison, what's goin' on? You all right? Where you been? You seemed out of sorts when you left yesterday."

"I was… come into the back room, I'll explain everythin'."

The two brothers went into the small back room, more like a large broom cupboard, to discuss matters. Harrison told Morgan a short summary of what Lenora had confided to him – the attack she suffered and her connection to Sam Walker.

"Jesus H. Christ, Harrison… She… She's *The Phantom's* daughter!"

"Keep your damn voice down, Morgan! Not by blood, she ain't, but… I believe she feels for him as a father, yes."

"What in the hell are you gonna' do? What should we do? Jesus, I can't believe this." Morgan was staring blankly at the ground for a moment, trying to process this revelation before he looked back up to his older brother, "Harrison, you love 'er, don't you?"

"That ain't got nothin' t…"

"Harrison! Mary, Mother of Jesus, come on now. It's me you talkin' to. I know you better'n anyone. God dammit, don't go givin' me any crap or avoidin' the question. I ain't a child no more; you said it yourself! I *know* you love 'er. You might not even think I know what love is, but I do, and I can see it in you… same way our pa looked at momma every damn day. But you need to get your stubborn head out of the clouds now and realise just how dangerous an entanglement with a woman like that might be. For all we know, Sam'll come lookin' for her in the night!"

"I have everythin' under control, Morgan. I don't…"

"No, Harrison! Listen t' me." Morgan grabbed the left lapel of Harrison's jacket in an attempt to convey the seriousness of the situation. "I know you got a few years on me, but you ain't thinkin' straight now. For once, it's my God damn turn to be the voice of reason." Morgan was now looking intently at his brother, with genuine and deep concern. "Watch. Your. Step."

"Morgan, I know y'…" Harrison sighed. "Look here, I'll admit my feelin's for her are true, and it was never somethin' I intended… But make no mistake, I still know what I'm here to do. I'm gonna' find that son of a bitch and deliver him straight to the hangman."

"What about Lenora, then? You think she might have somethin' to say about you hangin' her daddy? I'm tellin' you, Harrison, how is this gonna work?"

"Lenora is an intelligent woman. She knows why I'm here and she ain't once asked me to spare his life. I think she may have loved him as a father once, but at the end of it all, he abandoned her. She knows he's got a rotten core. He don't care 'bout her or nobody."

"Rotten core, don't half cover it, those fellas you mentioned? The ones that attacked Lenora? They came up in some of the letters we got back from other towns over. I think they was the first three people Sam ever killed. It was… pfft… I mean, Jesus, they was bad men in themselves, but… Sam Walker sure wasn't waitin' for

God to judge 'em put it that way. Morgan leaned back on the small window ledge with his arms folded.

"What did he do to them?" Harrison was looking stern now.

"I mean, he butchered 'em. One by one… No, you know what, honestly, butcherin' ain't even right, 'cause a butcher would have left most of the body intact."

Harrison stood forward now, and for the first time, Morgan could see an unfamiliar and unwelcome change in his brother. Harrison was always controlled and contained in his emotions, but now Morgan could see a fleck of twisted anger in the older James' brother that worried him. It was subtle. So subtle that maybe nobody else in the world would have noticed, but Morgan could see it.

"Morgan, what did Sam do to them? Tell me exactly," Harrison repeated.

"Well, the first two you mentioned, um, Albert and Nathaniel? I think they were cousins. Albert and Nathanial Calhoun. Sam… Sam killed Albert first, from what the letters say. I ain't sure on the details of how he captured him, but he managed to get a hold of him anyways and rode off to a secluded part o' the railroad. He, uh… he tied Albert to the tracks and well, witnesses from the train said Sam Walker sat right there on his horse and watched the train rip open the man's body, sprayin' all his parts into the dirt below."

"And what about Nathaniel?" asked Harrison.

"You really wanna know abou'…"

"Tell me, Morgan!"

"Jesus, all right... Nathaniel was drinkin' at some bar round abouts where they lived and supposedly Sam went in there posed as a... a farmer or some such, I can't remember exactly, but he told Nathaniel that his wife had taken ill in a field near the house, and he needed to get out to her right away. The man was drunk as ever, so I suppose he didn't find any reason to be suspicious of the tall tale. Nathaniel followed Sam and a co-conspirator into the night to an isolated field and uh, from what the local law could tell, he got his leg clamped in a bear trap and was blown up."

"What do you mean, blown up?"

"They found a detonator and some wire buried underground. Seems like... I don't know Sam and whoever was with him managed to walk this fella over a bear trap, then blew him up with some dynamite buried below. They found nothin' but a leg and guts splattered half a mile across the land with a note sayin' *Love From Sam*.'"

Harrison didn't react, just waited for the final story.

"The last man... uh, Wayne? Wayne Westerfield was his name. The Westerfield family was pretty well off; Wayne Westerfield's pa was close personal friends with the Texas Governor at the time, Governor Hamilton. I don't know how he managed to get into the Westerfield home without a soul seein', but Wayne was found lyin' dead in his bed and he... uh..." Morgan choked up a little. "When the sheriff of his town found him, his neck had a knife stickin' out of it... blood everywhere and..."

"And what?"

"His dick was cut off and shoved in his mouth."

The two brothers were silent for a moment until Harrison spoke up.

"And they were sure this was Sam, how?"

"Another letter, '*Love From Sam*'."

"I see."

"You don't seem all too bothered by this, Harrison? This dirty bastard is a ruthless son of a bitch and you ain't so much as twitched as I'm tellin' you about your woman's daddy cuttin' and blowin' up folk?"

"Why would I be bothered, Morgan? You said it your damn self, these were bad men. Three less piece's o' shit in the world ain't no skin off my back."

"I don't suppose you ever heard the expression two wrongs don't make a right?" Morgan was getting a little uneasy about Harrison's behaviour now.

"Don't lecture me brother you know there's some truth in it, three less cocksuckers for us to chase down."

"What in the God damn hell are you talking about, Harrison? You a lawman? WE ARE LAWMEN! You – I know you! You walk, talk and breathe the law! Since when do you see Judge, Jury and Executioner beholdin' to one man? There was a time when I might have thought that way, but not you! What in the hell has gotten into you?"

Harrison sighed. "I'm sorry, brother… I don't know why, of course you're right – the law is the law. Can't have no God damn lynch mob mentality."

Morgan looked to his brother and somehow knew, despite what Harrison was saying, that he had changed somehow, couldn't quite put his finger on it, couldn't quite say what it was, but it was there. He decided, however, to let the topic go, for now.

"Right… look, anyway, we're gettin' off topic here. Where do we go from here? I don't suppose Lenora gives you any leads on Sam?" quizzed Morgan.

"Not much of a lead, but she mentioned an old cabin where she lived with Sam, near Wolf's Pass. It ain't much, but we might find somethin'… I reckon it's worth a look."

"Ain't no harm in it. That's about a day or more ride from here at least; you gonna' tell Lenora we headin' out there."

"No, I don't wanna' bring up the whole thing again with her. I think it would only serve to distress her now. I'll just let her know we're followin' up on a lead out o' town. And Morgan? Keep what I've told you to yourself. Ain't nobody else needs to know for now." Harrison nodded towards the door to the sheriff sitting in the next room.

"You have my word. We ridin' out first thing tomorrow?"

"Yeah, at first light."

"I'll get on over to the general store for a few provisions."

Harrison nodded to his younger brother and the two men left the back room. Morgan could see the sheriff eyeing him suspiciously before leaning back into his chair and placing his hat over his eyes. Maybe the old coot wasn't as dumb and drunk as everyone took him for.

Morgan was pacing down the street, mulling over things in his mind. He was becoming fearful that his beloved brother, the last of his family, was getting wrapped up in bad business and was too blinded by a woman to see it. Was he losing his damn mind? The Harrison he knew should have immediately cut ties with Lenora as soon as he knew about her past connections. But the Harrison he knew had never been in love.

God dammit… Why her?

Chapter 16
Sam Walker – Notorious Outlaw

Sam awoke on that fine summer's morning to a note passed under the door. It seemed as though the gang had taken notice that the Marshall and his deputy had left town on business and there was potential for a train job.

The note was from Adelita. She overheard in the whorehouse some wealthy banker or such was going to be travelling back to the city after closing off a *big deal*. Adelita's thinking: big pay-out. In the note, she asked Sam to meet with the gang that afternoon to make arrangements – highly irregular, but Sam had to be smart about this. The gang was getting very uneasy of late and Sam needed to contain any doubts they might have brewing.

Sam, this time, was not the first one to arrive at the meeting point in the woods. The gang was all there, waiting. Sam dismounted and walked to the centre of the group.

"Well, do I have somethin' on my face? What the fuck are y'all lookin' at me like that for huh?" Sam snapped.

"We wasn't sure you'd show," sneered Bill.

"Watch your damn tone, boy," Sam retorted.

"You got Lita's note? 'bout the train?" questioned Javier.

"Yeah, I got the note. Are y'all out of your fuckin' minds? Another job here? The god damn federal law is in town or have you forgotten?"

"They're not here right now," said Michael.

"That ain't the fuckin' point, you dumb shit, we can't attract attention to ourselves before we get our money from *the woman* – it ain't worth it!"

"We could have had *el dinero* already, but you sent her off! *¡esto es una mierda!*" yelled Javier.

Sam had some of the fastest hands in the West, but not fast enough to grab either revolver before Clayton and Bill snatched them right out of their holsters. They planned this. Sam stared at them in venom-fuelled disbelief. Were these motherfuckers actually going to attempt a double cross? How dare they? What the hell was going on?

"What in God's fuckin' name do you think you're doin'? Gimme' my guns back RIGHT FUCKIN' NOW." Sam whipped a hunting blade out and threatened the two men in a state of pure anger… and panic.

Austin spoke directly to Sam now.

"No, for once you's gonna' listen to us. We're tired of bein' here, we should've been long gone by now, enjoyin' our spoils, but you keep us here workin' like God damn slaves. We're tired o' this, Sam."

"You'll regret takin' those weapons, motherfuckers."

"You still ain't even listenin'! Jesus H. Christ, Sam! The others ain't got the stomach to say nothin' to you 'cause they reckon you'd cut their tongues out for lookin' at you funny, but we's all thinkin' the same thing!"

"You all mighty brave now that I ain't got my guns, huh? Enlighten me here, Austin. What exactly is it you's all thinkin' 'bout me, hmm?" Sam stepped right up to Austin now, staring him dead in the eye, knife still in hand.

"Your *personal* relationships 'round here… we think you's goin' soft. You's gettin' a little too cosy with the law, Sam. We don't like it. *I* don't like it."

Just as Sam went to lunge at Austin for his outrageously audacious slander, Bill cocked Sam's own, personally engraved revolver and pointed it right in their direction.

"You can plunge that knife right into my neck, Sam, but I promise you, Bill will kill you right after… I know you're smarter 'n that."

The entire gang paused while Sam stopped to weigh up the options. The tension in the air had almost frozen time. Austin sighed and spoke again.

"Sam, I been with you since the beginnin'. We know you ain't led us wrong before, but you ain't right this time. You got your fuckin' head in the clouds. We agreed to wait for more money, like you said, and for your sake, I *do* hope it pays off. But you're gonna' do what we want now. There's potential for a fine haul on this here train that Lita heard 'bout and we want it all. Them Marshalls is out o' town. No better opportunity."

Sam stared him down for another minute before responding.

"Well, shit you know what? When we end up strapped in the God damn hangman's noose after this? I'll be sure to kindly remind you of this bright fuckin' idea in the forsaken pits of hell!"

"Are you in or are you out?" asked Bill.

The worry was setting in for Sam now; this was bold. Too bold. Sam needed to weigh up the options here. Maybe in this instance, revenge was a dish best served cold. Sam would have to agree to go along with this ridiculous plan for now.

Sam looked at each of the gang members now. "For each o' *your* God damn sake, *this* better pay off."

Tempers of the group finally calmed, and Sam set the gang their tasks to prepare for the robbery. They needed to plan the route to get there, plan to jump on the damn thing and plan the route to get the hell out of there. They would need to work efficiently to work their way through the carriages in the shortest amount of time.

Sam was nervous. Careful not to show even a sliver of it, but the feeling was there all the same. The gang had never challenged Sam's decisions like this before. They had never been so bold and that was out of fear, but that fear seemed to be growing less and less by the day. The more they believed Sam was losing touch, 'going soft', the bolder they would become. That could not happen. Six assholes against one was a fight that would surely end fatally for the one. Sam had to do this. Leadership had to be restored in full, but this was far, far more impulsive and downright risky than any other job, Sam was nervous that this might end up being the last one.

Death himself would be watching now, eager to see if Sam would manage to cheat him once more.

The train would be leaving Whitepost late that evening. There was an isolated spot a couple of miles out they would make their move at, the train would slow just enough on a bend for them to jump on. They needed to get moving fast now if they were to make it on time, the spot in question was a few hours ride out of town.

They got to the planned location on time. The train would be coming any minute. All of them except Adelita and Michael would be boarding the train, those two would follow the train down the tracks with the rest of the horses so they could make their getaway afterwards. The train was in sights, bandanas up over their faces – it was time to go.

Sam and the boys rode hard and fast along the train and, just like times before, made a successful leap onto the flatcar. They made their way through the train – Javier, Bill and Clayton were to clean house in the normal passenger cars. They would take any and all cash, jewellery… anything of value. Sam and Austin would head straight for the private, first-class cabin reserved by the wealthy banker.

Sam and Austin arrived at the door of the luxurious passenger car, the inside filled with lavish and ornate décor, upholstered chairs, curtains, and carpets. Sitting at a desk, a foot away from the safe they had their eyes on, was the banker. The banker had gone white and spilled his inkwell across himself and his desk in fright, now that the outlaws had come for him.

Austin spoke first, putting his hand on the handle of his holstered weapon.

"Don't you move from that seat there now, ya hear? We got ourselves some business to conduct."

"Oh, my… sweet Jesus… y… you're them, ain't ya? You're them! The Spector Gang! Please, oh God, no… no, please… I don't wanna die!" The banker's voice trembled as he tried to piece a sentence together.

Sam stepped forward now, right up to the desk, and aimed a revolver right at the man's crotch.

"P… please, Mr Walker. I'm beggin' ya, don't do this I…"

"Shut your mouth. I don't wanna' hear your damn squakin'! You will only speak when I ask you a direct question: You got that cocksucker?"

"Oh my God… Y… you're a…"

"WHAT DID I JUST SAY, GOD DAMMIT?" Sam whacked the man in the head with the back of the gun. He fell to the floor, clutching his head.

"Now, as I was sayin'. We heard tell you been doin' good business back in Whitepost, closed off a nice deal for yourself, hmm? Well, that's *our* nice deal now. Open the safe!"

"Okay, I will, please don't hurt me!"

"OPEN THE SAFE!" Sam roared.

The banker clambered to his feet, stumbled over to the safe, entered the combination and opened it. Austin cocked his gun and prepared to shoot the man before Sam stopped him.

"Wait! Hold your damn fire. I need to see what's in this safe first, gotta make sure he ain't holdin' out on us."

Austin lowered his weapon and Sam walked over to review the safe's contents. First glance revealed a number of gold bars, maybe about twenty or so, with a bill of sale sitting on top for what was left of the Laudergill estate.

"This it? This everything?" Sam spoke directly to the banker.

"Y… yes."

"Son of a bitch! This ain't worth my damn time! You better not be hidin' the rest of your riches elsewhere, you little motherfucker!" Sam was pointing the gun right at the man's head now.

At that moment, Javier, Bill and Clayton burst into the room.

"We gotta go, boss!" said Clayton.

Sam was looking at the three of them in disbelief.

"Is each of you deaf or just collectively stupid? I told you to take out everyone in the cab and stop the fuckin' train. How you expect us to get off? Two of you get your ass up there NOW! And you two grab the bars out of that safe."

Austin and Clayton ran off to the front cab of the train, Javier and Bill had sacks full of loot taken from the passengers, which they were now transferring the gold bars into. Sam spoke to the banker once more, the gun still aimed right at him.

"I'm gonna' ask you one more time now; where is the rest of it?"

"That's it, I swear! That's all there is; I bought property with the rest of it; I ain't have no reason to lie to you!"

Just as Sam was about to squeeze the trigger and put the man out of his misery, he dropped to his knees, hands clasped together and made one final, desperate plea for his life.

"Please, PLEASE, I am begging you, don't kill me! I won't say nothin' to nobody; please don't do it; I have a family!"

Sam was very agitated by now; for the first time in years, something very strange and unwelcome was happening. Just for a moment, Sam's conscience was acting up. The sudden and awful feeling of guilt swirled around like a typhoon inside. Sam must have killed at least fifty men over the years and never batted an eye. Why now? Why was the look in this man's eyes as he pleaded for his life different from all others before him?

"Shut the hell up, god dammit, I don't wanna fuckin' hear it!"

"Please, PLEASE! My wife is with child; we're gonna' start a family! I can't leave her to be a widow; I'm begging you to have mercy!" The man sobbed.

The train came to a sudden halt and Javier and Bill were now looking to Sam in confusion. "What in the hell are you waitin' for? Blow his head off!" said Bill.

Just then, the gang looked out of the train carriage window to see a bloody train driver riding off at high speed on one of their horses, he had gotten away from Austin and Clayton. Michael and Adelita were firing at him outside the train, but he was too far out of range.

"*¡Mierda!* We gotta go! Now! He'll have the law after us!" Javier shouted!

"Shit!" Sam exclaimed right before Bill shot the banker in the head.

They grabbed their loot and got the hell off the train. They rode as fast as they could for about two hours before reaching their pre-planned meeting point. Sam could not stop thinking about the man that had just died for the entire journey there.

Adelita started arguing with Austin and Clayton immediately.

"What is the matter with you two, huh? Couldn't manage one lousy train driver? *¡perras estúpidas!*" she shouted.

"Shut the hell up, bitch; you couldn't kill him either!" Clayton snapped.

"*¡Cállate bastardo!* You won't talk to my sister like that and live *hombre*!" Javier shouted before punching Clayton in the face.

"Jesus Christ, SHUT THE HELL UP!" Sam roared above all of them. "We ain't here for three seconds and y'all gotta tear each other up. Cut the shit right now! Open them, God damn bags and tell me how much money we got outta this."

Javier and Clayton had a scuffle for a moment before settling down. The gang trifled through their loot, gold bars included; they had only hauled about $1,500. They were not happy.

"What a God damn joke. Tall fuckin' tales from that piece o' horse shit bank man… 'a big deal' my ass… I would not have gotten out of my bed for less than five thousand!" exclaimed Austin.

"That rider that got away – he see any o' your faces?" asked Sam.

"Nah, we had 'em covered the whole time; he didn't see shit," Michael replied.

"Good, fucker got away, but at least he didn't see nothin' o' worth. I won't have the law chasin' my ass over less than two thousand God damn dollars. Michael stash that gold. I'll see the rest o' you cocksuckers back in town," Sam said before turning back towards the horse, preparing to mount the stallion once more and leave.

"Hang on one moment there now, before you go. I gotta ask you somethin'," enquired Bill.

"Bill, I ain't got time for your fuckin' pesterin', get back to town 'fore I make you regret it! The Marshall' be back soon, God dammit," Sam said sternly.

"Well, now, funny, you should mention the Marshall and the law *chasin' your ass*. I gotta say… seein' you hesitate back there, with the bank man? Well, I was surprised to put it thataway… You playin' us for fools?" As Bill finished speaking, the rest of the gang were staring in stunned silence, waiting for a dramatic reaction from their leader.

Sam slowly turned back to face Bill.

"What did you just say to me?"

"I wanna know… is you workin' for that, Marshall? You make some kind o' deal for a pardon? You didn't kill him!"

No words. Sam went straight for the gun, cocked it and squeezed the trigger – all within seconds. The shot left the barrel, and, in almost slow motion, the bullet was moving towards Bill's forehead. At the last moment, right before the reaper would have his next soul, Austin dove onto Bill. A desperate attempt to save his true friend meant the bullet instead entered Austin's shoulder as the two men fell to the ground. Austin cried out in pain.

"FUCKIN' CHRIST! MY ARM!"

"God Dammit, Austin! You son of a bitch, this ain't your concern; why would you go and do somethin' stupid like that?"

Sam genuinely did feel concern for Austin; the gang in general had to be kept at arm's length, but Austin had been with Sam since the beginning of it all and Sam did trust him for the most part. Almost considered him a friend, almost. Mainly, Austin was the most level headed and intelligent one (after Sam) in the group, so if he died, Sam would lose the gang's anchor.

"Just get on back to town, Sam, and the rest of you too! Bill will stay, get this slug out o' my arm and patch me up. There ain't no time for this mess; all o' you get goin'!" shouted Austin assertively as he winced in pain.

Sam was flustered. The right-hand man had just been shot by Sam's own hand, albeit by mistake, but still. Austin was loyal, but if he now feels betrayed by Sam, he might turn. He might start siding with the doubts of the rest of them. If Sam lost Austin's allegiance, then there was a very real possibility the gang would begin planning to downsize by one.

Things felt like they were crumbling a little more every day and the more Sam tried to do to contain the decay, the faster it fell apart. Sam's control was beginning to seem like nothing more than an illusion.

Sam rode away as fast as the stallion could travel. Sam was supposed to be travelling back towards Whitepost and getting back into the everyday routine and the everyday clothes, but… the situation was becoming overwhelming at that point. Sam rode back to a place from the past. A familiar place. A place Sam had not been in years – a place to think.

The cabin out by Wolf's Pass.

Chapter 17
Harrison James – US Marshall

The ride out to Wolf's Pass was challenging and long, but oddly peaceful. Harrison couldn't help but feel a little nostalgic on this ride out with his younger brother, it felt just like the first time he took Morgan out after he returned home from the war.

The James' parents were loving and good people, but both had succumbed to fatal illness by the time Morgan was only fifteen years old. Harrison had always loved and cared for his younger sibling, but there was a nine-year gap between them, so they weren't overly close in the early years – there isn't much a seven-year-old and a sixteen year-old have to talk about.

When Harrison was twenty-two, their father died, and he went off to fight in the war. Morgan, being just a boy at the time, stayed home with their mother. She passed away in 1863 and Morgan stayed with different, distant cousins and relatives until Harrison finally returned.

When Harrison came to find his younger brother after the war, he almost didn't recognise the man he saw before him. When Harrison last saw him, Morgan was scrawny, pale and barely thirteen. Now, he had grown up and out into a tall, muscular, eighteen-year-old man.

After an initial hug and greeting, they went to go for a ride. There was an awkward silence between the two brothers. Years had passed since they had seen each other and they were both different men now. It was only when Morgan decided to take a chance and play a prank that the ice was broken.

When they were riding along the path, Harrison hadn't noticed Morgan fell behind; it was only after a few moments the older James' brother looked behind him to see Morgan's horse standing a few yards behind without his rider.

Harrison, at first, was obviously confused and worried. He called out for Morgan, but there was no response. Just as Harrison was about to dismount to search around, Morgan leaped out from behind the trees and spooked Harrison's mare. She bucked up immediately and Harrison fell backwards into the dirt.

His initial instinct was to give out and protest as he clambered to stand up and calm his horse, but seeing the tears of laughter rolling from his brother's eyes, he just couldn't help but see the lighter side and laugh along with him.

Harrison had always treasured this memory and held onto it vividly. This was because not only was it the first time he had seen his dear brother in so very long, but it was also the catalyst for the close relationship they would have from there on out. No matter the trauma, hardship or difficulties of life that Harrison had or would have to endure, Morgan was always there to make him smile after it all.

Since that day, Harrison had many layers of closeness with his younger brother. He loved him very much as a brother; he valued and trusted him as a deputy; he felt protective over him like a son, and he needed him as a friend.

During their journey to the cabin, they told stories, laughed and joked. Neither of them were in a big hurry to get back to Whitepost and to reality, so they took their time. The two men made camp halfway, so they and their horses could rest before they would have to set off again in the morning.

They got a fire going and started cooking up some freshly caught rabbit and a can of beans.

"Harrison, you remember when Pa took us fishin' that time and I pushed you in the water?"

"Yes, Morgan, I lost my damn watch in that lake. What of it?" Harrison said as he turned the meat over the fire, gently cooking it.

"Well, you think Pa knew he was sick then? Lookin' back, he started to spend so much time with us all of a sudden. Maybe he knew 'fore we did."

"It don't matter. It was a nice trip."

"I guess… I just… sometimes I think it must be harder to have family, you know. If he knew he was gonna' die, it was probably harder knowin' what it would do to Momma. She was so heartbroken after he passed. I hated seein' her like that."

"Everyone dies someday, Morgan."

"I know that. I mean, if you knew you was gonna die before your wife, maybe it's easier not to put somebody through that. Maybe it's easier not to put yourself through it. What if I were married and I loved 'er and then she up and died? I cannot fathom why anyone would wish that upon themselves."

Harrison paused before responding. He was contemplating what his brother had just said and wondering why he was thinking this way. He also couldn't help the realisation that, up until he met Lenora, he used to feel the very same.

"You'll always think it's better to be alone 'til you meet a gal you don't wanna be away from."

"Like Lenora?"

Harrison didn't respond.

"Come on now… I know I said you need to be careful with her, and I do still think that, but I also think, *family history* aside, she seems like a real fine woman."

Harrison smirked ever so slightly.

"I mean any woman that can put up with your broodin' is somethin' to behold huh!" Morgan playfully shoved his older brother.

"I do not brood." Harrison objected.

"Oh, sure, yeah, you are a picture o' positivity, night and day." Morgan laughed. "But seriously, you… you think you gon' stay with her?"

"I… I've been thinkin' maybe I… Oh shit, rabbit's burnin'!"

Harrison jumped up to retrieve the barely salvageable meat.

"Haha! Jesus, brother, that is charred as hell. Len sure ain't with you for your cookin' skills, that's for damn sure!" Morgan chuckled.

The two of them forced their dinner down and settled in to rest for the night. Harrison lay awake for a while after Morgan had drifted to sleep. He lay there by the dwindling embers of the campfire, staring up at the stars. He stared up, reflecting on his past and imagining his future. His future had always been somewhat of a blank slate in his mind before, he spent his adult life living by the gun – a soldier, a Marshall. These were occupations that rarely allowed a man to live his life out to old age. With that in mind, Harrison thought it best never to settle, never to think on it, for his last day could be creeping around the corner at any moment.

But in crossing paths with Lenora Taylor and experiencing what romantic love could truly feel like, more and more he could not stop fantasising about the future. In this picture that became more vivid in his mind every day, he imagined a small ranch of his very own. Lenora would be his wife. He and Morgan would tend to the chores around the property, and when they grew old enough, maybe his children could help too. Two sons and a daughter. They could run around the land, free and unburdened by any of the troubles their parents had endured in their own lives. They would be happy.

Harrison drifted to sleep with this comforting dream swirling in his mind.

The two men awoke the next morning and got back on the road first thing. It was another few hours' ride across the countryside, up further into the mountains, before they reached their destination. They didn't know the exact location of the cabin, so it took some time to find the damn thing in the woods.

"Harrison! Look there! That it you reckon?" asked Morgan as he pointed at a small, old, dilapidated cabin hidden between the trees.

"Well, we's definitely in the right spot, so it might well be. Let's check it out."

Harrison and Morgan dismounted from their horses and waded through the overgrown weeds and debris from the trees above to the front of the cabin.

"Christ… I'm guessin' ain't nobody been here for some time," said Morgan, observing the old wooden panels of the cabin exterior, showing signs of rot.

"Morgan take a look around the property, see if there's anything 'round that might be of interest. I'll look inside."

"Well, you and I got different opinions on what the word *property* means, but sure, I'll look around." Morgan smirked before Harrison entered the small dwelling.

The inside of this place seemed eerie. Lenora had told Harrison that Sam left suddenly, but it seemed as though she herself must have left suddenly too. Everything was dank, dusty and falling into disrepair, but everything was left in such a way as if the residents had up and vanished without warning one day. The bed still had old linens on it and a timeworn dress thrown across. A pot hung over the small fireplace with remnants of what was once food inside. The small table had crockery meticulously placed on it, but some had fallen to the floor and broken. One thing Harrison took note of, in particular, was a very old-looking wooden chest that appeared to have been rifled through. The chest was open and its contents appeared to have been thrown out across the room, as though someone had been looking for something in a hurry.

Within these contents, Harrison found a journal laying on the floor. Some of the pages had water damage and were illegible, but there were still a few pages intact. He proceeded to read and within moments, he realised this journal belonged to Lenora. He took a moment to read a passage she had written:

September 3rd 1859

Sammy and I woke to find the crops desecrated by the hoppers once more. I wish he would listen to me. He is so adamant we stay away from town, but I heard tell when I was a young girl that were we to acquire some chickens or turkeys, we might be rid of this plague. We need only venture in for a short spell and purchase our required predators. Might also be a nice addition to our dinner some nights! I am tempted at times to disregard his instruction and simply go myself, but I then cannot bring myself to do it. I would just hate for him to be unhappy with me.

Today marks just over a year since I met him. Maybe that is why I am feeling so sentimental. I cannot fathom what my life were to be had he not saved me. God truly watched over me that day; he had seen my suffering and chose to reward my patience. He chose to save me from a horrifying existence. God watches over us still. If a blight of grasshoppers is the most we must endure, then I am still grateful. Maybe it was meant to serve as a reminder for us to appreciate all that we have.

Anyway, I will away now to begin my chores for the day. Maybe someday Sam and I will live in a beautiful big house with servants to do everything for us!

Harrison couldn't help but think how different this young girl seemed to the Lenora he knew now. She would have been all but seventeen or eighteen here. She hadn't experienced the horrors that were to come and she seemed so innocent. Harrison felt a sudden sadness wash over him. She had been so content here, so at peace. What an injustice it was to rid her of her happiness so cruelly. The sadness soon turned to anger as he reimagined the men who attacked her and led her guardian to become a vicious outlaw.

Harrison, in his moment of anger, was now reminded of why they were there. He needed to get his head back in the game and find something, anything, that would bring them a step closer to capturing Sam Walker.

"Harry, HARRISON! Come on out here I think I found somethin'!" Morgan shouted.

Harrison rushed around to the back of the cabin to find his brother standing beside something very curious. Morgan had cleared away some weeds and undergrowth to reveal two graves.

"What's all this?" Harrison enquired.

"The names marked on these here graves ain't familiar; well, one of 'em says Walker at least, but I don't know what the other one says."

"Well, this has to be the right cabin, I found Lenora's journal inside."

"Well, who the hell is this, then?" Morgan gestured towards the two graves.

Harrison leaned in to read the faded engraving on the first old, wooden cross erected at the top of each grave.

"Abigail Walker… Len said Sam's mother died here 'fore she met him. This is likely her."

"All right, that checks out okay but she mention anybody else?"

"No…" Harrison leaned in to try and read the other name on the second grave, "T. S. I… Tsiishch'ili."

"What in the hell does that mean?"

"It's a name, Morgan, I think it's native."

"Oh, right, so like Apache?"

"Not Apache, no… I think this might be the Navajo."

"Okay, so it's a Navajo name… So, who in the hell was this Navajo native and why is he buried beside Sam Walker's mama?"

"I don't know. Somethin' ain't right here."

"Lenora definitely never mentioned anyone else bein' here wit' 'em?" Morgan questioned.

"No, Morgan, this doesn't make sense."

"Harry! Holy hell, that pendant!"

"What of it?"

"Don't you remember? You said it belonged to Lenora, she took it from here after Sam left or some such."

"Get to your point, Morgan."

"There's a damn 'T' carved on the back of that! You think that 'T' is for Tsiishch'ili?"

"I had forgotten… You may be right… This does not make sense."

"What are you thinkin' brother?"

"Lenora said… Lenora told me that pendant had originally been a gift to Sam from his mother, who we now know to be Abigail… So if that pendant had 'T' carved in the back of it then Tsiishch'ili must have been someone important to Sam and his mother…"

"Maybe his father?"

"Maybe… no, that still ain't right though. Look here at the condition o' this wood." Harrison pointed between the two crosses. "Abigail's grave is older judging by this – it's more rotted at the bottom, more faded in the name… Tsiishch'ili's grave is more recent… Lenora told me Sam lived alone after his mother died until he met her… somethin'… somethin' is not addin' up here."

Harrison was growing more concerned by the minute… who was this? Why would Lenora lie… did she lie? There was a big piece missing in this puzzle and they needed answers.

"Harrison, I know it's a long shot here, but… you think we could find someone who hails from the Navajo tribe 'round here and see if they know the name? We might find out who this is?"

"If we even could locate them, I do not think they would be much inclined to answer the questions of two federal lawmen, not since the walk to Bosque Redondo anyway."

"Bosque Redondo was their camp, right, their uh… reservation? How far'd they walk?"

"'bout four hundred miles to Fort Sumner."

"Jesus… Well, why don't we see if there's anyone else livin' 'round here – at least, anybody somewhere nearby – that might shed some light on all this? A distant neighbour or anythin'."

"All right, we can look around at least; won't do no harm."

The two men trekked through the woods in an effort to find anyone who might hold some answers. They roamed for some time before they saw some light breaking through the trees from an open field of land. From a distance, they couldn't see much, but as they walked closer to the forest's edge and emerged from the trees, the only way to describe what they saw before them was pure and absolute horror.

Chapter 18
Morgan James – Deputy Marshall

Morgan had never seen such a sight. Harrison had experience in these matters, but not Morgan. One or two convicted criminals hanging was one thing, but when the two men emerged from the forest borders, what they saw before them was a massacre.

Across what felt like miles of land, all they could see were mangled corpses. With the exception of a few scattered uniformed soldiers here and there, the majority of the dead they could see were natives. Morgan's stomach was knotting and churning as he and his brother stood there in revolted silence. They could smell the sun's heat beating down on the decaying bodies. So many looked to have been ravaged by animals, but there was no mistake; their cause of death was a battle.

Morgan was struggling to keep his composure, but knowing Harrison had seen war was driving Morgan to keep it together. He did not want his older brother to perceive him as 'lily livered' in the face of such a bloody atrocity.

"Harrison… what…"

"I do not know, Morgan."

"Was this… was there some kind of battle… is there a fort 'round these parts they might've attacked? Fort Defiance is the nearest one t' here, ain't it? Harrison, this is… this is wrong. All wrong."

"Yeah, that *was* the closest… Kit Carson changed the name Fort Canby a couple years back, but they abandoned it. I heard tell the old fort was turned into the Indian Agency just about a year ago, so I cannot understand what in God's name is goin' on here."

"The natives hardly attacked the agency… would they?"

"Morgan, it is their own agency; to what end would they attack?" Harrison slowly stepped towards the nearest dead soldier and kneeled down to examine the body. "Why would these soldiers be out here? They couldn't have been defendin' anywhere because there is nowhere near to be defended. Why would they be sent then? What could have prompted such violence? I had not heard of any major troubles with the Navajo, so why all this bloodshed?"

Morgan knew these questions were posed more to Harrison's own self, as Morgan could not possibly know the answers, although he desperately wanted to.

"Morgan, come here."

Morgan took a deep breath in and approached the corpse.

"Morgan, how did this man die?"

"Fightin'."

"Don't be smart. What exactly was it that killed him? Look at the body; look at where he was wounded."

Morgan hesitantly examined the corpse. The dead man's cloudy eyes seemed unnervingly fixed towards Morgan, as if this departed soul was watching the young James' brother determine the cause of his untimely end.

"It looks… it's hard to tell, but looks like he was shot… a couple times."

"You are correct, sir. Which means the man who shot him had a gun, and I would wager his fellow soldiers were not likely to cut him down."

Harrison stood up and walked further into the scene of horror. Making his way past multiple dead men. Morgan followed his trail.

"Harrison, these natives must have shot 'em, they got guns here, right beside!"

"What type o' gun?"

"A rifle o' sorts."

Harrison turned back to examine the weapons laying scattered around the blood-soaked earth. He picked one up for a closer look. "This, here is a Springfield Rifle. They were used a lot in the war."

"Why would the Indians have 'em? If they were used by the soldiers, I mean?" Morgan questioned.

"I do not know… this here ain't right. This was a damn slaughter, why? We ain't near a fort; the Navajo were allowed return to these parts, so they ain't trespassin'. Why do they have these rifles? Where did they get 'em?"

"Harrison, maybe we should be on our way; the natives might come for their dead. They might not be so welcomin' to us at the sight of this."

"You're right. Let's make our way back."

The brothers left the sight of that atrocity and re-entered the relative safety of the woods. They began the walk back towards the old cabin where their horses were hitched.

"What do we do about this, Harrison?"

"We need to inform the Governor about what we've seen."

"You think it's got somethin' to do with Sam?"

"It is an odd coincidence that we came across this so close to Sam's cabin, but I do not believe he had anythin' to do with that. Sam Walker is a cold-blooded outlaw, but his angle is money and murder for the most part. This was somethin' on a bigger scale. There's a bigger reason for this and I could not imagine what motive there would be for Sam to engage in such nefarious dealin's with the Navajo Indians."

"Why are we tellin' the Governor then?"

"Morgan, we are tellin' the Governor because he ordered us to keep him informed as our investigation continues. You are gonna ride back to Whitepost and get a letter to him. Inform him that we have found Sam's original residence and are followin' on some leads from there. You will also tell him of our discovery. Tell him what we found and inform him that, whilst we do not believe it to be the work of Sam Walker, we thought it important and appropriate to bring it to his attention."

"*Me* ride back to Whitepost? Pray tell Harrison, what're you doin'?"

"I'm goin' to have another look inside that cabin; there's somethin' I wanna have a better look at; Lenora's journal is inside. I might be able to find answers in it about Tsiishch'ili. I'll only be an hour or two behind you."

The two men waded back through the forest floor until they eventually reached the cabin. Morgan couldn't place why, but he was suddenly feeling uneasy. They were far from the stench of rotting flesh cooking in the sun, so he knew it wasn't a feeling that stemmed from anything physical; it was an ominous feeling that something was amiss. He stepped over to his horse, preparing to mount his saddle, when he stopped and looked to Harrison entering the cabin.

"Harry, before I go, I... Doesn't this all seem strange to you?"

"It was... curious, but the Governor may have an explanation that we do not."

"No, I mean, not just that, this whole thing. Since we got here, we got to Whitepost... I don't know it's different than any case we been on 'fore now. I... God damn it, I don't have enough words to explain it, but... I don't know my gut is tellin' me somethin's wrong. Like... kinda like as if I have this feelin' that we're in danger."

"That feelin' will pass. It is the weight of the death you have seen now sittin' on your shoulders. It'll be long since faded by the time you get t' Whitepost."

"No, Harrison, it ain't that... I mean, that was horrible, ain't no denyin' it sure, but I swear somethin' is tellin' me we gotta be real careful here."

"You will be fine, Morgan."

Morgan scoffed and climbed onto his saddle. He pulled the reins to move his horse away before giving Harrison a final word.

"I know you don't see it now, but hear me, brother, there is somethin' off about this whole damn thing. Ever since we set foot in Whitepost, I feel like it's buildin' up to somethin'. I don't know what it is yet or how I know it, but my gut is tellin' me we need to think real carefully about the moves we make."

Harrison stared at him for a moment, contemplating in silence, before making his final response.

"Be on your way, Morgan; I'll see you back in town."

Morgan rode away. Frustrated and unable to shake the unnerving thoughts swirling in his head.

In an effort to settle his nerves, he light-heartedly made a pact with himself. "As soon as Harry's finished his term, we're buying a fuckin' farm and livin' in God damn peace. I'm sick o' these fuckin' outlaws."

Chapter 19
Harrison James – US Marshall

Harrison watched his younger brother ride out of sight before re-entering the cabin. Harrison probably should have fixated more on Morgan's unnerved feelings and tried to understand why the younger sibling might be speaking this way, but now all he wanted was to get that journal and find answers.

He picked the journal up from where he left it and took a seat just beside the one small window of the cabin. It was dusty and grubby, with a few cobwebs scattered around, but you could still get a clear enough view of the woods outside. Harrison began flipping through the pages, looking for legible paragraphs with anything of interest or any mention of Tsiishch'ili.

He came across one entry that was mostly ruined, but two sentences were still legible:

... Found some lavender, so I'm going to go back and gather what I need to make the dye. T said he doesn't mind me dyeing the dress, said they all belong to me now to do with as I...

Surely *'T'* had to be Tsiishch'ili. And if she went to him for permission or a blessing to do something, it means he was important to her or an authority figure. Harrison's mind was starting to spin a little faster and faster each moment. If Sam was her guardian, her chosen father, who was this man and how did he fit in here? This wasn't making sense. Why did Lenora lie or rather neglect to mention his existence, if he was someone of importance…?

Harrison's heart was starting to beat faster, adrenaline was beginning to drip through his body as he started to feel agitated and tense. This whole thing didn't make sense. The more he discovered, the more questions he had. If Lenora would go as far as to confess her devastating past, her deep connection to a notorious outlaw, wanted for multiple murders, what was it about this other man that had to stay hidden? How was he worse?

Just then, Harrison became alert to the sound of something coming from outside. It was in the distance but seemed to be getting closer. Hooves pounding on the ground; someone riding hard and fast. Had Morgan come back? Was something wrong?

Harrison vigorously wiped a patch on the window to ensure a clear view outside. He kept staring, trying to get a glimpse at who the mystery rider approaching was, until they came into view.

Harrison froze.

Time seemed to slow to an almost stop; each hard thump of his heart beating against his ribcage felt minutes apart and louder than a crack of thunder in his ear. His eyes didn't dare blink once as he tried to process what he was seeing. If he *was* seeing what he thought he was seeing.

The Phantom himself riding past. Within two yards of the cabin. Right past…

Harrison had never seen the man in person, but it had to be him. Harrison knew it in his gut. Same black hat and a black bandana covering his face – exact same as the Wanted poster. The rider had weapons holstered on either side of him too, roughly about the same height… riding a black stallion. Harrison knew it. It was Sam Walker. Why else would this rider of the same description be coming past here, Sam's cabin? It had to be him.

In the few seconds it took for Sam to gallop past, Harrison was weighing up his options: ride as fast as possible back to get Morgan and outgun him for sure, but risk losing him for God knows how long… Or go on after him now, alone, with a chance of catching him and ending this.

He made his choice. This was going to end here and now.

Harrison dropped the journal and ran out to his mare. He mounted her so fast he almost flew up to the saddle. He swiftly followed the trail of hoof prints left in the dirt, riding fast for a few moments, when suddenly he jerked the horse to slow right down. Harrison spotted the prints left in the mud were getting much closer together; Sam's stride was slowing. Harrison wanted to maintain the element of surprise, so riding in hard wasn't an option. He dismounted and decided to proceed on foot; the further into the woods he went, the slower the pace at which it seemed his opponent was travelling.

Just as it seemed Sam's horse may have slowed to a walk, he looked across the woods, through a thick cluster of different plants, leaves, branches, and spotted the rider in black, still mounted on his horse but moving slowly. The horse gently stepped deeper into the woods. Harrison could not help but think it bizarre that only moments ago this man was riding like the devil himself was chasing him, but now, just a gentle stroll.

Harrison needed to be on guard. It may be that *The Phantom* is waiting for someone; if that was the case, Harrison's chance of surviving this meeting had just dropped somewhat. If he was going to do this, it needed to be now while he still had an equal chance.

Harrison silently moved across the forest floor until he found a spot with an open view of his target. He put his back to a large tree and quietly loaded his gun. Just as he loaded the last bullet, he took a deep breath and prayed he would return tonight to see his brother and his love.

Harrison peaked his head around the tree and just in the split second he raised his arm to aim and fire, he was stopped in his tracks. Harrison's mouth dropped.

The confusion of what he was seeing before him almost had him drop his weapons.

Sam Walker had dismounted, sat onto a tree stump and appeared to be crying.

What could this possibly mean? One of the most hardened and intelligent criminals he had ever been sent to find, going from the stories everyone told, and here he was, alone in the woods, crying. This couldn't be right?

Harrison could not help but stare at the outlaw, in curious disbelief at what he saw before him, when, in just one blink of his eyes, his entire world began to implode and burn around him.

Sam Walker was still crying and then abruptly removed the hat and bandana. From under the hat fell out the long dark hair he knew too well, and under the bandana, a face he wished he never laid eyes on.

It was Lenora.

Harrison felt like he was drowning, suffocating… panicking. He desperately struggled to catch his breath as his soul felt like it was scorching inside him.

No, no, no, no, not her. Please, Jesus Christ, no. Harrison was falling apart. The only woman he had ever truly loved… a liar. The only woman he had ever dreamed up a future with… a thief. The only woman he ever truly wanted… a vicious murderer.

The despair, the severe heartache and the emotional torture he was cycling through in these mere moments boiled up to a breaking point. The medley of destructive feelings came together into pure, uncaged anger.

He blurted out a scream before he could contain himself.

"LENORA!"

She raised her head from her hands and turned to see him, her eyes red and welled up with tears. She was paralysed with shock at the sight of him here, now.

"Harrison? Jesus…? How did…?"

Harrison started moving towards her, she flustered to wipe the tears away before he got too close.

"I trusted you. I believed you! Jesus Christ… I can't… It's you, isn't it? This whole fuckin' time, IT WAS YOU!"

"Harrison, please, you don't understand I…"

"Shut the *fuck* up! I do not want to hear any more god damn horseshit out o' your mouth, you lyin' piece of shit! Answer the God damn question! Are you the fuckin' *Phantom* or not?"

She sighed with sorrow and nodded.

"I'm sorry, Harrison."

Harrison felt cold. A cold knife of betrayal into his heart.

"You… you used me… I can't… You used me you GOD DAMN WHORE! WAS ANY OF IT REAL? WAS ANYTHIN' YOU TOLD ME REAL?"

Lenora just stared at him, silent. She didn't say a word. Just tears fell one by one from her eyes.

"Just some fuckin' pawn in your twisted game! You think you was always one step ahead; thought the stupid fuckin' Marshall would be blind to your true self this whole time! I wonder how many other damn jokers you pulled this shit on! Did you have 'em fooled as well as me, huh…? You're a cold, vicious bitch! I believed your stories! I believed the horrible things that happened to you! What you think you could just hide right under my nose 'til you were good and done with me?"

Lenora remained silent.

"Ain't you got nothin' to say for yourself? Ain't got no words to justify your evil soul! ANSWER ME, GOD, DAMMIT!"

Harrison pulled out his revolver and aimed it directly at her head. His rage was coming to a head now: he couldn't control his free fall of emotion.

"You're comin' with me; we're goin' back to Whitepost right fuckin' now!"

Lenora sniffled and then spoke. "And then what, Harrison?"

"You'll answer for every God damn rotten thing you've done!"

"No. If I go with you now, all that awaits me in Whitepost is a noose around the neck. Well, I choose to die right here if that be the case. Go ahead, do what you came here to do – kill Sam Walker."

Harrison pressed the gun right at her temple now, his eyes welling up, but he refused to allow himself to release the tears. She never moved, never even twitched as the weapon pushed against her head.

"Get the fuck up and walk, Lenora, NOW! I ain't gonna' tell you twice!"

"No Harrison. I am not gonna' die in that town. Or any town. If today is to be my end, I choose it to be right here."

Harrison was twitching, almost ready to squeeze the trigger, while his heart and his mind screamed internally at each about his next move. In that moment, a cold breeze whipped past him through the forest, and he found he had one last question he needed to ask.

"You didn't know I would be here… So why were you crying just now?"

"Harrison, you don't want the true answer to that question, nor will you believe it, so just be done with your business here. Get it over with!"

"You owe me the God damn truth, Lenora: if I have ever meant anythin' real to you, answer the fuckin' question!"

"You… you may be the first man in a long time that I have ever truly cared for. For that, I truly do not wish any more burden on you, just finish the job!"

"I got no more time for your horseshit and your lies! They will make no difference for you now."

"Believe what you want, Harrison. I ain't have no more strength for lies any more. I've carried 'em around for too long. I'm done with all of it. I'll go if now's my time… I'm…" She hesitated; her voice wobbled as she attempted to hold back her crying. "I'm just… sorry I crossed your path. I pray you will forget me before long. If God still listens to a sinner's soul as dark as mine."

"Why. Why were you crying? What God awful deed has finally broken your cold heart?"

"Harrison… please, I promise you, you don't want to know this."

"So help me, God, I will drag you back to rot in a cell right fuckin' now if I have to, LAST CHANCE!"

Lenora sighed. She looked up at the sky for a moment, looked back to the ground, then raised her eyes to meet his.

"… I'm pregnant."

Chapter 20
Lenora Taylor/Sam Walker –
Notorious Outlaw

Harrison's hand was shaking as the gun was pressed to her head. He was falling to pieces and the truth was, it broke Lenora's heart to see it. To know that she was solely responsible for this brutal torment of a man she loved. To know she consciously brought them both to this moment and never tried to stop it. Her illusion of control had shattered.

Harrison was speechless as he heard her confession – as he found out she carried his child. The turmoil must have reached its limit within him as he dropped his weapon and released a primal scream across the reach of the woods.

He dropped to his knees and stared at the ground. After a long pause of silence, he spoke.

"How… how can I trust you? This is more lies to twist my mind! You'll say anythin' to save your own skin!"

"Harrison, I was ready for you to end my life without tellin' you. You could have pulled the trigger right then and there and never known. You wanted the answer; you demanded it! And I have provided it. It is the truth, and I warned you that you would not want this weighin' down upon you."

"Why… why God, dammit… why you?" The defeat in his voice was icy as he posed this question to the world.

Lenora's tears still dripped one by one from her blue eyes. She could feel herself cracking under the weight of all her crimes in the years past. She had been so consumed by bitterness and rage in the past that she thrust herself on a path of vengeance, but in carrying out her personal justice, she was left numb for years. Numb and disconnected from any true happiness, from real love and from her true conscience. In falling for Harrison, a man on the opposite side of the law, her guilt had finally found her. In discovering she carried his child, something of pure innocence, the guilt had finally ripped her open.

She knew she was playing with fire the moment she kissed him for the first time. She knew, deep down, this would only end in pain, but she never stopped herself. She wasn't hurt by the insults he screamed at her; he felt betrayed… conflicted by an impossible choice he had to make now. Uphold the law and everything he stood for by killing her, or forsake his duty for the life of his unborn… saving a murderer. No, she wasn't hurt by his insults, but she was hurt that she would never see him look at her the same way again. The eyes that once beamed with true caring now burned with hatred.

Harrison spoke again, but this time he dwindled down from fury, to a man crushed.

"Was anythin' you told me true?"

"Most of it was. Sam and I really were attacked, and you are the only person who knows that. But the real truth is, when I made it back to the cabin, Sam wasn't just gone; he was dead." She sniffled and sobbed a little more. "And I simply could not bear that reality."

Harrison began to raise his voice once more. "So what that's it? And let me guess now you're so sorry for what you did, huh? Jesus Christ, you still think me a fool?" Harrison stood back up and stared down at her.

Lenora stopped, stood up and stared him right in his eyes. This time, the venom and fury were in *her* voice.

"Make no God damn mistake, Harrison; I ain't sorry for a single fuckin' thing I did to those three *animals*." She took a step closer to him, squared up to him now. "I would kill them again right here right now if I had the chance – worse than before. They got off lightly."

Harrison was looking at her, almost stunned. This was the first time Lenora was speaking to him truly as herself – no more masks of innocence.

"Let's say I could manage to forget about that; let's say then I surmised that to be justice… God awful justice… but justice all the same on the three men that so brutally wronged you… what about the rest, Lenora? You murdered more innocent folk after that! You and your vicious gang have been wanted for years! You ain't sorry for that? They ain't done nothin' to you!"

"What the hell was I supposed to do, huh? I didn't seek out that gang, they came to me! I was in too deep; if I didn't keep 'em in line, they would have killed me a long damn time ago! I know their names and I know their faces; they wouldn't keep me alive if I tried to leave God, dammit! Fear was all I had! I ain't ever killed a man that didn't deserve it anyway; every single piece o' shit that you heard tell of dyin' by my own hand was an asshole, I promise you that! Ain't no God damn innocents; that's a sure fact!"

"What about the pregnant girl? From outside of town… Was she an asshole?"

Lenora froze up. Her gut wretched and she dropped from her self-made pedestal into a deep hole. She turned away from Harrison and wrapped her arms around her own stomach, staring at the ground.

"Well! Was she an asshole? Was she a piece of shit? Come on, Lenora, tell me how much of a horrible person she was and how she deserved it!"

"Stop."

"Oh, I'm sorry. Is this hard for you?"

"Harrison, stop, please."

"No, come on now, Lenora, you must have some justified reason for murdering a young wife and her unborn child! Two people that did noth'…"

"I DIDN'T MEAN TO!"

He stopped at her scream. Lenora dropped back down to the stump and stared off into nothing. She felt cold and broken as this memory came back so vividly to haunt her once more. Profound sorrow filled her as she visualised and explained the nightmare that tortured her.

"I see her face every night before I sleep. I see her face in my sleep. I see her everywhere. I didn't know she was there. We thought the house was empty. The boy came down the stairs and into the hallway; one of the others shot him, but… I heard the floor creakin' in the next room, and… I panicked. I thought it might have been another boy runnin' for the law. I fired without lookin' and…" She struggled to get her words out through the tears: "I heard a body hit the floor."

She paused. "The others went lookin' for the money and I… I don't know why I went to see… I saw her body draining out all that blood… and her belly."

She paused again and looked back up to Harrison, who still stood looking down at her.

"She did not deserve her fate… I am sorry for what I done to her. I am truly sorry. I know for certain that even if God could forgive and overlook all my other sins… all my other crimes… killin' that gal has secured my passage straight to Hell."

Harrison stared at her with a cold look on his face. He stayed silent before finally deciding to interrogate her further. Lenora was a dead woman now, so what use were lies from here on out? Harrison knew this too.

"Who was Tsiishch'ili?"

"You found the grave, huh? … That's Sam's real name. The real Samuel Walker."

"What?"

"Sam's mama was a slave who escaped her masters'; she found refuge with his daddy's people. She stayed and got pregnant. His father named him Tsiishch'ili."

"Where did Samuel come from, then?"

"His father died fightin' with some soldiers, I think, when Sam was a child, 'bout eleven or so. His mama didn't think they were safe there any more, so they travelled here up into the mountains. The cabin back there was a shell – practically nothin'. She and him, built it together over time. There was a lot of tension buildin' up atwixt the government and the natives and I think his mama was afraid they'd get separated. They were already forcing natives off their land all over and there was rumours startin' of reservations. Abigail was also afraid that her previous masters might still be lookin' for her. She figured if someone in the nearest town were to hear of a boy with a name like Tsiishch'ili, well, it might attract the wrong kind of attention, but Samuel? Well, nobody would give two shits about a Samuel, so that's what she started callin' him."

"How do you know all this?"

"He told me."

Harrison sighed and turned to face a tree. He placed his right arm against the trunk and looked down. He suddenly spun back towards her, agitated once more.

"Well, what am I supposed to do now, huh? What *the fuck* am I supposed to do now, Lenora? You're a God damn criminal. You're a murderer! How can I just forget all that? I was sent here by the God damn Governor to kill you! I'm askin' you now: What would you have me do? You're supposed to hang! You deserve to hang!"

Up until now, Lenora felt as though she was drowning in the reality of her black soul. True, there were some men that she did not regret killing, but she hated knowing that if she never had experienced the trauma that set her on her dark path, there never would have been a reason to kill. She felt sad that she would never be herself again. She felt great guilt now and sorrow for the harm she inflicted on most of her victims and she could never come back from that. She could only attempt to repent and ask God for mercy. She also felt great sadness knowing she now carried life inside her after taking that away from that young woman all those years ago. Yes, all these emotions of remorse had been swirling inside her, but as Harrison spoke those words just then to her, she was triggered by something else. She was flipped from her own guilt into anger. She would accept the truth about herself, but she would not accept a God damn hypocrite. She stood up dramatically and squared right back up to him. She looked him right in the eyes with that same unhinged look that had, in the past, only been used to control her gang.

"Hold up, just a motherfuckin' minute here now, Harrison…"

He interrupted, "What do you thi'…"

She pointed her finger right into his face and kept her sinister eye contact.

"Shut the fuck up, it's my God damn turn to speak now and you count your fuckin' lucky stars that I ain't got a weapon on you!"

Harrison looked severely aggravated, but he reluctantly stayed quiet to let her finish.

"I've done some bad things in my time, real bad. I know who I am. I see the woman I've become. But I got good in me too: I ain't heartless and I've done some good in my life too. But make no mistake, I see the monster starin' back at me in the mirror and I'm acceptin' that. But you, Harrison, I will not sit here and continue to have you preach at me about my evil deeds while you feign innocence! You as much of a God damn murderer as I am! Don't DARE claim that I deserve a noose and act as if you do not!"

"What the hell are you rantin' on about woman? I'm a US Marshall!"

"Yeah, you a US Marshall… Tell me, *Marshall* — how many people you killed in your time?"

"I kill criminals. Wanted Men… *and* women."

"And *allllll* those people you probably killed in the war they was criminals too, huh?"

"That's war, Lenora. It's different! You killed for money!"

"Oh, it's fuckin' different, is it? Yeah, it is, I killed for vengeance and then I killed assholes for their money. You killed to keep people like MY SAM IN FUCKIN' CHAINS! You had a hand in killin' how many hundreds of sons, fathers… brothers!"

Harrison was dazed. He stammered to get his words out; maybe this truly was the first time he was being shown his true self.

"I… that's not why I went fightin'… I, we… I couldn't let my friends, my cousins, my family… I couldn't let them go and fight the Yankees and me stay behind; I had to protect them! It was expected of me. It was a war, Lenora; it's not the same!"

"You went and killed folk to protect your asshole friends then, friends who thought people outta' be property… you killed to protect ones you cared for, I killed to protect myself and I killed to avenge the one I cared for… You kept killin' 'cause an officer told you to; I kept killin' 'cause I'd die if I didn't. Either way, for both of us, it was kill or be God damn killed. Only difference between the two of us is I see myself for who I am; you do not. You just so happened to land yourself on the right side of the law. You ended more lives'n I ever did; remember that when you drag me to hang."

Harrison's face dropped. His temple started twitching as this revelation vibrated through his mind. His eyes looked to be revolving through all the memories of his past. He couldn't find words, but this truth seemed to cut him deeply. He stared back at Lenora as if this bubble he'd been living in for his whole life had burst, as if he had never seen his actions for what they really were. He finally spoke up, quietly and seemingly emotionless.

"Why did you pursue me?"

"I… the first night we met, I knew you were a stranger and I could tell you were a lawman… I wanted to know why you were in Whitepost; I needed to know what you knew. But you were damn stubborn."

"So it was all just for information, then."

"It was just for information at the start; that's what I told myself. I thought I could find out what I needed and be done with you…" Her eyes softened, and welled up with tears once more. "But then I came to know you more… Every time I was near you, I could forget everythin' that brought me here. I couldn't stop myself from… Harrison… truth is, I love you… It's true, I didn't intend it at the beginning, but… I haven't felt any love like this since my daddy was killed; you're the only one in the world I care for now."

Harrison stayed silent, just staring back at her.

"I will not go back to that town to die, Harrison, but if you choose to do your duty here and now, I understand, and I won't fight you."

Lenora turned from him and sat back onto the tree stump.

"Be done with it now, Harrison; I've said all I need to say."

Harrison stepped over and dropped to the ground in front of her.

"Duty?… What if you are right… maybe I am more of a monster'n I ever allowed myself to see… what is my duty? To kill a killer? And be a killer? How can I hold peace with God if I put an end to my own flesh and blood, my own child…?"

Lenora was surprised at this epiphany. She wanted Harrison to know the truth about himself; she wouldn't let that go, but she hadn't expected it to save her from her fate.

"My duty. My duty has been somethin' I struggled with my whole life… I knew the things I did were ruthless, but I did 'em anyway, and I got rewarded for it. Maybe… maybe the only duty that matters is a duty to the ones that mean the most."

Harrison paused for a moment and raised his hand, very gently placing it on her belly.

"What would you have me do, Len?"

Chapter 21
Harrison James – US Marshall

Harrison had been trying to come to terms with an intense moral and emotional dilemma. True at first, he felt enraged, disgusted at the real truth of Lenora, but now he had opened his eyes, maybe for the first time in his life. His sense of moral superiority, his entitlement to bestow justice, was all an illusion, a lie. In reality, what right did he ever have to bring a woman such as her to hang when he had committed sins equal, if not worse, than her? He had never imagined himself to be an overly religious man, but in the face of such a monumental choice, he felt powerless to stop the influence of the Almighty in his decision.

In the eyes of the only eternal judge that mattered, she and him were equal. They were both sinners; they were both murderers. And if there was one act he was sure God could never forgive, it would be to knowingly send his own child to die when they had not yet even lived.

And if he was truly to be honest with himself, in his heart he knew he still loved her.

"Why don't we just leave?" he asked her.

"What?"

"Let's just go. Now. Let's leave and be a family. Forget our past and carve a new future; we can run and we can start again!"

"Harrison, I know you ain't that naïve."

"Well, what's naïve about it? We stay, then I'm likely to be found guilty by association with a wanted criminal and we'll both be sent to die. Then what's the point of all of it?"

"Ain't a soul knows all this truth but you and I."

"For how long? How are we to continue a charade? I was sent to kill you… What do I tell the Governor when he asks weeks from now why the trail suddenly went cold?"

"Harrison, have you lost your mind? How exactly do you suppose we ride off into the sunset without a God damn pot to piss in? Use your head. Well?"

"Well, what's your plan then, huh? What do we do here? Ride back on into town, pretend ain't a damn thing's different and just keep runnin' circles round folks 'til one of us is caught?"

"No. I don't reckon that'll work either… I think my gang is fixin' to kill me."

"What?" Harrison was a little blindsided by this sudden confession.

"They can see me gettin' soft. They can see me getting' wrapped up with you, and they think I've cut some deal to save my own skin. They won't risk bein' sent to hang… and before I came here, I-I accidentally shot the one man in the damn gang that mighta stopped 'em from plottin' against me."

"Christ on the cross, Len… You ain't makin' this easy. He dead?"

"No, but… he sure as shit ain't happy I'm bettin'."

Harrison was about to initiate a line of questioning about how exactly the woman managed to 'accidentally' shoot one of her men, but honestly, at this point, it really didn't matter.

"… I mean, if that ain't reason enough to get the hell outta here, what more do you need to convince you?"

"What more? I'll tell you what more – cash, dollars, currency."

"How is it that you don't have money? I thought you'd have cleaned out half o' the damn West by now."

"Money doesn't last. We split it when we dig it up. I mostly spent mine on guns, horses and nice rooms to stay in. We always need another job."

"You only just did a job? That's why I'm here in the first place. The damn stage? Wait, hold up a minute… Did you say dig it up?"

"We bury the loot 'til the heat is off."

"All right, so I'm assumin' there's some reason you can't just go on and get it? Some reason we can't use that money to be gone from this God damn town for good."

"I don't know where it's buried. Couple years back, some of the boys were gettin' riled up, thinkin' each time I buried the loot, I was hidin' away some in my own pockets. To keep the peace, I set a new rule – every time we do a job, a different person buries it. I mean, I'm sure each of 'em still stashes a little somethin' of it away now for themselves when it's their turn, but at least no one person would be gettin' all the spoils, equal opportunities."

"Who buried it this time?"

"Man called Clayton."

"And you can't get this Clayton to dig it up now?"

"Oh yes, Harry, my goodness, now why had I not thought o' that? Oh, silly old me, I am such a silly little woman!" Lenora tutted and rolled her eyes.

"Don't get smart with me: I'm explorin' all the damn options."

"We only dig it up when it's time to high tail it. Plus, that ain't a whole lot between all of us."

"Well, why can't it just be time t' go then? What are y'all hangin' 'round here for?"

"Jesus, you know what… I almost forgot about all that, ha! My God… We're waitin' on the big money."

"What?"

"We're waiting on someone. A woman. And 'fore you ask, no, I do not know her name, and I have yet to ascertain who her secret employer is."

"What's this woman and her mysterious employer got to do with you and *big* money?"

"She hired us to rob that stage. Said we could have everythin' we wanted 'cept a letter she needed, that needs to be delivered to her and we'll get paid a handsome sum to the sound of seven… maybe even eight thousand American dollars."

Harrison was struck silent for a moment. All the pieces were coming together. Harrison wasn't originally sent to kill 'Sam'. He never even knew about the Spector Gang until after his arrival. Harrison was sent because that letter was stolen. That letter was supposed to be quite valuable, and here Lenora was telling him she'd been sent for the exact same reason… and whoever hired her apparently thinks it to be *extremely* valuable.

"Hold up now. Eight thousand dollars? Eight thousand in hard cash? And this woman is just bringin' it to you?"

"Well… no, it ain't so simple. Whoever she represents had originally offered us six thousand, but I read that letter and to be honest, I think it's worth a damn sight more'n that. Some biiig shit is goin' down. When she came to collect the letter, I… uh… politely told her that we wanted more'n she wasn't gettin' the damn thing until we got it… now we are waitin' for her return."

"Yeah, I'm sure it was real polite." Harrison smirked. "What's in that letter? What does it say?"

"I can't remember word for word, but it's in my room back in Whitepost. Hidden. But the summation of it is, I think someone is planning on startin' up trouble with the natives 'round here. And I think one of the two 'someone's' is Gabe Hammerton. And I think whoever hired us wants to blackmail 'em."

"Gabe Hammerton, the man who beat the whores? Did he write the letter?"

"I reckon so. It was signed off GH, and he's the only GH anywhere 'round here with any money worth blackmailin' for. He addressed it only to 'A'."

"A? Just *A*? And you have no idea who the blackmailer is? How did this woman find you and your gang, I thought nobody knew who you all really are?"

"Now that I do not know as of yet, and believe me, I will find out."

Harrison suddenly felt sick to his stomach; a deafening realisation rang through his skull and he couldn't believe it even took him this long to make the connection. He muttered under his breath as he stared off in disbelief.

"The massacre…"

"The what? Speak up, Harry, what is it?"

"Can you remember exactly what it was in the letter that made you think the natives were involved?"

"Well, there was somethin' in there about givin' 'em weapons and getting em all riled up. Next line said they were gonna' '*send in the cavalry'*. Whatever that is supposed to mean, I'm not exactly sure."

"Len… sweet Jesus… aw hell…" Harrison began pacing back and forth, with manic, anxious energy. "No, no, no, this is big Lenora, this is a big God damn problem!"

"Why? What're you ramblin' 'bout?"

"Lenora, I think that was meant in a literal God damn sense. I think that it was the actual motherfuckin' cavalry!"

"Where you pullin' all this from?"

"I… we saw it. Morgan and I… a slaughter." Harrison paused and took a deep breath before speaking again. He stopped pacing and looked back to her. "A ways walk from here, we found it after findin' your cabin back there. We was lookin' for more answers. Jesus, Len, this is too big. You… you can't be wrapped up in this Lenora; it was God damn soldiers fighting the natives!"

"Soldiers… like American soldiers? Horseshit! You saw this?"

"I'm tellin' you! We saw it clear as day. Whoever's entangled in all this, they are connected. Connected to folk who will have all our heads for just knowin' about it. Lenora, you can't wait for this woman; you have got to take it from your mind. We need to leave. I'll write to Morgan and tell him about your condition and say I've taken you to the next town to see a good doctor."

"Harrison, ain't a damn thing has changed; we can't leave without money! If I am gonna' have a God damn child, I ain't livin' on the streets in filth; can't stay at the damn cabin 'cause the gang *will* find us and they *will* kill us. You can't just go back to work; you're supposed to be findin' and killin' me!" Lenora took a deep breath and her voice lowered and calmed. She stepped up to him and placed her hands gently on each of his arms. She looked deeply and lovingly into his eyes. "Listen t' me. We are gonna ride back to Whitepost. We are gonna go about our days like ain't a damn thing is changed. I will be sure to avoid death at the hands of my gang; I know how to keep at least one step ahead o' those bastards, and you will continue your investigation. Just as normal. You will keep all o' this to yourself until we hear from the woman. Soon as I have that money in my hand, then we're leavin'."

"And how exactly do you plan on just pacin' off away from the men you said are already suspicious of you, with all that money?"

"That's pretty simple. You will be waitin' about two miles up Persuader Path on the day; that's the route we'll take outta here. I'll convince the gang that I've been playin' you all along. I'll tell 'em we're leavin' right that second. The simple bastards'll be too damn excited to care about their previous suspicions. We'll ride away, you'll be hidden with a good line o' sight. Shoot the three at the front; I'll pull back on my horse and shoot the three at the back. It'll all be over 'fore they even know it. You'll have your criminals and your letter to give to the Governor and we'll have our money and our freedom."

"And how exactly did I suddenly find the gang, huh? Seems a little strange; I just happened upon them?"

She paused for a moment, contemplating her ideas.

"Tell folk the gang kidnapped me; tell folk they got nervous cause you was gettin' too close, so they were gonna blackmail you; use me as leverage. You went to meet me in our spot in the woods somewhere, saw 'em take me and took chase. There was a shootout and you won. Simple as. You'll be a damn hero. Finish your term on a high. Choose one of the dead fuckers to be Sam and there's your wanted man with the letter in his pocket."

Harrison didn't respond straight away; he broke her gaze and looked down to the ground. Whatever about lying to the Governor, the stupid sheriff, all the townsfolk that didn't matter, how was he going to lie to his brother? How was he now to become a criminal, officially?

"Len, what am I to say to Morgan of all this?"

"Harry." She raised one hand off his arm and stroked his cheek with it. She then softly placed her finger under his chin and raised his head and eyes back up to hers once more. "You can't tell Morgan about this, any of it."

"He's my brother; he's my family; I have to tell him."

"Darlin'… he hasn't done the things we've done; he hasn't lived the life we've lived. He won't understand… and if you tell him, then he's guilty too. I know you love 'em… so leave him out of all this. Harrison he's still young and by all accounts that matter, he's innocent. Keep him that way. If our plan works out, he won't ever need to know. You'll both have done your job here and we can all leave Whitepost. If he asks about why we suddenly have money to spend, tell him it is my inheritance from my estranged family."

"I've never kept anythin' from him… but maybe you're right… I do not wish to burden him with all this. I just want it all to be done with."

"It will all be done with soon, my sweet love, and we can be together. Morgan, you, me and our child." She placed his hand on her belly.

For a fleeting moment, mere seconds, Harrison fell back into the fantasy he imagined for himself while travelling with Morgan the day before. His own ranch with all those who meant the most to him in this world. He had just one thought, one plan for when all of this was over: 'Mrs Lenora James'.

Lenora smiled and kissed him. "I'm gonna' change into my dress and then let's be gettin' on back."

Chapter 22
Morgan James – Deputy Marshall

Morgan had been riding back towards Whitepost for a few hours before stopping to make camp. Once he had settled and lit his campfire he expected Harrison to be along after an hour or two. While he sat in front of the growing flames, waiting for Harrison's arrival before opening his can of food, he found he had a moment to reflect. He pondered the death he had witnessed. He was pondering the soldier that Harrison questioned him about. The soldier who died at the hands of army weapons. He was younger than Morgan himself, or at least he looked to be, as much as you could tell under the blood and dirt on his face.

He also thought about Old Bill's son once again. The one who died at the hands of the Spector gang. He probably looked just the same when he was killed – when he was murdered.

It felt so wrong to him – so wrong that these young, southern boys were dying for no good reason. He felt bad about the dead Indians, for sure, but if he was being honest with himself, he felt worse about the young soldiers. For reasons within him he couldn't quite explain, his true sympathy fell with them. Maybe he saw a bit of himself in them; that's what he told himself anyway. Had he not been on the road with Harrison, in another life, one of the dead could have been him.

He wanted answers. The gnawing feeling in the back of his mind since he heard Bill's story all those weeks and months ago was getting bigger and bigger. Every day that passed, every dead body they found was slowly twisting his innocent sorrow and horror into festering resentment. Resentment that those who directly had a hand in so many good, young American men dying are still walking free. Living the lives the dead men should have had. He wanted answers and he wanted justice.

Time went on and the night grew darker. Morgan was getting uncomfortable that Harrison had not shown up yet. If he had left the cabin an hour or so after Morgan did, he definitely should have been there already. Just when Morgan was beginning to debate whether he should ride back and find his brother, he heard someone approaching.

Morgan cocked his weapon and called out.

"Who's there? Make yourself known or I'll be forced to cut you down!"

"You gonna shoot me, Morgan? I surrender." Lenora laughed as she came into the light.

"Miss Taylor, what are you…"

Harrison came into view behind her.

"Sorry, Morgan, Len came looking for me; she suspected I was at the cabin, and we were…" Harrison cleared his throat. "Held up with some things'." Harrison dismounted and hitched his and Lenora's horses to a tree.

Morgan looked over to Lenora and then back to Harrison.

"Well, is everythin' all right?"

Harrison looked slightly uneasy; Morgan couldn't put his finger on it, but something about his body language was off.

"Of course, brother, why wouldn't it be?" said Harrison.

"Well, I mean… what was so urgent that Lenora had to come find you?"

"Morgan! You…" Harrison was just about to protest when Lenora interrupted.

"Morgan, I came to find your brother because I had some excitin' news I just couldn't wait to tell him." She smiled.

Harrison looked at Lenora and then back to Morgan.

"Len is, um… well…"

Lenora interrupted once more. "Morgan, your brother is gonna be a daddy." She put her hand over her belly and smiled again.

Morgan was suddenly disarmed; he was in shock, but mostly in a good way. He couldn't believe it. Harrison, the broody, serious Marshall… was going to have a baby. The man who'd never put *anything* ahead of his job now practically has a wife and a child. If he was being honest with himself, there was a voice in his head that couldn't help feeling frustrated – of all the women in the world, it had to be the criminal's daughter… But right now, what was important to him was celebrating with his dear brother. Morgan walked straight over to Harrison and gave him a massive hug.

"Congratulations, Harry! Holy shit, you're gonna be a father! I'm gonna be an uncle! And Lenora, I'm real sorry, I was blunt before; I was just, I don't know, tense. Congratulations!" Morgan turned and gave Lenora a hug.

"Tense? Haha! You turnin' into ol' Mr Stern and serious over here?" Lenora nodded towards Harrison and laughed.

"Not if I have a damn thing to do about it!" Morgan joked as Harrison grumbled, "Harrison, I can get a tent set up for you and Lenora – help me here."

Lenora piped up before the two brothers got the tent out of the saddle bag. "Boys, I've been on the road longer'n any woman you know; I don't need no tent, just a blanket and a good view o' the stars."

"Well, I guess *pops* over here can keep you warm, huh?" Morgan playfully nudged Harrison and winked.

Harrison broke a little smile before shoving his younger brother. "Shut up, Morgan."

The three settled down around the fire. Morgan told funny stories about him and Harrison growing up, much to Harrison's delight. Harrison told stories of their own parents. Lenora sat there, soaking up all of their tales with her beaming blue eyes.

Morgan resolved to himself that he felt glad to see Harrison with her. She was definitely boisterous for a woman, but she did soften his edges, she brought him out of his shell, and she made him happy. Most importantly, seeing them both together, in that moment, Morgan could not only see that Harrison loved her – he knew that already – but he got a glimpse that maybe she truly loved him.

Eventually, after the excitement of Lenora and his brother's news simmered down, they decided it was time to rest. They got some sleep, ready to make their way back in the morning.

The next day brought with it radiant sunshine. The three awoke and set out on their way back to Whitepost. Morgan couldn't help but feel a lightness in the air, a sentiment of excitement and hope. They all rode back together, enjoying the delight of this new day. They laughed and chatted as they travelled, and Morgan realised this was the first time he had spent some real time with Lenora.

She was quite a good-looking woman, despite being a bit older than him, but definitely not his type. Morgan tended to enjoy the fair-haired, sweet, doe-eyed, mostly silent type. He found it a funny irony that his brother, of all people, would end up falling for such a live wire.

He pulled back a little on his horse's reigns to allow Lenora and Harrison to ride in front of him. Morgan was watching the two of them, seeing them flirt and dally with each other warmed his soul. He could almost soften to the idea of settling down himself… almost. Mostly though, he was just giddy at the thought of teaching his future niece or nephew all kinds of ways to wind up their daddy… (He secretly hoped for a nephew.)

As they descended upon the town of Whitepost once more, Morgan was looking forward to the three of them finishing up their business and leaving sooner rather than later. Making plans for a life somewhere else – no more travelling, no more outlaws, just him, his family, and a busty blonde every now and again.

"Hey, y'all gonna get married?" Morgan asked as they approached the sheriff's office.

Harrison was seemingly caught completely off-guard, judging by his stammering to get any words out. Lenora answered instead.

"I haven't decided just yet." She chuckled and winked at Harrison. "I'll see you boys later – I've got some business to attend to."

Harrison was suddenly composed and overly serious. "Lenora, wait!"

"What?" The two were now staring so intently at each other for a couple of moments, as if trying to communicate without words.

"Well, 'er, just… be careful, look after yourself."

Lenora chuckled awkwardly. "Well, of course, Harry, what else would I be doin'! Come find me later, Bye, Morgan!" She rode off towards the stables.

Morgan turned to Harrison, who was still watching her ride off.

"Jesus, Harry, she's just pregnant, not dyin'; what's got you twisted all of a sudden?"

"Nothin', I'm just… I just want her to look after herself," Harrison abruptly replied.

"She's been on the road for quite some time now. I mean, I'm sure she knows how to look after herself. Relax! You's grittin' your teeth like you could bite the sites off a six-gun!"

"I'm fine, Morgan. Let's get the horses hitched and get into the office here."

The two brothers did as Harrison suggested and made their way into the sheriff's office.

"Well, look here now. I was startin' t' think you boys had left Whitepost for good. You find what you was lookin' for?" the sheriff asked as they entered the room.

"We found out more'n we knew before, so yes, I would say so; wouldn't you, Harry, 'er, Harrison?" said Morgan, in a condescending tone to the sheriff.

"Right. Morgan, get to workin' on that letter."

"What letter's this? Who y'all writin' to? Is your letter concernin' news from your travels?" quizzed the sheriff.

Harrison grunted a little under his breath before reluctantly resolving to answer.

"We are writin' to the Governor to inform him of our progress. We found The Phantom's cabin and a few more clues."

"And what were these *clues* you found, huh?"

Morgan responded this time before his older brother got the chance.

"The clues and information we discovered, Sheriff, will be detailed in our letter to the Governor, the details of which are not your concern. This here is between me, the

Marshall, and the Governor. I suggest you return to your own work now."

Both Harrison and the sheriff were both a little taken aback by Morgan's assertive behaviour. Where Harrison was looking at him with a flicker of pride; however, the sheriff showed only disdain and contempt. Morgan was just sick of this nosy, lazy joke of a lawman butting into their work and more importantly, talking down to him simply for being the youngest in the room. He was a Deputy US Marshall, and he was finally opening his own eyes enough to realise that he deserved respect. Should he not receive his due respect, he would demand it.

The sheriff seemingly decided to change tactics and work on the older James' brother, now that he had seen Morgan would no longer be an easy target to antagonise or provoke.

"Tell me, Marshall, why then did you have your woman out on your travels with you? Or is it *actually* all between you, the deputy, the Governor, *and* Lenora Taylor?"

"As my brother has already made clear, I would pay no mind to that which does not concern you, sir."

"All's I'm askin' is why Miss Taylor rode out after you. It's my job to keep folk in this town safe, so I got a right to know if she is all right. Pfft, I mean… nobody has seen her for couple days… you's were probably the last ones 'round her. How'd I know you ain't done somethin' suspect?"

Harrison stormed over to the sheriff's desk and slammed his hands down on the surface, staring the stinking lawman dead in the eyes.

"You know what, Sheriff? I swear to God if all your brains were dynamite, there wouldn't be enough to blow your fuckin' nose! Keep Miss Taylor's name out of your God damn mouth from here on out – she ain't ever your concern, you understand? Keep to your own business and stay the hell out o' mine; I will not tell you again!"

Morgan was suddenly worried. What in the hell was going on, Harrison was normally straight to the point, fair enough, but this was different. He was acting… on edge, tense. It wasn't like him to blow up at someone like that? Felt like he was slowly snapping. Surely it wasn't the investigation that had him like this, they had been doing this job together for years and it hadn't ever affected Harrison like this. Was it impending fatherhood? Was the news upsetting him for some reason? Morgan still felt that wasn't right. Something in his gut was telling him it was something else.

Harrison stormed out of the sheriff's office and Morgan followed him out. Harrison was marching down the steps when his younger brother placed a hand on his shoulder to gently pull him back.

"Harry, you all rig'…"

"Don't call me Harry! God dammit, Morgan!"

"Jesus, will you ease up? What is wrong with you? You was fine all but a few hours ago! Tell me what is goin' on?"

Harrison paused. He just stared at Morgan, but there was something behind his eyes. Sadness. Harrison finally spoke and lowered his tone as he affectionately placed a hand on Morgan's shoulder.

"I'm… I'm all right. Morgan, I'm sorry… I-I have a lot to think about right now is all. I apologise for my behaviour. You head on back in, pay no mind to the damn sheriff and just get that letter drawn up."

"Where are you off to?"

"I just have some things I need to follow up on. I'll see you later."

"Harrison wait, you swear you're all right, there's nothin' you gotta' tell me?"

Harrison gave him a faint smile, a smile that was probably meant to portray that things were all fine, but Morgan could see it was a mask.

"You go on back inside and I'll read over the letter 'fore you send it. I'll see you later."

Morgan could feel it; something was not right.

Chapter 23
Harrison James – US Marshall

Harrison was agitated. Trying to act normal was making it worse. How could he keep this up? He was already feeling the weight of this dishonesty towards his brother and they had only been back for a short time. How could he keep this game going? This lie? He felt uneasy and sick to his stomach as he rushed back to his rented lodgings. He could feel a tightness growing in his chest as beads of sweat began forming on his forehead and around his body.

He climbed the stairs to the first floor and felt dizziness thrust upon him as he stumbled to the door of his room. He fumbled the key in his hand before finally making it inside, slammed the door closed behind him and practically collapsed on his bed – almost fully in the grips of his panic now.

Harrison had no idea what was happening to him; he had never experienced a feeling like this. He had seen gruesome war, lost his parents to illness, seen many horrors in his line of work, but now, more so than ever before, it felt like the world around him was crumbling, like he had mere seconds before the ground itself would open and swallow him whole. Like he might be having an honest to God heart attack.

As he lay there on the bed, clutching his chest, he started to sternly try and calm his hyperventilating. He inhaled deeply and slowed his breath. After a few moments passed, he finally regained his composure. No sooner had his body been calmed, a profound feeling of remorse, shame and sadness befell him.

Harrison couldn't understand what exactly had just happened, but he instinctively knew it must be something to do with the fact that his life has suddenly turned upside down.

He sat up on the edge of the bed, wiped his forehead with his sleeve before placing his head into his hands.

What the hell was going on? Two murderers to become parents. A brother betrayed. A lifetime of believing himself to be a man of the law, a man of honour, a good man – nothing but a tall tale, a falsehood, a lie.

It felt deeply conflicting to act as if nothing was wrong – a sin to pretend he was still the same man, knowing what he knew now. Knowing the choice he had made to abandon all that he thought he stood for… but… then again… he began to remind himself of why he made that choice. He wanted to be a true father to his child. He wanted to live a life of peace with his future wife and try to make amends for their past wrongs. He wanted to raise a child with a good heart, a child who would grow to live an honest, simple and happy life. He wanted something good to come from all this. Above all, he wanted her.

He stood up and walked over to the grubby mirror and looked at his reflection. After a few moments, he moved over to the window and looked out at the town below. Harrison had a knotted feeling inside him that things were not going to go according to plan. It appeared all too easy.

Okay, yes, they would have the element of surprise when it came time to put an end to Len's gang, which gave them a considerable upper hand, but it was still going to be two against six… and that's assuming they haven't caught on before that. What if they figure it out? They'll kill her.

Harrison didn't like this; he didn't like it one bit. They needed a better solution. He truly wanted to keep Morgan out of all this, less he suffer the same torture of conscience as his older brother, but Harrison's logical side could not deny the fact that an extra set of guns, guns he could trust, might tip the scales fully in their favour. Their chances of success would increase dramatically.

He needed to convince Lenora that they could tell Morgan, he would understand… Of course, he would? They're not just brothers; they are true friends and partners.

Harrison straightened himself up before making his way out again. He was going over to Lenora's room to see her and talk through this.

He marched straight over to Calvin's, up the stairs and to her door. He knocked but found no answer. He found himself yet again becoming increasingly distressed. Where was she? She said her life was at risk from any one of those rotten shits she associates herself with; why is she not safe inside? What if she was already dead? Harrison descended the stairs with vigorous haste and went straight over to the bar, interrupting one of the patrons to speak with Calvin.

"Has Lenora been here? Have you seen her?"

"Jesus, you's lookin' a little green around the gills just now, Marshall. You feelin' all right?" Calvin responded.

The drunken patron perched at the bar included himself in the conversation too. "You look like…" He hiccupped. "You could use a rest, I'd reckon. Bein' a lawman in these *err*… parts' bound to wear a'." He hiccupped again. "Wear a man out."

"Have you seen Lenora?" Harrison said much louder this time.

"No, Marshall, I ain't seen her in a couple days. I wasn't sure if she'd just left or what, but I must say I didn't think she'd up and leave without sayin' goodbye."

"She hasn't left; she arrived back today. If you see h…"

Calvin suddenly interrupted the Marshall as he spoke over towards the doorway of the saloon. "Well, look what we have here! My word, the lovely Miss Lenora, you are a feast for tired eyes madam! We thought you had up and left us without so much as a word!" Calvin smiled.

"My dear Calvin, you know I would never dream of rushin' off without seein' you first." She playfully smiled. "I just went to see some distant relatives I found to be stayin' a ways outside o' town. I… Harry?… *err*… I mean Marshall?" She abruptly became aware of him. "What are you doin' here?" Lenora's sweet demeanour suddenly became a lot more serious. "You look to be quite flustered;

is everythin' all right?" She looked at him now very intently, as if what she was really saying was 'what *the fuck* are you doing here?'

"I-I just needed to speak with you is all. I wanted to know where you were, so I asked the gentlemen here."

Lenora walked towards them and placed the basket of various goods she was holding on the ground. "My good gracious this seems mighty serious, I take it you are not here to see me on personal business then – must be about your investigation yes?" She stared him down and he understood she meant for him to follow along.

"*Uh*, Yes, Miss Taylor. I need to ask you some questions relating to the search for the Spector gang."

Lenora portrayed herself to be highly offended. "My God, Marshall, I ain't a criminal if that's what you think?"

Calvin and the other man at the bar both laughed. "Oh, Miss Taylor, you're a sweet soul ain't you? I don't think anyone could believe a woman such as yourself to be involved with the likes of the Spector gang. That Sam Walker does the devil's business! I reckon the Marshall here probably wants to know if you seen anything suspicious while you was outta town – on account of the train robbery a couple days ago!" Calvin nodded towards Harrison with a superficial notion that he was 'clued in' on the Marshall's work.

"Is that it, Marshall? You lookin' to know about the train robbery? I didn't see nothin' I'm sorry to say."

"Well, Miss Taylor, if it would be all right with you, how's about we go somewhere to talk properly? – I have a few more questions."

"Well, all right. Follow me upstairs I need to get these things unpacked. Calvin, darlin', I'll be back down in a bit with the rent for another week if that's all right?"

"Take your time, Miss Taylor!" Calvin smiled.

Harrison proceeded to follow Lenora upstairs to her room once more. They both went inside and no sooner had Lenora closed and locked the door, she swung around to Harrison and aggressively whispered,

"Are you out o' your fuckin' mind? Did you hit your Goddamn head on the way over here or what?"

"Don't you talk to me like I'm an idiot, Lenora!"

"Well, forgive me for thinkin' you are! What in the hell has gotten into you? You can't go runnin' around all twisted up like that runnin' your mouth, askin' about where I am! Folks will get suspicious; you look like your stomach is upside down! What the hell happened to acting goddam normal?"

"What is wrong with me asking where you were?"

"You look nervous; you look anxious; you look like someone who knows somethin'!"

"Oh, what? You're worried the bar man and the goddamn drunk are gonna find us out? All I did was ask, Had they seen you?"

"Harrison, you need to get your fuckin' head out of the God damn clouds. You don't know who my gang members are, and you don't know what in the hell they look like. I have taught most of 'em well. So well, we ain't ever been caught. We know how to hide right under everyone's noses. Now, for all you God damn know, that could have been one of my guys sitting right there at that bar. You bust in there flustered, demandin' to find me? Well, you might have just made him a little too suspicious, you might have just given the whole God damn game away. Act normal."

"Act normal? How in the hell can I act normal? This don't come fuckin' natural to me, Lenora!" Harrison started to raise his voice.

"Shhhh! Quiet, God dammit, there's too many folk around; it's the middle of the day!"

"How am I to do this, Len? I thought you were dead earlier. Where were you?"

"God, Harrison, I went to the general store and whatnot to pick up some essentials. I need to make sure my saddlebags are stacked with whatever we might need if a quick getaway becomes necessary. I like to plan for all outcomes."

"You can't go marchin' around the place; what if one of them does decide to finish you off, Len? I need you safe!"

"Harrison, I just told you, my gang ain't stupid; they may be thinkin' of killin' me right now, but they will not risk doin' it in the plain light of day, in the middle of town with the fuckin' federal law around. They won't risk the hangman like that. Relax… please. We just need to keep everythin' together until we get the money. It won't be long; any day now the woman will come around; you'll have your letter and folk will be none the wiser."

"Speakin' of money, what was that downstairs they were talkin' 'bout – did you rob a fuckin' train while I was out of town?"

"I had to; I tried talking them out of it, but it came down to, if I didn't agree to it, I'd have signed my own death warrant right there and then. I had to show strength."

"I thought you wanted to be finished with all that! Are you takin' me for a damn fool, Lenora? My recollection was that we would finish off *your* gang, then that's it – no more death, no more murder! We make our way to leadin' a better life! Why in hell would you go and do that?"

"Harry, will you stop? *I* didn't kill anyone. I do want a better life, but there wasn't gonna' be a better life if those bastards thought I was changed. They would have killed me then and there. You need to trust me, Harry, please. I know what I'm doin'."

Lenora took his hand in hers and looked deeply into his eyes.

"This will be over soon, and then we won't ever have a damn thing to be fightin' about, nothin' but you, me… and our son."

"Son? What makes you so sure it ain't gonna' be a daughter? How'd you know?"

Lenora smiled and looked down to her stomach and back up to meet Harrison's eyes.

"I just have a feelin'… but seriously, Harry, you need to stay relaxed; you need to stay calm around town;

nobody can know anythin' is up. You looked more nervous than a long-tailed cat in a room full o' rockin' chairs when I walked in here."

"I'm sorry, all right? I'll act *normal*. The reason I came lookin' for you is 'cause… well, I wanna tell Morgan. He should know about all this."

"Harrison, we've been through this – he won't understand!"

"Why not? I trust him with my life – I ain't ever hidden anythin' from him. He's a grown man now; he can handle the truth! He won't turn his back on me."

Lenora took a step back and spoke with intensity.

"But he will turn his back on me. He may even kill me, Harrison."

"Like hell, he would! Morgan is my brother!"

"Yes he is your brother, but he is also a deputy Marshall workin' on behalf of a Governor. Harrison, you almost killed me when you learned my truth. The only thing that stopped you was your heart. Morgan holds nothin' for me, so why would he spare me?"

"He wouldn't do it; he knows the depth of my feelings for you! He is a deputy only because I brought him into this line o' work; he never chose it for himself; he would stay loyal to me!"

"If things were the other way, if it was your dear brother who had fallen for someone you believed to be evil – someone you believed to be corruptin' and vicious – and you had the means to remove that person from his life, wouldn't you take it? He could live to love another, someone better."

"He doesn't think that of you."

"He will if he finds out. Please, Harry, you cannot tell him anythin'. We stick to the plan."

Chapter 24
Morgan James – Deputy Marshall

Morgan stood outside the sheriff's office for a couple of minutes as he watched his older brother rush in the direction of the boarding house they had been staying at.

He turned to go back inside and draw up the letter. He sat at Harrison's desk, directly across from the now sleeping (and snoring) sheriff. He wrote about the cabin they found, the massacre of natives and, to his mind, more importantly, the massacre of soldiers.

He stopped writing for a moment and contemplated adding more to the letter. Should he tell the Governor of the connection between Lenora and Sam Walker? Was it wrong to keep it from him that they had found *The Phantom's* ward? Harrison was too entangled with her personally to realise the importance of this fact in relation to the case. The Governor *would* want to know this surely?

He almost went to write about it; he could just send the letter himself without allowing the Marshall to see it. No. Harrison would kill him for going behind his back like that. He couldn't do it to him. He left the letter as it was, signed it off and sealed it up in an envelope.

When the work was all done, Morgan sat at the desk, staring off into nothing. Worrying.

He couldn't shake his older brother's odd behaviour; why would he not tell Morgan of his troubles? – perhaps it was because they had not had a chance to speak alone, in private, since they were at Sam's cabin and Harrison may have worries he doesn't wish for others to hear? That still felt like a stretch… Harrison was tougher than that. A few daily troubles wouldn't have a man such as him on edge.

Morgan resolved to just go and confront him. Harrison wanted to look over the letter anyway, so it was the perfect opportunity to lay everything out on the table. Just the two of them.

Morgan packed up his things and left the office. He made his way over to the boarding house and up to Harrison's room, but to his disappointment, Harrison was not there. He went back downstairs and asked the young woman at the desk had she seen where he went.

"I seen him marchin' over to Calvin's not too long ago in a fluster – someone in trouble over there or somethin'?"

"No, ma'am. Just workin' on the case is all. Thank you kindly." Morgan gave the woman a quick smile before not so subtly checking her out.

Now how did I miss her until now? he thought. As he was walking out, he turned and gave a cheeky wink and a tip of his hat. The woman blushed.

"A red head an' everythin' – wild card,'" he whispered to himself as he stepped down onto the street.

Morgan made his way across the town to the saloon. He walked in and made his way to the bar.

"Howdy Calvin!"

"Morgan! We was beginnin' to almost miss your sorry face 'round here!" Calvin joked. "Don't normally get you in here this early, specially 'fore our dear sheriff has awoken from his daily nap!" Calvin and the other men sitting at the bar laughed.

"I ain't here for the usual just yet, boys, here on business." Morgan held up the envelope in his hand and shook it. "You fellas seen the Marshall come in here?"

"You actually just missed him; he and Miss Taylor just went upstairs. He had questions about your case for her or some such."

"You mind if I head on up? I need to confer with him."

"Sure, sure. You back later on for the usual?"

"Ooh, I dunno, boys, there's a red-head dyin' for my attention elsewhere, you see?" Morgan flashed his cheeky smile once more.

"Look at him – grinnin' like a weasel in a hen house!" Calvin and the men laughed.

Morgan chuckled to himself as he ascended the stairs. He made his way down the hallway when he started to hear voices. Tense voices coming from inside Lenora's room. It must be the two of them.

Morgan didn't want to disturb them, but suddenly he heard something. His mind was telling him it was wrong to eavesdrop, but his gut was telling him to listen.

Morgan silently moved up closer to the door and listened.

"*... What if one of them does decide to finish you off, Len? I need you safe!*"

Harrison I just told you, my gang ain't stupid; they may be thinkin' of killin' me right now, but they will not risk doin' it in the plain light of day, in the middle of town with the fuckin' federal law around. They won't risk the hangman like that. Relax... please. We just need to keep everything together until we get the money. It won't be long; any day now the woman will come around; you'll have your letter and folk will be none the wiser..."

Morgan stepped back.

No... no...

He couldn't think. He couldn't process what he was hearing. His mind was petrified... He needed to get out of there; he could think to do nothing but run.

Morgan fled from the saloon. The patrons at the bar tried to speak to him as he dashed by, but he couldn't register a word they said.

He hurried back to the boarding house. He burst in the front door and the young woman at the desk was startled but pleasantly surprised.

"Oh, Deputy James, back already? Seems you mighta' missed me a little, huh?" She playfully quipped.

Morgan stared at her with sinister eyes, just for a moment, but enough to intimidate her to look back down at her desk, pretending to work. He charged up the stairs and into his room. He slammed the door closed.

"My gang... *my* gang, she said... her *fucking* gang..."

"*Her* gang... no... NO... I do not believe this..."

Morgan was frantically pacing, horrifying thoughts and realisations swirling in his brain faster than he could comprehend them.

"Until *we* get the money, she said, he's a part of this… he's a part of this? No. No…"

Morgan stopped moving. He stood there in the middle of the room, frozen.

They've been playin' me this whole time. It was all horseshit, rotten HORSESHIT! He's known who Sam God damn Walker was this whole time… and he's been FUCKIN' HER!

Morgan erupted into a furious rage. He smashed, kicked and threw any furniture he could move in the room. He screamed with wrath as the room was vandalised.

The woman from downstairs was frantically knocking on the door.

"Please, Mr James, sir, what's goin' on in there – are you all right? I can hear you screamin'!"

Morgan swung the door open for the woman.

"GET THE FUCK AWAY FROM ME!"

She scurried back downstairs faster than her legs could carry her.

Morgan turned back into the room and sat on the floor, trying to catch his breath.

How could he? How could Harrison do this to him… how could he do this to people… has he murdered people in cold blood? How long has he known about that retched filth of a woman? All that horseshit about her being attacked… nothing more than a vicious manipulation, an excuse for her killing spree.

Morgan's soul felt crushed. His brother, his only family, his best friend, his hero – an outlaw? A wretched liar? He then started thinking of old Bill's son and the wife once again, only this time, Morgan started picturing Lenora's evil grin as she stood over their cold corpses, laughing.

Now he thought he could see things very plainly. Harrison's not on edge because something's wrong; he's on edge because the bastard doesn't want to get caught. He and the woman spat from hell. How did she twist her rotten claws into him? It didn't matter… He was as bad as her. If he hadn't killed her the moment he found out, he may as well have done those evil deeds with her as far as Morgan was concerned.

There was venom in his veins now. This betrayal ran deep. How could Harrison stand to breathe the same air as that beast, knowing what she did… knowing what she is. Did he even know his brother at all?

Morgan stood up. And made a resolution for himself. As God was his witness, Lenora Taylor will die.

If Harrison tries to stop him, then he has no choice but to end him as well.

He needed to think carefully about this, though. He was going to need evidence; otherwise, folk will just think he murdered a woman, a popular woman.

He was going to have to come up with some way to expose her… and him.

Morgan started attempting to fix up his room; he couldn't arouse any suspicions until the moment was right. He finished fixing the room up as best as he could and he went downstairs. He could hear the woman from the desk crying in a little side office. He gently opened the door and leaned his head in.

The woman jumped out of her skin at the sight of him.

"You stay away from me!"

"Miss, Miss, please, I came to beg your for—"

"I'll… I'll get the sheriff… o'… or the Marshall! Stay away!"

"NO… no, please, please, miss…" Morgan was using his softest tone of voice. "Please, there's no need for the Marshall; I'm truly very sorry for my outburst. It wasn't right – not right at all. I… I had just received some very upsettin' news, see? And I was not myself. Please, I didn't mean to take it out on you, ma'am."

"You scared me half to death, sir… How am I gonna fix all that damage? My daddy is gonna kill me… I didn't know what to do." She cried into her hands.

"May I come in?" Morgan asked softly.

She sniffled and nodded.

"Now look here, see?" Morgan took out some money and left it on a little table by the door. "That should cover a new lamp, and mirror and such for the room. I am truly sorry, miss. I admit I feel a fool for allowin' my emotions to get the better of me like that, and to upset a sweet gal like yourself. I assure you, it will never happen again."

The young woman looked up at him, down at the money and back up to meet his gaze. She wiped her eyes with a handkerchief.

"Thank… thank you, Mr James. Are… are you all right? What was your terrible news?"

"Oh… It doesn't matter now; I… I have made peace with it… Forget about me though, are you all right? What is your name, darlin'?"

"Holly."

"Well, Miss Holly, I cannot thank you enough for your kind and understandin' heart, but I must ask a favour of you."

"Okay, um… what is it?"

"I'm… well, as you can understand, I am just horribly embarrassed by all this. I feel such a fool for behavin' as I did, and… I would just very much appreciate it if you would keep this whole business to yourself, please."

"Well… before now, I had seen you to be a calm and decent gentleman, so… I believe you. I will keep this to myself, Mr James. I'll try and get the room fixed up 'fore Daddy gets back from his travels."

"Miss Holly, I cannot tell you how much I appreciate your discretion, and please call me Morgan." He smiled sweetly at her and kissed her hand.

Holly smiled and blushed once more. "Are you stayin' in town for much longer, Mr Morgan?"

"I'll be here for a short spell longer. I'm just headin' back upstairs now, Miss Holly. Thank you again for your kindness." Morgan deliberately leaned in very close to her gullible face and said sweetly, "And we'll keep this just between the two of us."

She sniffled and smiled as Morgan left and returned to his room.

He calmly closed the door and sat on the edge of his bed. His face deadpan and emotionless, but inside he was festering with resentment. He sat contemplating his next move as the revelation of Lenora *and* Harrison's true selves gnawed and embedded into his brain – rotting away the love he once carried for them. He sat there like this for almost an hour when suddenly his eyes fixed on the letter he had drawn up for the Governor.

He had an interesting thought.

Perhaps I should write a new letter…

Chapter 25
Sam Walker/Lenora Taylor –
Notorious Outlaw

A few days passed and things were going surprisingly smoothly. Lenora kept to the beaten track, stayed in very public spaces just to be on the safe side. She had successfully managed to curtail Harrison's unrealistic urge to tell his brother and any day now, this *woman* should be back.

She was almost… excited. She was mostly staying over in Harrison's room each night, living in a bubble of secret delight and anticipation of their forthcoming future of family bliss. True, the future of family bliss would not come too easily; there were significant risks and obstacles to overcome between this point and then, but she was feeling… hopeful.

She awoke one particular morning early, with a certain spring in her step. It was going to be a good God damn day; she could feel it. Even the dull weather outside could not sway her mood. She rolled over to kiss the half-asleep Marshall before jumping out of bed.

"Where're you off to so lively, hmm?" grumbled Harrison with his face planted in the pillow.

"What's wrong, Harry? Worn out from last night?" She giggled as she playfully threw her pillow at him.

Harrison rolled over and sat up a little to see her.

"Well, now I didn't say that." He smirked.

"C'mon, get up! You's movin' like molasses in January!"

"Why damn it? Hens ain't even cluckin' yet. What's gotten into you?"

"Today's the day, Harrison. I can feel it. I can smell money."

Harrison rolled his eyes and turned over under the blanket to go back asleep.

"Fine! I'll make the preparations myself. Oh, by the bye – did I tell you what I heard 'bout Morgan last night?"

"What you talkin' bout? What's wrong with Morgan?" This time Harrison sat up in bed properly, back to his serious self.

"Well, I was speakin' with some o' the gals from the whorehouse at the bar and one of 'em said she heard some all-mighty shoutin' comin' from one of the rooms here. I asked her which one and she said it was the first window on the left at the back. I didn't say it to her, but I knew right away that's Morgan's room, ain't it?"

"Why was she at the back of the lodging house?"

"Well, I don't know; she was fuckin' some guy who didn't want his wife to hear about him payin' a trip to a whorehouse I'm bettin'."

"This was a few days ago? He hasn't said a word 'bout any o' this; in fact, he ain't said more'n two sentences to me in days. Somethin's off with the boy."

"Well, why don't you go and ask him 'bout all this?"

Harrison sat there silently, contemplating for a moment before getting up and proceeding to get dressed.

"I'm gonna go see Morgan and get down to the sheriff's office. I'll see you later."

"Hey!" She grabbed Harrison by the belt buckle and pulled him in for a kiss. "I love you."

Harrison smiled, kissed her again and left the room.

Lenora took her time getting herself together. She wanted to make sure everything was in order in case things didn't go exactly as planned. She packed up the essentials they would need for the road that she had purchased a few days earlier; these would be stashed away in her saddlebag.

Even if things did go to plan, she still wanted to get all of her non-essentials packed. One way or another, as soon as this business was all dealt with – Lenora wanted to leave Whitepost and start a whole new life as a whole new person.

After a couple hours of getting organised, she went downstairs and across town to the bar. Calvin would usually have a freshly brewed pot of coffee ready by now and Lenora liked to enjoy it whilst she had a quick read of the local penny rag.

No sooner had she sat down to enjoy this blissful and quiet moment to herself, she saw a familiar face enter the saloon, a face that was frantically looking around, a face that she was acutely annoyed to see.

It was Austin.

He clocked her and hurried straight over.

"Sa…*err*, Jesus, sorry, I mean Lenora… Miss Taylor!"

Lenora subtly grabbed him in closer to her and spoke in a very hushed voice.

"Austin, what the *fuck*!" She was livid. What in God's name was he doing, bursting in here like this?

Austin replied at normal volume, in an attempt to appear somewhat normal whilst they were in a public space.

"Miss Taylor, I need a word. If you wouldn't mind, I… *uh*… have some news from… your family." Austin was staring at her keenly as he spoke, presumably attempting to indicate this was important.

She glared at him.

"Well, sir, I take it this is all a touch sensitive judgin' by your conduct here. Come and take a walk with me. I assume this news is of great consequence?"

"It is, ma'am."

"Well then." She took a final sip of her coffee and stood up from her seat. "Let's go, shall we?"

Lenora led the way to the back door of the saloon, with Austin closely following. She was composed and elegant as she exited the building. Rather than go for a walk, however, she pulled Austin into a dirty little side alley between Calvin's and the next building, pulled a small knife from under her dress and pinned Austin up to the wall – the knife just at his neck.

"You studyin' to be a fuckin' half-wit huh! What is the one God damn golden rule when we are layin' low?"

"I *know,* Sam, will you drop the knife?"

"Clearly, you don't asshole. When we're hidin' out in a town, you, or any o' the other shits, DO NOT know me. You do not approach me for any fuckin' reason! How many times do I gotta remind y'all that is how connections will be made – when they see we all fuckin' know each other!"

Austin grabbed a hold of Lenora's wrist to try and pull the knife back from his throat.

"Sam, you fuckin' shot me last time you seen me, and I ain't here with a grudge now. The least you can God-damn do is hear me out, huh? *Jesus*!"

Lenora reflected for a minute and then lowered the knife.

"Well, somebody better be fuckin' dyin' Austin, I swear t' God."

"You should know I wouldn't have done this if it weren't an emergency; I was lookin' for you all mornin', time is of the essence here."

"Spit it out then, go on!"

"The *woman* who hired us for all this? She's workin' for ol' Mrs Laudergill."

"The hell you say?"

"I swear it. She rode out to Javier and the boys camped out in the woods. She told us and said, wait 'til you hear this. She told us that she will pay us twelve thousand *motherfuckin'* dollars – every penny she owns – if we ride out to her ranch right now and kill a man called Arthur who's on his way. He was spotted in another town over, so she said he won't be long now."

Lenora stumbled back in disbelief. Twelve thousand. That's money to buy their own house; that's everything they need... everything *she* needs. She was overwhelmed. This was suddenly happening so fast. Just kill this Arthur when he shows up and that's it – job done? So easy – too easy.

She needed to get out to that ranch as soon as possible, but she needed to tell Harrison. He had to help her kill the rest of them as soon as the old bat had paid up.

"Austin, where the rest of 'em at now?"

"The boys and Lita are saddlin' up to get on over to the ranch."

Lenora's conscience started to eat at her. Whatever about the rest of them, they were no good bastards mostly. Greedy sons o' bitches... but Austin was good to her. In his own way, he had always respected her and right from the very beginning, when she recruited him to help her finish off the rotten pieces of festering shit that killed the *real* Sam, he didn't ask questions; he just knew it was personal and he stuck with her since.

She didn't want him to die. He didn't deserve it. He at least deserved the chance to try and get away. If he was spared, he could just disappear, same as her, and start a fresh new life.

"Austin, listen t' me. I've got a plan: get everyone over to that ranch. I got a feelin' if this Arthur fella is worth twelve thousand dollars, then he surely will not be comin' alone."

"You not comin' to the ranch now?"

"No, I gotta grab some things first; I'll be right behind you… and… Austin?"

"Yeah?"

She took a deep breath. "Listen t' me. When I tell you to go, you ride back into town. No questions you hear? No matter what is happenin' at that ranch, you ride back."

"What are y…?"

"I want your God damn word, Austin, just…" She took another deep breath and exhaled. "Just please trust me."

"All right, you got my word." He looked at her a little puzzled, but, as was his way, he decided not to ask questions.

"Now, c'mon, we ain't got no time t' spare! Get your sorry assess to that ranch; it's pay day, cocksucker!" She jokingly punched Austin's arm and laughed.

"All right, I'm gone – see you soon!"

Just as Austin was about to leave the alley out of sight, Lenora called over to him.

"Austin wait! I just… I'm sorry about your arm; last time I saw you. You know I didn't mean to…"

"Woman, this money's got you all kinds o' twisted; you ain't *ever* this nice!" He smiled at her.

"I'll see you there, Sam."

She smiled right back as he left.

Holy shit. This was happening. This was happening right now. The plan had to change; she needed Harrison hidden behind the walled entrance to the ranch, then they could catch the rest of the gang by surprise after this business was over. She needed to go and find him right fucking now.

Her heart was racing, pure adrenaline coursing through every vein. She grabbed her dress in her hands and ran out to the street, down to the sheriff's office.

She burst in the door to find each of the three men silently working at other corners of the room – Morgan at a desk facing the wall, his back to all of them. Harrison at his desk on the opposite side of the room and the sheriff perched at his own desk in the middle. The sheriff was, surprisingly, working.

"Miss Taylor?" Harrison stood up immediately and walked towards her. "Are you all right? What's happened You look flustered?"

"Oh, Harr… 'er… Marshall I'm fine. I just need a quick word is all… in private, if you wouldn't mind." She looked attentively into his eyes, an attempt to let him know, without words, that this couldn't wait.

"Of course, step on into this back room here."

They both went into a small back room beside the jail cells. It was more of a glorified broom cupboard, but there was a stool in there and one small-sized window.

"Len, what's happenin'? It's not somethin' to do with the baby, is it?" he whispered as he gently placed a hand on her stomach. She didn't have an obvious bump just yet, at least not through her clothes, but he could feel it.

"No, no nothin' like that; baby's fine, Jesus. Harry, relax, will ya? This is much more important than that right now!"

"What is it then?"

"It was old Mrs Laudergill this whole time – she's the one that hired us!"

"The widow Laudergill… what? How you know all this?"

Lenora explained what happened with Austin. She also informed him of the new plan.

"Who is this Arthur? What did he do? What could the old lady Laudergill have possibly done that this Arthur is comin' after her? How did it end up involvin' me and Morgan?"

"Who gives a shit? We kill him and we have our money. Harry, we kill him and the rest – we've got our ticket out of here." She grabbed hold of both of his hands and looked into his eyes with loving exhilaration.

"Lenora, what if he's an innocent party in all this? What if he ain't done a thing wrong? You can't just kill an innocent man like that. It ain't right."

She dropped his hands and stepped back. "Harrison – it's them or us. Make your choice."

"It ain't that fuckin' simple!"

"YES, IT IS. You start thinkin' like that, like a lawman, then we sure as shit won't be lastin' too much longer. You want to leave here and be a family? You want to finish up a life of violence same as me? Well, this is the price. It's a high price, for sure, but I am sure as shit going to pay it to get what I need. Now I am going to do this with or without you. I am done with all o' this; I've been on this road too God damn long and this is the final one, the last job. You in or not?"

Harrison stared at her. If she was being honest with herself, she was nervous. Nervous that he might actually leave her now, when she needed him the most. When they were so close. Every second that went by without a word felt like an hour. She couldn't take it any more, and she was too stubborn to let him know she needed him, so to hell with him then.

"You know what, Marshall? Forget it! I see how it is. Just do not get in my way…"

She turned to leave and as she did so, he grabbed her wrist and pulled her back.

"I told you already, back in the woods that day. When I found out about all of this."

"What?"

He sighed. "I told you the only thing that really matters is a duty to the ones that mean the most. Lenora… for now, and always, I am gonna be with you."

She couldn't help break a smile before proceeding to scold him again.

"You wastin' time now come on, I need to go, you need to make an excuse in about an hour and follow us out to the ranch – stay out o' sight, I don't need to remind you what'll happen to me and to you if any o' the boys spot you 'fore it's time."

"Hold up… One last thing…"

"What?" Lenora was getting impatient now she needed to get moving.

"The letter that started all this – who was it addressed to again?"

"It wasn't a name, just a single letter."

"Yeah, I *know* that. What was the letter?"

"Just A… wait… holy hell, I didn't even think o' that myself; 'A' is obviously this Arthur fella?"

Harrison's face fell and he suddenly looked vexed and troubled.

"Len… I don't like this. If this is the same 'A' from the letter, then this is the man who had somethin' to do with that massacre out by the cabin. This man may have influence that would attract a lot of God-damn attention were he to be killed. He may not be ridin' to the Laudergill ranch alone, neither. This could be real dangerous; I can't let anythin' happen to you."

"Harry, I got six trigger happy assholes to cover me; it won't be anythin' we can't handle. Now come on, I *need* to go."

"Oh my God… Shit… oh FUCK!" Harrison pressed his hand to his head as he appeared to have a dramatic revelation.

"Jesus, what now?"

Just in the split seconds before Harrison had the chance to answer her, a banging knock came on the door. It was the sheriff.

"Marshall, you best come on out here. Your Governor has just arrived in town; he's on his way over here right now. Be here any second."

Harrison was twisted into a flustered state of stress.

"Right, I'm comin'!" he shouted back to the sheriff before grabbing hold of Lenora's shoulders and looking her dead in the eye. She had never seen him so serious; he was staring at her like it was a matter of life and death.

"Len, listen, stay here. DO NOT MOVE, you understand? I swear to God, do NOT leave this room until I come back."

"Harrison, I have t'…"

"LENORA. DO NOT MOVE."

"Okay, fine, Jesus." She was admittedly a little unnerved, what the hell had gotten into him. She was also decidedly anxious to leave by now; she was running out of time. Her impatience was likely going to get the better of her if he didn't come back very soon.

Harrison left and closed the door behind him. She pressed her ear against the door to listen to the happenings on the other side.

She could hear Harrison pace back to his desk and sit down.

She then heard the office door open and a man step inside.

Lenora heard Harrison speak first.

"Governor Lewis, Good to see you, sir. I must admit I wasn't expectin' you here."

The Governor spoke. He had a deep and commanding voice, but there was something about it that seemed… shaken, tense.

"The formalities are not necessary, Marshall; I've told you a hundred God damn times – Call me Arthur."

Chapter 26
Harrison James – US Marshall

As soon as Lenora mentioned the story about Morgan that morning, Harrison was immediately concerned. He had noticed Morgan was acting unusual, quiet… not his normal self at all. He hadn't seen too much of him in the saloon playing cards with the other men or down by the river fishing… or even chasing the local skirt.

He had initially dismissed it; he figured Morgan was probably just bored of the folks around here; he could imagine the old coots in the saloon are probably only good for so much conversation. Maybe Morgan was just *really* ready to move on from here… but upon hearing that he was seen to be screaming in his room? What in the hell could that be about? What was so terribly awful that would lead a happy-go-lucky young man such as Morgan to erupt like that *and* not say a word to Harrison about it?

Harrison was nervous. Did he know?

No, how could he possibly…

No. He would have confronted Harrison. He would have wanted the truth if he was suspicious of anything, and they would have spoken by now surely. When Harrison jumped from the bed to get dressed, he resolved that he was overthinking it all; it was probably nothing, but he should check on his brother all the same.

After he left Lenora to her business, he went down the hall and just as he almost had his knuckle to Morgan's door for the first knock, the door swung open.

Harrison was startled; he had never known Morgan to be an eager early riser, but there he was, dressed and ready for the day.

"Morgan, you all but gave me a damn heart attack; what has you up and ready at this hour?"

"Could ask you the same thing." Morgan's tone was cold and unreceptive.

"I just wanted to come by and let you know I'm headin' down to the Post Station to see if there's anythin' back from the Governor. I'm assumin' you posted that letter? You ain't never showed it to me."

"You don't trust me to write the letter myself?"

"Morgan, you know that ain't true. I just wanted to have a look was all. Doesn't matter now anyway; point is it was sent and I'm gonna' check for a reply. Are… are you all right?"

"Why would I not be?" Morgan was still just standing there in the doorway, staring Harrison down. Emotionless.

"Len told me she heard tell of you screamin' and hollerin' in your room here the other day? You ain't said anythin' to me, so… I wanted to know if you was okay?"

Morgan's body language dramatically changed. He suddenly broke into a big grin and put his hand on Harrison's shoulder. Seemingly in a gesture of familiarity but something about this seemed… weird, strange… fake. He chuckled as he spoke, but it felt forced.

"Oh, that, HA! Would you believe I found a snake."

"A snake? In the room here? That's what had you screechin' like that?" Harrison was a little confused. He couldn't shake off this gut feeling that this was bizarre.

"Well, you'd be screamin' too… if things were the other way 'round, although, maybe not. You'd probably never let a snake rattle your cage like that, would you? The tough old Marshall would *never* give in to something as worthless as a rotten little snake!"

Morgan laughed in that strange, forced way again and Harrison awkwardly gave a slight chuckle alongside him.

"So, you sure you're all right then?"

"Peachy. You get on down to the post station now and I'll see you later." Morgan weakly smiled one final time, closed the door behind him and brushed past his older brother.

Harrison went to the edge of the stairs and could hear Morgan mumbling something too quiet to decipher to the woman at the desk down below. She giggled before Harrison could faintly hear her say, "Will I see you this evenin' for dinner?" Morgan mumbled a response and then left.

Harrison stood there contemplating to himself, he thought. Okay, Morgan is still chasing the local skirt after all; maybe Harrison was overthinking everything. Maybe it was just as he thought before – everything's fine… But why would he be acting strange and 'stand-offish' with him then?

Harrison couldn't fathom it, but suddenly an idea crept in. The last time he spoke with Morgan, and his brother didn't seem to be acting odd, was the day just after he found out Harrison was to be a father. Could it be possible, now that the news has sunk in, Morgan believes he and Harrison may grow apart? That he may have no purpose if Harrison becomes focused on his own family. Could that be the reason for Morgan being so distant?

Harrison thought more about it as he walked downstairs and out the door to the post station.

When he arrived at his destination, Harrison was disappointed to find no response from the Governor. There was, however, an older woman frantically fussing and nagging at the clerk behind the office counter about a missing letter or some such. Her eyes were bloodshot and full of tears, her hair frazzled and untamed as she pleaded with the post master to take another look.

"Please, sir, there has to be a letter… He wouldn't have left it this long to write. He… there has to be something I'm beggin' you to just please try again; it could be addressed to Montgomery instead?"

"Ma'am, I can't keep goin' through this with you; there ain't nothin' here for you. Now, I'm sorry but there are other customers needin' my attention. Once again, I'm gon' have to ask you t' leave."

"You can't just dismiss me like this! I bet you's workin' for them, ain't ya? I've given my whole goddamn life up in this rotten town and not one o’ y’all gives a damn about me! I gave your momma work in my house; you had food on your table ’cause o’ me!”

Harrison interrupted in an effort to calm the woman.

“Ma’am, I’m sure you’ll get your letter in good time. Best to head on home now.”

“You stay away from me! I know who you are – I know who you work for! I want nothin’ to do with you, ya hear? Stay away from me!”

The woman pushed past Harrison and left the building in a tizzy.

Harrison was almost going to ask the clerk who that was, but to be perfectly honest, he didn’t care all too much – probably just some crazed old woman expecting a letter from her kid or something.

He then left himself and made his way over to the sheriff’s office; he wanted to write another letter to the Governor. In this letter, however, he wanted to outline his wish to retire as soon as this case was over with.

When Harrison arrived at the sheriff’s office, the atmosphere was tense. The sheriff and Morgan were sitting on opposite sides of the room. Harrison attempted to greet them both, but neither were all too welcoming.

“No news from the Governor yet.” Harrison spoke towards Morgan, who had his back facing the older brother.

“…hm…”

“When did you post the letter? He would have received it by now, yes?”

"He surely would."

"You gonna' look at me when I'm God damn talkin' to you!"

Morgan turned halfway around in his chair and looked at him.

"I'm sorry, *Marshall*. Anythin' else new?" There was almost a vitriol in his tone.

Harrison glared at Morgan. "No. Get on back to whatever it is you were doin'; we'll talk properly later."

"Sure thing, boss."

Morgan turned back around to face the wall once more. He didn't seem to be doing a whole lot, so Harrison was a little curious as to what he was doing here… He could have stayed in his bed, gotten some breakfast or something… Why come and sit here watching the wall?

He thought better than to bring it up with his deputy now; best left for later on. Harrison got to writing and finishing up a couple of other bits of work that needed tending to. It was only after an hour or two that Lenora came bursting in.

When they went into the back room together and Harrison heard all she had to say, he was in full panic, sweat trickling down his brow. Just seconds before the sheriff knocked on the door, a truly deadly and alarming thought rang through Harrison's mind… was it possible, could it be possible… that the Arthur Lenora wants to kill is the same Arthur that governs the entirety of New Mexico Territory? The same Arthur that commissioned him to the investigation in the first place?

Whoever kills the Governor will become the most wanted.

This was escalating way too fast; Harrison couldn't let Lenora go out to that ranch. To hell with the money, he didn't give a shit about that. None of it mattered if she died. She would stay here, Harrison would accompany the Governor to the ranch and end all of this. The gang would die, Lenora would live, the case would be over and they would be free.

That was all dependent on Lenora staying in that room… which, if Harrison knew Lenora, was a fifty-fifty fucking chance.

Harrison walked back to his desk and sat down just before the Governor walked in. He was a tall man with a stocky build. Harrison knew him to normally be quite well put together, as one would expect of a Governor, but when Harrison saw him just then, he looked worn out, stressed and slightly hostile in his body language. His eyes were bloodshot, and bags hung underneath as though he hadn't slept in days.

Harrison jumped up to greet him, being careful not to mention his first name for fear Lenora would hear this and reach the same conclusion.

"Governor Lewis, Good to see you, sir. I must admit I wasn't expecting you here."

"The formalities are not necessary, Marshall; I've told you a hundred God damn times – Call me Arthur."

Shit.

Harrison's stomach twisted. He knew that Lenora was sharp enough to put two and two together now, but he couldn't exactly go and check on her. He didn't want the Governor to know anything about her, especially that she was right there behind the door, listening.

The Governor spoke again; he was not pleased.

"Marshall, Deputy Morgan, gather your things; we're goin' on a ride. Sheriff, you're comin' too."

Harrison couldn't help but notice something odd: both Morgan and the sheriff immediately stood up and began to holster their weapons and prepare to leave; neither of them asked where or why.

"Sir, if you don't mind my askin', where abouts are we headed?"

"Well, Marshall, seems as though I have to do your God damn job for you; y'all been out here weeks on weeks, and I ain't any closer to getting my fuckin' letter back. But lucky for me, the bitch responsible has unknowingly revealed herself."

His letter? He just confirmed it. He couldn't have known Harrison was aware of the highly sensitive content within this letter, but what really triggered Harrison was the final sentence. 'The *bitch* responsible'… a woman. He knows a woman is responsible; it's not possible.

There's no way he could know Sam's true identity, could he?

No.

Harrison's heart was beating out of his chest. How much did he know? How could he know? It felt like the ground was crumbling underneath his feet, like the air itself was being pulled from his lungs, but he had to appear calm. He could not let any of them know he was panicking; his external presence had to be normal. Harrison had to make sure he did not give the game away.

But… what if the Governor knows he's wrapped up in this now? What if this ride they're going on is to serve him his last rites?

No. Overthinking this could be his end. Harrison needed to remain composed and remain confident. It's not possible the Governor knows; he kept reminding himself that over and over as he collected his things, preparing to leave.

Harrison gathered his thoughts and responded.

"I'm sorry you feel that way, sir. We have been diligently followin' any lead presented to us and kept you informed at all times. How did you ascertain the identity o' this perpetrator?"

"Well, now would you God damn believe it? the head house nigger. That fuckin' black bastard had been goin' behind my back and writin' to an old bat that lives 'round these parts 'bout my private business. She then took it upon herself to steal somethin' of mine. I was suspicious of him fo' a while and then… well, my suspicions were confirmed."

The men were all ready to leave and just as they stood around the door, Harrison took a deep breath and spoke again.

"And I'm assuming we're ridin' out to find this woman now, who is it?"

"You assume correct, Marshall. We're ridin' out to the widow Laudergill's ranch."

Harrison may have been relieved for a short, sweet moment that the Governor did not know of Sam's true identity… but the crushing weight of reality soon dragged him right back down as he prayed to God that Lenora was still in that back room.

The four men exited the sheriff's office and began making their way to the stables. The air was tense. This wasn't just in Harrison's head, something felt off. There was something going on here, hidden from view. Unspoken unease and distrust.

They saddled up and rode out of the town towards the old Laudergill ranch.

The Governor rode beside Harrison with Morgan, and the sheriff was directly behind, riding two abreast.

Harrison couldn't stop the thoughts and judgements swirling around his mind faster than light. How could this man do it? A highly respected representative of the county, a man chosen to govern an entire territory, a man who is supposed to uphold the same morals as the president himself… in cahoots with this family driven by greed – The Hammertons. Slaughtering natives in secret – what conspiracy was happening here? Harrison could not fathom why… Why would a Governor be involved at all with this family?

The apprehension and friction between them kept building as they trotted down the road. Every minute of silence seemed to reinforce Harrison's suspicion that something was not right at all.

He couldn't shake the awareness that Morgan hadn't said a single word since the arrival of the Governor, nor had the Governor addressed him at all… not even to greet one another. It seemed so strange considering they had usually gotten along in the past.

They were about a mile out from the ranch when the Governor spoke up.

"Listen up, I do not believe the widow will be alone here. She's paranoid these days; been actin' like somebody went an' stole her rudder. When we go in, keep your eyes peeled and your wits about you. Me and the Marshall will head in first; Morgan, you and Robert will follow behind us."

"Robert?" Harrison looked at the sheriff with surprise.

The sheriff seemed embarrassed or… ashamed almost when his name was revealed.

The Governor laughed a little; even a small chuckle from him sounded menacing though.

"Well, now I'm not surprised he never mentioned his name to y'all. You ain't never gonna guess what his family name is, why don't you go on and tell 'em, *Robert*?" Arthur flashed an evil grin towards the sheriff in anticipation.

The sheriff didn't lift his head to make eye contact; he remained silent.

"Well, come on now, ain't no time to be shy… oh hell, I can't take the suspense; I'll tell 'em myself! This here, boys, is Sheriff Robert E. Laudergill. HA! And this ranch we're comin' on up to belongs to his *dearly beloved* Aunt Amelia Laudergill! But you know what, that's a story for another time. Get ready, boys, we're here."

The four men descended down the long entrance path that lead directly up to the front door.

Harrison took a deep breath.

This was it. Game on.

Chapter 27
Sam Walker/Lenora Taylor –
Notorious Outlaw

"Call me Arthur…"

Holy *shit*.

Those words glistened through Lenora's mind like a thousand gold bars bouncing the sun's light right off them. 'Arthur' is the God damn Governor.

This was *the* pay-out. This was the future she believed she had always deserved, now being served to her on a silver fucking platter. Just one more job.

Within seconds after hearing this revelation, she was immediately rattled. She needed to get out to that ranch now. Lenora frantically looked around the tiny room, trying to figure out how she could get the hell out of there, when her eyes fell upon the little window. She pressed her hands against it and using as much control as possible, gently pushed the window up and opened it, taking every precaution to be quiet as a mouse. The window was very small; it would be a tight squeeze, but she had to do it. Lenora held the window up with one hand and stretched across as much as she could to grab a broom in the corner with the other. She grabbed the broom and jammed the brush right under the window to prop it open.

As soon as she cleared the window, she picked up her dress and sprinted. Lenora raced as fast as possible across town, straight to the stables. She could see random townsfolk looking at her in confusion, but she didn't care; she didn't have time for cover-ups and niceties – it was now or never.

Lenora practically flew onto her horse as soon as she reached the stables. She kicked her feet back into her stallion and tore the ground up beneath her to get out to the woods. She was riding like her life depended on it, because for her, it did.

As soon as she cleared out of sight in the woods, she quickly dismounted to change her clothes; her disguise was in the saddlebags of her horse. She got her trousers on, shirt, belt, waistcoat, heavy jacket, hat, holstered her two engraved LeMat Revolvers, and finally tied her bandana right over her face. All that was visible now were her eyes – *The Phantom's* eyes.

She mounted her stallion once more and rode like a violent storm out towards the ranch. Waiting just outside the walls for her when she arrived was the gang.

Austin spoke first as she approached.

"We wasn't sure you was comin'."

"What y'all thought I had somethin' better t' do?"

Javier responded to her. "What he meant was, we were not sure you were coming *alone*; thought you might have brought your lawman."

Normally that would have been a little too cheeky for Lenora to tolerate, but at this point, she really did not have the time for that bullshit.

"Listen here, you dim-witted sons o' bitches." She looked across to each and every one of them, "I have just *finally* uncovered the last piece of this fuckin' puzzle; y'all ain't got no idea what we're gettin' into! While you were all so convinced that I'd turned, you never stopped to think for one *fuckin'* minute that I was just damn good at my job! I was late here, because I have just learned that this Arthur motherfucker we're about to finish... is a God damn Governor."

The group was stunned, staring at Lenora in disbelief.

Adelita stepped forward slightly and spoke, "Are you for fucking real?"

"You bet your ass. And we are runnin' out o' time; he'll be here any minute. We gotta get inside that house and we need every piece of everything that Laudergill bitch has to offer. Let's go make some real bank boys, y'all ready?"

The gang was too lost in their own exhilaration to question her further. They hollered and yelled in excitement. They, like Lenora, were fixated on one thing only: cold, hard cash.

They all rode down the long entrance path that led directly up to the front door, leaving their horses round the back to keep them out of sight, for fear Arthur would see them, turn tail and run.

Lenora knocked on the large front door first and an older, distressed looking woman opened it.

"Get inside, he'll be here any minute!" The older woman, whom Lenora recognised to be Mrs Laudergill, frantically ushered them all inside. She was wringing her hands with nerves.

"Calm yourself, ma'am, 'fore we get into anythin' here, why don't you come on in here now and take a seat?" Lenora gestured towards the drawing room, just to the left of the entrance hall, through a large archway.

"Take a seat? Don't you understand? He's comin' here now! I think he mighta' killed George, my sweet George," she started to sob, "and now that rotten bastard is comin' to finish me off! This wasn't supposed t' happen!"

"Listen up, old woman." Lenora stepped right up to the widow Laudergill. Lenora was a few inches taller, so this alone was more than intimidating: "I ain't in the habit of repeatin' myself; sit your fuckin' ass down… Now."

The widow looked around at each of the gang members, now standing in a semi-circle around her. She was nervous as hell. She stumbled back slightly as she turned towards the drawing room. She rushed over to a chaise longue and immediately sat.

Lenora looked at Bill and Austin. "Keep an eye out; I wanna' know the second he shows up at that gate." She then proceeded into the drawing room with Javier and Adelita, towering over the seated Mrs Laudergill.

"Now look here, you old bitch; I'm gonna make this real quick and simple for you, seein' as though we're pressed for time – two questions. First, how did you come to find our *merry band* here? I am curious to know how it is someone like you happened to discover who and where we were."

"My cousin, on my mother's side, she… she lives in Red Lake. She had given her housekeeper a night off for service well done, see? Well, her housekeeper ended up havin' a drink with one o' your boys there; he got so intoxicated that he started braggin' 'bout '*knowing Sam Walker*' to her. I had confided in my cousin of my troubles with the Governor's family, so when she told me her maid happened upon one o' your gang… Well, I… I made my plans."

"The little bird you had meet us back in Red Lake, one who told us 'bout the stage, was she the maid?"

"Yes."

"I see. And which one o' my boys was it that drank with her that night at the bar?"

"I don't know… I didn't think to ask."

"Your cousin's maid didn't mention anythin' 'bout him? Anythin' at all?"

"I don't know, I… just that he had a funny kinda' accent."

"Funny how?"

"She thought he might be from across the sea, Irish maybe?"

"Irish, you say?"

Lenora took five steps back into the hall and pulled out her revolver.

BANG!

One bullet went right through Michael's head. His body hit the floor faster than anyone could blink. Lenora felt nothing for Michael. He was loud, mouthy and she never trusted him for a second. Now that she had confirmation that he was a liability, there was zero question, zero debate. Michael dies and that's it. His blood began pooling out across the floor as the realisation of what had just transpired rippled out to the rest of the gang.

Clayton was standing in front of Michael's lifeless corpse, his mouth hanging wide open. Bill immediately pulled his gun and aimed it at Lenora. Austin shouted, "What in the hell did you just do? What the fuck! Jesus, you killed him!"

Lenora calmly holstered her weapon once more. She looked at each of the men in the hallway. "Bill, put down the fuckin' irons. Michael was runnin' his God damn mouth around the place, and that shit will not be tolerated." Lenora walked right back into the drawing room and continued her line of questioning with the widow as if nothing had happened.

"Now that we have that business dealt with, I'll move onto my second and final question: where is the money? And not just the twelve thousand; I want every piece of gold, silver, jewels… everythin' you got."

"I'm… I-I can't tell you 'til after the job's done… what's to say you won't just kill me here and now yourselves and make off with it?" She was fearful, shaking, but trying to hold firm in her resolve. Considering she had just witnessed Lenora kill one of her own men, Len *almost* admired her guts.

"Ha! Now that's funny. See these two here?" She gestured to Javier and Adelita. "Now these two are twins, see? And I don't know if you ever heard, but some folk say twins can hear each other's thoughts." Lenora leaned down, close to the widow, "So right now those two are tradin' a hundred different ways they are gonna' make you suffer worse'n death, if you don't give 'em what they want right fuckin' now."

Lenora stood back up straight, still staring the widow right in the eyes.

"Now, if you want my advice? Me and the twins here tend to treat those who give us what we want a lot better than those who don't. Make your choice, ma'am, and make it quick."

The widow took a moment, but then she spoke.

"I'll tell you, but please… please, if you have any heart left in you, any decency, you'll kill that bastard comin' down here! He and his family have taken everythin' from me; I don't even care if I die; I just want that demon killed, and I wanna see him sent to hell!" Tears were falling from her eyes as she voiced this final request.

Lenora was taken aback. Looking into the widow's eyes for that split second, she could have been deep in her own reflection. Lenora was witnessing misery spilling from this woman's heart as the last shred of love she held in there had been ripped away. The venom twisting inside her was all too familiar, the sinister lust for the one responsible to suffer had become a part of Lenora too, all those years ago.

"Who's his family?" Lenora asked.

"Who gives a shit?" Javier leaned in to the widow and pulled out his knife to threaten her. *"¿Donde está el dinero, puta blanco?* WHERE IS THE MONEY?"

Right then, Austin ran over. "Sam, Sam! – they're comin'."

"Don't let her move!" Lenora left the twins with the widow as she rushed over to one of the front windows.

As she peered through the window, her calm, her self-control and her composure all splintered out into a million pieces. Her stomach knotted up tighter than a bowline.

Arthur was not alone.

Not only was he riding up with the sheriff, he was also riding with Morgan… and… God Almighty… Harrison.

How could she have been so stupid? She was so caught up in the money, she never thought of how many ways this scenario could play out. What was Harrison doing? What in the hell was he doing riding up here? There's no way he would be naïve enough to think she was still in that back room…

Harrison knew that she was going to be there, and that she had to kill the Governor. He also knew that they weren't going to get the upper hand on her gang without the element of surprise, without him waiting for them outside the wall after she had gotten the money. This suddenly felt a lot more like a death trap. Why would he not have made some excuse? Why would the Governor bring him? Surely Arthur could not know that she and the gang were there? What in the hell was happening?

She was in a tailspin. She couldn't process this. How the hell was she going to keep Harrison alive? Lenora was so caught up in her rapidly deteriorating plot and the anxiety that grew alongside it that she took a few minutes to realise Austin was talking to her.

"Sam, Jesus! Are you listenin' t' me? What do we do here?"

Lenora spoke for his ears only first. "Austin, remember what I said back in Whitepost, when I tell you…"

He nodded to her before she called out to the rest of them. If there was any chance of success here, it all depended on her staying in control.

"All right, motherfuckers, its show time! Get out o' sight but stay close, and do not, I repeat, DO NOT fire one God damn shot unless I give a signal, you understand? When you have a chance, get a gun on each of 'um, but DO NOT fire without my say so! Y'all hear me? And somebody get Michael's body outta here. Right, let's do this."

Chapter 28
Harrison James – US Marshall

Harrison and the Governor ascended the steps onto the porch of this once grand manor house. They approached the large front door and the Governor knocked three times.

Knock...

Knock...

Knock...

With each bang on the door, Harrison's heart jumped. The moment that door opened, all their fates were in the Almighty's hands.

Just before the door was answered, the Governor spoke to Harrison.

"You know, Marshall, *real* shame you weren't more successful on this job. You were one of the best I had. Real shame." He kept his eyes on the door the whole time, never had the decency to make eye contact whilst he belittled Harrison's efforts.

Just as Harrison was about to respond, the door opened. When he saw the woman standing in the doorway, he realised it was the same lady he had seen frantic in the Post House, but now she looked even worse. He couldn't help but notice now, she looked frightened.

The Governor spoke.

"Well now, at long last – Amelia, it's been too long! You look… well, you look like you've fallen on hard times now, Mel. No servants to greet your guests any more, no?" He smirked as he taunted her.

"It's Mrs Laudergill to you! What do you want, you wretched man?"

"Mrs *Laudergill,* you say? But you always wanted it to be Mrs Clarke though, didn't you? Or would you have preferred to stay Montgomery… See, I'm not quite sure if you was just feedin' my house nigga lies to get information or if you really did love the bastard…"

"What have you done with him? Where is George?" What have you done, you monster!" She cried.

"Now, now, no need for your hysterics, woman; why don't we all go inside and sit down – this ain't no way to treat your guests now, is it? Have you forgotten your manners? Southern hospitality says you outta bring us inside and fetch us a drink. A woman of your… *standing* should know this."

Harrison was horrified. He tried not to show this on his face, but he had never seen this side of the Governor… He was a wicked, spiteful bastard.

Mrs Laudergill was shaken and aggravated, but she stepped back and allowed them to enter her home. Harrison noticed the sheriff avoided any eye contact as the widow Laudergill stared at him with detest.

"Now why don't we sit on down in the front room here and have ourselves a little *discussion,* but first you can fetch me a drink? I'll have a… a nice bourbon… if you still have anythin' decent in this place that is." Arthur spoke to her with a distinct condescending and patronising tone.

Amelia Laudergill had an expression of pure loathing as she stared at him for a moment before heading away, presumably to adhere to his request. The Governor made his way into the drawing room; Harrison, Morgan and Sheriff Robert all followed behind. The room had lavish furniture inside, but it was dusty and untended; there were no servants or staff around to maintain the place from what they could see.

The Governor sat down on an opulent-looking sofa in the centre of the room, but just as the men went to sit, he objected.

"No! You boys, keep on guard. Marshall, Morgan – stand over by that archway there." He gestured to the entranceway out to the hall. "Robert, get your ass over by the other doorway there."

The men stood in position as Mrs Laudergill returned with a drink. Morgan, now standing beside Harrison, still hadn't looked at or spoken to him.

The widow proceeded to hand the Governor his drink.

"Ah, ah… you first, Mel."

She practically growled at him before taking a sip of the drink.

"Can't be too careful, you know; poison does have a kind of '*womanly*' feel to it, don't you think?" He took the drink and savoured a sip.

"Now sit down; I wanna talk about my letter."

Amelia sat on the opposite sofa.

"I won't tell you a damn thing until you tell me what you've done with George! Where is he?" She wailed.

The Governor raised his voice to her now. "Your little black bastard would still be alive if you coulda' just kept to your own business, Mel, but you went and got all crotchety and just *had* to have your way. So I'll tell you where your precious George is, you nigga lovin' bitch – he's buried in a hole in the middle o' God knows where, and you will soon join him if you don't answer my questions, right fuckin' now."

Harrison could see it now. Of course, this man wouldn't think twice about massacring natives and killing his own soldiers. He was a brutal, evil, grasping and greedy son of a bitch. But, that wasn't Harrison's only concern; he suddenly had another deeply troubling thought… This man has no problem in killing anyone and covering his trail behind him. And here he was, revealing all his secrets to Harrison, his brother and the sheriff. Was he planning on letting them leave here with that information? His gut was telling him, No.

Tears flooded from the eyes of the widow as she stood up.

"I hope you and every last Hammerton rot in the worst pits of hell. I hope every generation of your family that comes after you is cursed with misfortune with every breath they take. And I hope you know… that *you* are nothin' but a greedy dog who didn't know when to quit."

Even Morgan also looked surprised by this revelation. Harrison couldn't hold his tongue; his words came out before he knew he had formed them.

"Sir, what is she talkin' 'bout? How is it you know the Hammerton's here?"

"Well, the cats outta' the bag now, ain't it, Mel?" The Governor turned his glare from Amelia to Harrison.

"You know, normally, Harrison, I'd tell you that was none of your God damn business, but seein' as we're havin' a party here, why not! *Lewis*, which you have always known me by, is my mother's maiden name. But my father's name – my true family name – is Hammerton. And every move I make is for the benefit of my family. That is the *only* thing I care about in this world."

In a split second, the Governor's face dropped and he jumped up from the couch, dropping and smashing the glass on the floor. There was alarm splattered across his face as he looked out towards the hallway. He took a step or two backwards.

The door beside the sheriff burst open and Harrison heard guns cocking all around him. Two men had burst through the door beside Sheriff Robert, one with a gun on the sheriff; the other, a Mexican man, had his aimed at the Governor. The sheriff managed to get his own pistol pointed right back.

Harrison looked slowly to his right and could see a woman with her gun pointed right into the back of Morgan's head. Harrison immediately cocked his gun and aimed it right at her. She must have been hidden in the hallway, along with the final man, who suddenly now had a gun pinned right into the back of the Marshall's skull. This man spoke to Harrison.

"Eyes front, *Marshall*."

Harrison had seen one or two of these people around Whitepost, wandering around under everyone's nose the whole time. Wandering around under *his* nose. Why did he not see them? Killers. Murdering bastards. Living normal lives around town. They just blended in, as if that was pretty much what Whitepost was all about.

Suddenly, there were footsteps approaching from the hallway.

Yet another man walked in with Lenora.

The man accompanying Lenora approached the widow and aimed his gun at her, whilst Lenora walked past everyone and approached the Governor. She was entirely in disguise, but he knew it was her. It was surreal, unnerving… nail-bitingly tense. This was the other side of her. The dark side of her soul was now in full control of the reins.

It was so quiet in the room you couldn't even hear a breath. Nobody dared move; everyone so still as though to move would detonate a block of dynamite. Lenora slowly raised her weapon until it met the Governor's eyes.

The Governor spoke.

"Well, well, well… as I live and breathe. The *notorious* Phantom Walker, here in the flesh, come to finish me off." He stared right into her core.

Lenora armed her revolver.

Harrison's forehead was dripping sweat. One wrong move and that was it. His heart was pounding out of his chest.

The Governor spoke once more.

"Not feelin' talkative, I see? Well, I'll make this short then, one question…" In the blink of an eye, with one hand, he slipped an armed Philadelphia Deringer handgun from his sleeve, directed it right at her chest and smirked. "You absolutely sure you can make that shot faster 'n me?"

Lenora took a sharp inhale in and froze.

"I gotta hand it to that Booth fella; he had more'n one good idea in his time." Arthur sniggered.

"You slimy motherfucker," Lenora uttered.

The Governor appeared to be pleasantly surprised at the moment she spoke. He laughed in excitement before speaking again.

"You know, I didn't believe it all when I first heard, I thought to myself there's no God damn way! Then, seein' your eyes up close just now, I was thinking, my… my… they do look real girly now, don't they? But here we have the proof now! The *notorious Sam Walker*… a woman!" He laughed at her, and Harrison could feel her rage brewing from across the room.

Lenora cut off his enjoyment. "Enough! Even if you kill me right now, my boy over there has got you in his sights. You ain't leavin' this place alive, you fuckin' bastard. You got one round in there."

Every set of eyes in the room were swapping back and forth, waiting for the first shot.

Arthur edged in ever so slightly closer to Lenora.

"Here's the thing though: I think you're bluffin'… 'cause I think, in the past, you mighta' taken your chances with me; you mighta' been bold enough to think you could dodge and take this one shot in the shoulder… or the arm if you were quick enough… but I know your secret, see? I know the one reason a little rotten bandit like you can't take that risk no more – the one thing that would make *The Phantom* lose that brash and merciless spark." The Governor slowly lowered his handgun from her chest, hovering just over her womb.

"You's gonna' be a momma now, ain't ya?"

Each member of her gang looked back and forth at each other in disbelief and horror. Harrison could no longer hold his emotions back; this had gone too far. The very second that man, Governor or not, held a gun to his unborn child, he could not stand for it. Harrison went to lunge forward in fury and disgust. That man was nothing more than a malicious piece of shit and Harrison could not watch this unfold.

Before Harrison could get anywhere near Lenora and the Governor, the man behind him and the man by the widow both grabbed him and held him back.

Harrison struggled relentlessly but couldn't break free.

"Don't you touch her, you motherfucker! DON'T TOUCH HER!" Harrison roared as the two men kept a firm grasp on each of his arms. Harrison still had his weapon clutched firmly in his hand but couldn't raise it high enough to aim at anyone.

"Ha! Finally! I was wondering how long it would take you to break Marshall. Or I suppose it should just be *Mr James* now, really; I mean, you are a criminal after all." Arthur stretched a sinister grin across his face.

"He ain't got nothin' to do with this. He's nothin' to me and my gang." Lenora said sternly, still with her back to Harrison.

"*Tut, tut, tut…* Now see, that is a God damn lie, *Miss Taylor*, 'cause he is definitely somethin' to *you*. I mean come on now, we have just offered out congratulations to your baby's daddy!"

Harrison abruptly had a moment of clarity, an epiphany. At the very moment, the Governor said the words, 'Miss Taylor'. Harrison witnessed something that crushed him… Morgan didn't react. No surprise, no shock, no astonishment. Not when Harrison himself had started shouting, not when it was revealed that Sam was a woman and not when the woman turned out to be Lenora. This should have been a massive revelation, unless… he already knew.

Harrison hadn't been able to understand up until that moment how the Governor could possibly have known these things. It wasn't possible that he knew who she really was, unless Morgan found out and told him. Why else would he have been acting so strange? The growing realisation that his flesh and blood, his own brother, his best friend may have just stabbed him in the back was too much. It surpassed rage; it was more than wrath; it was the most overpowering and profound, crushing betrayal. The most penetrating heartbreak.

Harrison's head dropped and he turned to look at Morgan.

"How could you do it?" The sorrow rang clear through Harrison's voice.

Morgan would not turn to meet his gaze when he spoke; despite a gun still fixed behind his head, he was almost… calm.

"You didn't give me a choice now, did you?" he said emotionless, but for the vitriol.

Harrison tried to struggle from the two gang members' grip but was once again unsuccessful.

"Didn't give you a choice? Are you out o' your God damn mind? I'm your family!" Harrison shouted.

Morgan finally turned his head and faced his older brother.

"You turned on your family the minute you found out what she was and left her alive."

The Governor interrupted before Harrison had the chance.

"Now that actually brings me to my final point, just on the subject of turnin'." The Governor now spoke to the room. "As it stands right now, I think it's plain to see that I may be somewhat outnumbered, huh? Now that *Mr James'* true colours are showin' I seem to be down to just two men… but before most of us go to meet our maker, I've got somethin' of a proposition for y'all."

"Hold your tongue, you son of a bitch, or you'll regret it," Lenora uttered to him.

"You know, Harrison, this one's got real fire in her; I'd say she's quite the ride." The Governor sneered. "But as I was sayin', I've got a proposition. Any o' you willin' to side with me right here and now, not only do I promise you any loot you can carry from this property plus a thousand dollars each, but you will also receive an official pardon from me. You will no longer be wanted men… or women" – he looked at the woman behind Morgan – "and you will walk away from here free and rich. No longer takin' orders from a *woman* who's turned soft."

"He's lyin! Don't any o' you listen to him; he ain't nothin' but a dirty liar!" the widow pleaded.

The room stayed silent for a moment until the Mexican spoke to the Governor.

"You swear this? We will have money and a pardon?"

"Yes, my good sir, that is a guarantee. And if you're still unsure, I'll leave y'all with one final thought: this bitch you call your leader is with child, and my faithful Deputy Morgan has informed me that she and the father of her child were plannin' on makin' off with the spoils o' this job themselves and likely leavin' all your sorry asses in the shithouse."

Lenora didn't move, keeping her head fixed towards the Governor as the Mexican moved his aim from the Governor to Lenora.

One of the men holding Harrison let go in haste to aim his gun back towards the Mexican.

"What do you think you're doin', Javier? Put your gun down. Put it down!"

"*Austin, siempre has sido una pequeña perra.*"

"I don't speak Spanish, motherfucker."

"You've always been a little bitch…" The Mexican, Javier, pointed his gun towards Austin and spoke to the woman behind Morgan. "*Lita, nosotros hemos terminado con esta mierda y nos vamos.*"

Lita turned her gun from Morgan to the man still holding onto Harrison. He let go and aimed right back at her.

"Lita, what the hell?"

"Sorry, Bill, it's nothing personal."

In a matter of minutes, the room had shifted. The Governor had dripped his poison into everyone's ears and now it was a stand-off. If Harrison was fearing for their lives before, he was terrified now. Morgan was now free of his captor and raised his weapon towards Lenora. Harrison had no choice; he couldn't bear to let her die, so he raised his gun to face Morgan. Who would make the first move? Who would pull the first trigger?

Who was going to survive?

Chapter 29
Lenora Taylor/Sam Walker –
Notorious Outlaw

As the Governor hovered his handgun over the child in her womb, Lenora's sanity was fracturing. There were too many thoughts swirling in her mind to grasp onto. The instinctive and biological urge she felt to protect this unborn life was powerful, which meant that bastard was right. He was right about everything he said; she couldn't jeopardise her child. That thought alone was conquering and crushing the confidence she originally held when they first walked in.

If this had been a year ago, he'd already be dead by now and she'd likely have survived with surface wounds at best, or so she believed… but now? She could not bring herself to risk it. She felt weak, she felt powerless, and she loathed this feeling, abhorred the fact that it made her feel just as she did on the worst night of her life. That night, when men took from her all that she'd ever cared for.

Every word that spilled from the Governor's mouth filled her with anger. Every word he spoke not only felt like hot oil spilling all over her, every word made her feel more and more betrayed… Had Harrison told Morgan? How did that little rat bastard know all this? How did he know everything? She asked Harrison to say nothing, she told him to say nothing... He *knew* how dangerous it would be for anyone to know the truth about her. She had walked into that room, fully sure that they had the upper hand. Now... they were going to need a miracle.

She should have known Javier wouldn't think twice about stabbing her in the back when the opportunity arose, and of course Adelita would follow his steps. Lenora just assumed, or rather hoped, they'd be dead before he got the opportunity. A stupid gamble that could cost her dear.

For the first time since the night her Sam, her Tsiishch'ili, was killed all those years ago, she feared this day could be her last.

As they all stood there in the room waiting to see who would join the reaper first, each of them could almost hear each other's hearts beating. Suddenly, there was a break in the achingly nervous silence. The widow spoke so quietly, almost under her breath.

"You can't get away with this... You ruined me... You and your family have ruined my entire life... You can't just get to leave here." She was staring into nothingness as she spoke, as if she were speaking to everyone and no one at the same time.

The Governor responded, but without taking his eye off Lenora, "Will you quit the dramatics? Mel, your family ruined their damn selves – Jacob and your son, whatever his name was... Wyatt? They drank and gambled themselves to death; that's on them. What a father and son choose to do with their free time ain't got a damn thing to do with my family."

The widow was staring at him now, almost twitching.

"This was a beautiful town 'fore you and your rotten kin came here… you came here with your new money and brought the whores, the gamblin'… the fightin'… you brought horrible sin to a God-fearin' town, you brought evil here. Jacob and… my darlin' Wyatt, bless his sweet heart, fell victim to these terrible vices… but I know… I *know* you and yours had 'em killed! They didn't pay their debts, so you got rid of 'em! And my poor daughter… my poor Eudora." Her eyes were streaming tears once more, she sobbed as she spoke these words.

"Eudora died on the birthin' bed; well that there's God's will." He grinned.

"God's will? GOD'S WILL YOU SAY? Your bastard brother raped her! Do you think I don't know that? She was twelve! A child! And you did nothin'!" She was screaming at him now, eyes wide with burning hatred.

The Governor simply rolled his eyes and, in an effort to taunt her further, mockingly looked up and spoke to God.

"Dear Lord, I humbly beseech you; deliver me from the ravings of this old hag."

Suddenly the widow's demeanour shifted, and then, in almost a whisper, "And then my George… my sweet, sweet George… he was the last person in the world I had – the last person who gave a damn about me… and you killed him."

The sinister grin on the Governor's face had finally dropped; his patience had seemingly run out.

"I killed that piece o' shit because he was a no good, nosey little nigga'. I found out he was goin' through my private things and feedin' it all back to you. You tried to scheme up some half-brained plan to cheat me out of my money, turn my family into criminals and *that*, ma'am, I could not abide. What you think you and that dirty black bastard was gonna' run off into the sunset? Grow the fuck up, Mel; I win – you lose. That's how this story was always gonna' end."

The widow gulped and took a deep breath. She took a moment and then seemed to stand up tall and proud. She sniffled, wiped her eyes and looked him straight in the eye when she said her final piece. Calmly now, with almost a smile creeping across her face.

"I take great solace in knowing George is in heaven now, caring for my children, bein' with them now and forever in the Lord's kind and lovin' embrace… but you, Arthur? *You*?… I'll see you in hell."

Like a spark that ignites a barrel of oil, a detonator that explodes mounds of dynamite, the widow pulled a long, sharpened knitting needle from her sleeve, dived onto the Governor, buried it deep into his neck and started a chain reaction that could not be stopped.

Shots began firing in every direction across the room. From the moment the widow lunged for the Governor, Lenora dived behind the sofa on her right, taking cover from the fire between this piece of furniture and the wall.

The Governor fired his one shot straight into the widow's chest in an effort of self-preservation; no sooner had she jammed her needle into his neck, she dropped to the ground with a bullet in her heart. The Governor also collapsed to the floor. He desperately clutched and pressed on the neck wound as he dragged himself over beside the fireplace, frantically trying to avoid a gunshot. His other firearm had fallen from its holster during the fatal scuffle. His blood was spewing and spilling all over him.

Lenora could just about get a good shot at him; she wanted to finish him off once and for all, but no sooner had she edged out to make the kill, a bullet came within an inch of the tip of her nose. Morgan fired on her, and she pulled back immediately.

She saw Harrison dash behind a grandfather clock positioned beside the archway to the hallway, on the side nearest to her. Morgan retreated to cover in the hallway; the two brothers were exchanging fire.

Harrison was shouting at Morgan; there was such pain in his voice.

"What you runnin' off now? This too fuckin' much for you, Morgan! You ain't have the guts to come and talk to me like a God damn man; when you found out, you ran and told that piece o' horseshit!"

"I don't owe you a God damn thing, Harrison, least of all respect after what you done!"

"I'm your *brother,* you son of a bitch!" Harrison leaned around in fury from his cover and shot at Morgan, but this time he hit him right in the arm.

Morgan wailed and Lenora heard him stumble out in the hall. She heard him get to his feet and run further through the house, out of sight.

Harrison went after him.

Lenora couldn't see who was alive and who was dead. Bullets were still flying across the room. It was panic, and chaos.

Morgan was gone, so Lenora was now free to put an end to the Governor. She stayed down on her knees as she edged over to the side of the couch. She was still safe from bullets coming from the opposite side of the room, but in the perfect position to see him.

He was still alive, but judging by the amount of blood on his shirt and the paleness of his skin, she reckoned not for much longer. She could have sat there and watched him bleed out, but that didn't feel personal enough for her. She wanted – no, she *needed* to be the one to do it.

He threatened her child, made her feel weak, and now he'll pay the price.

She raised her LeMat Revolver and aimed it square between his eyes.

He smiled at her, blood covered his teeth. He acted like he didn't give a single shit about the destruction he had caused or the prospect of his own death. He winced and spluttered as he tried to speak one last time.

"I wouldn't waste my bullets if I was you… I'm sure to be clockin' out any minute now, Miss Taylor… That old bitch had more fight in her, 'n I thought."

Lenora took a very short moment to soak up his last words before she relayed her final message to him. She pulled her bandana down from her face to let him see her.

"Love… from… Sam." *BANG*. She shot him dead, right between the eyes.

The satisfaction of sending that bastard to hell didn't last long as she heard Bill groaning and Austin called out to her.

"Sam, Sam! What's our God damn plan here? We gotta go!"

"Austin, what did I tell you? Get your ass back to Whitepost! I got your back!"

Austin was trading fire with the sheriff, who was well covered behind the doorway to the kitchen. Bill continued to groan, and Lenora could just about lean around the couch and see Austin and Bill taking cover behind the second sofa.

"You know I ain't leavin' without Bill, Sam!"

"God fuckin' damnit, Austin, get the fuck outta here; Bill ain't gonna' make it!"

"Fuck you, Sam!" Bill groaned as he clutched the gunshot wound on his leg, rocking himself back and forth.

Lenora pulled herself back behind the sofa, ignored Bill, and called back out to Austin, "Who's left? I can't see a fuckin' thing."

"Clayton, Javier and Lita are gone, dead!"

Just then, Harrison appeared back behind the archway. He looked like he had gotten into a brawl with someone – black eyes, a bloody nose, a busted lip. He shouted over to Austin.

"Can you take his weight?"

"What?" The two men looked to Harrison as he swapped between looking at them and firing back at the sheriff.

"Can you help him move and get him out of here? Do it now!"

Lenora edged herself up over the sofa and aided Harrison with covering fire as what was left of her gang made their escape. Austin put his arm around Bill, lifted him up and they stumbled and staggered out as fast as they could, narrowly avoiding a shot. They went through the archway and were gone from sight.

The shooting stopped. A dead, eerie silence filled the room once more. The carnage and pandemonium had left the place destroyed. Feathers from soft furnishings, wood chippings and fragments, broken glass from the windows all littered the room. Pools of blood splattered everywhere, bodies still lying where they fell. Harrison called out to the sheriff now, still behind the kitchen door.

"Robert, come on… I know you must be near outta' bullets by now. The Governor's dead; Morgan's gone. You on your own. Ain't no point in draggin' this out."

"I ain't gonna die here; I ain't dyin' in this God damn house!" The sheriff cried back.

Before anyone realised, some fallen candles had set fire to the window dressings. The flames were starting to spread and grow in the room. There was a clock ticking now on the old, dry house. It would not be long before the room would be devoured by a blaze and there was no means of stopping it.

"You come out to the hallway here and I swear I'll let you go. You go your way; we go ours. Ain't nobody ever has to say a word 'bout what happened here. We won't ever see each other again." Harrison actually sounded sincere in his offer, but equally tense.

Silence. The sheriff hadn't responded.

"Robert, you ain't got much choice; come on now! I know we ain't exactly seen eye to eye since we met, but that ain't a reason for you to die! I'm offerin' you a way out! Come on, we don't got time for this!"

"You… you swear it?" The croaky voice of the sheriff came from the kitchen.

"I swear it." Harrison called back as he started to cough at the smoke billowing through the room.

Lenora heard footsteps back away from the door. The flames were moving closer to her. She jumped up from behind the sofa and immediately ran over to take cover behind the archway, just across from Harrison. She looked at him briefly before turning her gaze to the kitchen entrance in the hallway, where she could hear steps hesitantly coming through.

She aimed her weapon. Harrison protested and tried to push the gun down. He agitatedly whispered, "What are you doin'?"

"Don't be stupid, Harry!"

"I swore to him he could go; we don't have any fight with him!"

No sooner had the sheriff taken one step outside the kitchen into the hallway, Lenora pushed past Harrison and…

BANG!

She shot him right in the head. The red-faced, overweight sheriff slammed down to the ground. He was dead before his body even reached the floor.

Harrison angrily grabbed her arms; he shook her and shouted.

"I swore to him he could leave; he didn't have to die!"

The blaze was growing in the drawing room, and most of the furniture was now engulfed in it. Lenora whipped her arms free of his grip and stared at him.

"You swore to me you wouldn't tell Morgan anythin' 'bout me! Your swears don't mean shit! Do you know what kind of person you can guarantee will never open their God-damn mouth? A fuckin' dead person. Don't be so motherfuckin' naïve, Harrison; he *knows* us; he saw my face. He was never going to leave here!"

"I never told Morgan a fuckin' thing, Lenora. Now, Jesus Christ, we do not have time for this; we need to get out of here, we need to go NOW!"

Harrison tried to drag her towards the front door. She wriggled free once more.

"Wait, we need to get the…" Lenora suddenly looked around the hall and felt alarm. "Harrison, where is Morgan?"

Harrison now looked even more visibly distressed; he was on the edge.

"I don't know."

"What the fuck do you mean you don't know?"

She coughed as smoke filled the room; soon she wouldn't be able to see him.

"I mean, he God damn vanished okay; he got away; I do not know where he is, which means there's every fuckin' chance he has gone for help and we're about to burn alive, so we need to go NOW!"

"What about the money?"

"Are you out of your fuckin' mind, Lenora? Jesus H. Christ, do you not see what is happenin' here? It's nothin' short of a divine wonder that we are escaping here with our lives! We need to go! FORGET THE MONEY!"

"It's twelve thousand dollars, Harrison!"

A beam directly above the front door collapsed and blocked their way. They had mere seconds to get to another room before the hallway would be engulfed. The heat coming from the drawing room firestorm was now almost blistering their skin.

He grabbed both arms again, desperately trying to shake sense into her and pull her out.

"How do you know it even exists? That woman had nothin' to lose; she could have lied to get you here! It's not worth it. Please, Lenora, I'm beggin' you… We need to go now!" She could see the desperation in his eyes.

She was so torn. Her entire adult life, she had twisted and moulded herself into a person entirely motivated by robbing and killing those she deemed to 'deserve it'. She had created this seemingly emotionless, ruthless persona that only cared for the next job, the next *financial opportunity*. Every bone in her body was shaped this way… so to walk away from the money this time, when it felt like it could be just at the tip of her fingers… to just forget about it and choose life, choose the risk of happiness… to choose *Harrison*… was going against everything she thought she was.

She took a deep breath, looked at him, saw him and said, "Let's go."

He smiled and they both ran past the bodies of Adelita and Sheriff Robert, which lay in the main entrance hallway, through the haze and clouds of smoke wafting everywhere. They made their way, hand in hand, through the house, out to the back, where some of the horses remained hitched.

They both mounted, kicked their heels in and were away. Just as Lenora's horse took off, she felt the greatest rush of her life. Holy *shit*, they did it!

This was it; she was free! They were free! It was incomprehensible! She whipped off her hat and threw it into the air in exhilaration. Harrison looked at her, smiled and laughed a little. This was the beginning of her dream – *their* dream. He was right, who gives a shit about the money? She just needed to let go. She needed to let go of that part of her life. She never thought that was possible, but she could see now that she was blessed to be alive, her and her baby. This was the beginning of the rest of their lives, and she had never felt so light in all her time on this earth.

They hastily galloped down the long entry lane away from the house towards the main stone pillars where the gate was open.

It was symbolic in a way, in crossing the gated threshold of this dilapidated, old house – the final remnants of her old life and the trauma that forged *The Phantom* Walker were disappearing now in the most glorious inferno. She was going to be a new woman, a good person, a good wife and a good mother. Like the Phoenix, she would rise from the flames.

Harrison was riding just ahead of her; he was nothing more than a head past the gate when he screamed.

"NO!"

Before Lenora knew what was happening, she heard a rifle fire… and she felt a pain like her insides were split open.

She crunched down, recoiling, as the pain was almost blinding. She touched her stomach with her hand and she knew she had been shot. She tried with all her will, all her might to stay atop that horse. She was bleeding badly. She and Harrison kept riding when Lenora looked back once more to see the gunman stood on the horizon behind them. He stood in front of the gate with the entire house now almost entirely swallowed in the flames.

It was nothing more than a silhouette of a man clutching his arm, but she knew…

It was Morgan.

Chapter 30
Harrison James – Outlaw

Harrison could see Lenora struggling with everything she had to stay on her horse; she was getting paler by the minute. They rode hard for a few minutes until they were out of sight in the cover of the trees and the foliage of the forest floor.

Harrison called out to her,

"Len, stop! Stop! We're safe!"

He pulled hard on the reins to slow his mare to a halt. Harrison jumped and ran straight to Lenora's mount. She was faint; were they to ride for a moment longer, she would have toppled off and collapsed to the ground.

"Here, grab onto me; come on, I'll get you down."

As soon as he reached up to try and take her weight, his heart crunched up inside him and his stomach dropped to a cold depth. Her stomach was covered in blood. The baby…

No. He couldn't think like that, no, no, no…

No, that was incomprehensible right now. He needed to help her; he needed to save Lenora. He saves her; maybe he saves the child… He couldn't think about anything; nothing else mattered. Just save her…

He struggled to pull her down and place her on the ground; she flinched, gasped and groaned in agony.

Harrison ran to her saddlebags and pulled one of her garments from them. He ripped it, attempting to make some gauze.

"Len, keep your hands down where it hit ya' as much pressure as you can!"

She was as white as a ghost, but so was Harrison. The fear and panic coursing through his body was making his hands shake uncontrollably.

He had seen so, so many people die more gruesome deaths than this, but he had never loved any of them. He couldn't fail her; he couldn't let her go like this. He refused.

He knelt down and tried to pull her body up towards him to get the bandages all around her tightly. It was breaking Harrison's heart as she sobbed with the pain.

"I'm sorry, I'm so sorry, Len. I need to get you bandaged up. We can get help!"

As he was wrapping her up he could see blood all over her lower back too; the bullet had gone right through.

"I've got you wrapped up, now, okay." He gently placed her back down on the ground, lying flat and sweetly touched her face. "you hang on, you're gonna' be fine… You hang on now, you hang on!"

He swiftly removed his jacket and folded it to make a pillow for her. He lifted her head and placed the jacket just underneath. Her eyes were glassy and red with tears.

"I know it hurts now, but I'm gonna' go get help; you just hang on, you hear me!"

Just as he went to stand and leave for help; she grabbed his hand.

"Don't go."

"Len, please, I need to get help, we need to find a doctor, someone!"

"Harry, please don't leave me here." There was such hopelessness in her voice.

"I can't get you up on the horse, Len. I need to get you help now!"

She squeezed his hand a little; it was weak, but he could feel it. She sniffled and winced as tears gently dropped down her face, one by one. She looked so deeply at him, as though she could see the world in his eyes.

"Harrison… I'm so frightened… Harry…" She really started to cry as she placed her other hand on her bloody stomach. "The baby…"

Harrison was trying so hard not to cry himself; it was almost as though for him to shed a single tear would be to admit defeat. To admit this wasn't going to end the way they dreamed it would. He couldn't do it, NO. This couldn't be happening. Was he being punished? Was this divine justice? What cruel God would take a mother carrying a truly innocent life before they had taken their first breath? His child, his beautiful child, murdered by his own brother.

How could he stop this? He couldn't bear to leave her, but to stay… meant the end.

"Hush up now, don't worry 'bout the baby, you're gonna' be all right, okay? Everythin' is gonna' be all right!"

"Harry… I'm so scared to die."

"Stop, Len, please; it's gonna be okay. Come on, I know you can fight harder 'n this!" Harrison started frantically looking around, trying to see anything – any cabin or something – where someone could help. "I'll only be gone for a few minutes; there has to be some folk nearby that can help!"

"Please… don't go." She was so quiet compared to her normal self, so defeated.

He saw it, he saw it in her. He was trying to block it out, ignore it. But it was sinking in. He knew, she knew. She was dying, and there was nothing he could do. To be so helpless, so useless in stopping this now inevitable fate, Harrison's soul was fracturing.

He started to cry. She reached her hand up to place it on his cheek. He placed his hand over hers and looked at her kindly.

"It's okay, my love; I ain't goin' anywhere."

"Harry… I'm sorry I left the room. I'm so sorry. I…"

"Len, don't; it don't matter now, darlin'."

"I shoulda' listened to you. We shoulda' just gone when we could…"

"Hey, hey, stop… It don't matter. You're who you are, and… and I love you for who you are." He squeezed his eyes shut in a futile effort to force the emotion down before looking up at the sky.

"Harrison, hold me, please."

He looked back at her.

"I don't wanna' hurt you."

"*Please*."

Harrison sat her up, she whimpered with every movement. Harrison propped himself against a tree and gently laid her down on his chest. He wrapped his arms around her.

They sat for a moment in silence until Lenora faintly spoke.

"Harrison, I want you to do somethin' for me…"

"Anythin'."

She sobbed and winced as she responded.

"Bury us by the cabin, with Sam…"

"Len, stop, don't talk like that…"

"Harry, please… Bury me beside my daddy and I don't want my cross to say Taylor, I want James."

He squeezed her and kissed her head.

"Okay."

She was taking deep breaths, trying her best to make each remaining one count.

"Harry, I wanna' tell you how much you…"

"Hush now, I know. Save your strength; I know what you wanna' say; it's all right."

"… Talk to me, will you?"

He softly stroked her hair. "What you want me to talk about?"

"I just wanna'… just wanna' listen to your voice… Talk about us."

"Us? Hell, I don't even know where to start," he gave a tiny chuckle and squeezed her a little once more. "When I met you first, I thought you were the boldest woman I had ever conversed with. You were audacious, even… I thought it best to keep my eye on you, for good reason, as it turned out."

He could see her cheeks rise a little as she smiled faintly.

"In truth, at the time, I did not know why, but I found somethin' curious about you, then I heard you sing. You got a real lovely voice, you know… I don't think I ever told you that… You were surrounded by a kind of a mystery. And I guess it was in my nature to investigate such mystery. I think I've spent so much of my life followin' orders blindly, doin' things I was told to do and doin' what was expected of me, but you? You're just… wild. Beautiful and unyieldin'." He struggled to keep his speech clear as the tears continued to fall from his eyes. "I don't care 'bout the past. I don't care 'bout what you or I did. I love you, and I know you're a good person in your soul."

He kissed her head once more and his world finally collapsed. She wasn't breathing.

Harrison tried to shake her a little, despite knowing in his head that it was too late.

"Len? Len? Len, please… no… wait!"

He was frantic now, accepting she was probably going to die did not make him ready for it to happen. He couldn't bear this pain, this splintering ache inside him. He didn't know what to do but keep shaking her, hoping she would open her eyes and they could even have just a few more minutes together.

"Please come back! Len… please! Please…"

He grasped her entirely in his arms, rocking back and forth with her.

He was crying inconsolably now. His screams and wails sounded haunting – that of a man broken entirely, a man cursed.

He wept for his lost love; he wept for his lost child – a baby never born; he wept for his lost family – a brother who bitterly betrayed him. His mind, his soul, his entire self felt like it was imploding around him.

The air was still, the animals and the insects quiet. The woods themselves could feel the tragedy that was Lenora Taylor's life and Harrison James' profound grief.

Time passed or did it? He no longer knew. Harrison's screams turned to sparce tears; his explosive emotions turned to crushing, devastating defeat. There was nothing, no one. Silence. Deathly silence. Stillness. Not even his heart was beating.

Staring into a void, he sat with her as she grew colder. Though pale and bloody, it still felt like she could just be sleeping. He didn't know how long he sat there; he couldn't think any more. He could barely breathe.

He stood up, took a blanket that had been packed up on her horse and gently wrapped her in it. He lifted and placed her body atop his mare and began the ride back to her old cabin, as was her last request.

It took quite a time to get there, but Harrison never stopped riding. Didn't stop to eat, didn't stop to sleep. He had to do this; he needed to. Harrison felt like he had failed her; he felt the weight and responsibility of her death lay with him entirely, so he needed to at least grant her last wish.

He arrived at the cabin, found an old shovel inside and started to dig. He dug for hours, through the night, with only a small, timeworn oil lamp to see with.

He lowered her body into the ground, still wrapped in the warm blanket. He went inside the decrepit cabin and took her old journal from it. Harrison placed the journal in the grave with her.

He stood there, staring at her. There lay her body, and with it, his dead heart, his broken soul. This would be the last time he would see her – the last image of her in his mind. A woman he knew to be so fiery, fierce and passionate lay cold and lifeless in the ground.

Harrison filled the hollow and pulled some panels from the cabin walls to make her cross. With an axe and some nails, he finished and erected it at the head of the grave.

He finished shortly before the sunrise. Harrison sat and watched as the sun's light broke through the trees, illuminating the three crosses at the back of the old cabin.

Abigail Walker. Tsiishch'ili. Lenora James.

Harrison stayed by the grave for some time. He sat, trying to understand what it was he felt now. He had railroaded through so many powerful and extreme

emotions – grief, devastation, fury, hopelessness, wrath –
but now what he held inside him was… nothing…

Empty.

In meeting this woman, as their lives and their stories
entwined, it was a seismic event for Harrison. In the weeks
and months he grew to love her, to be overwhelmed and
shattered by her, to devote himself entirely to her, he
became a new man. He imagined a new existence, a new
future.

Harrison had many chapters in his life: he was a son
until it came time for war; he was a soldier until it came
time to lay down arms; he was a Marshall until it came
time to meet *her*. What hurt Harrison the most was how
much he truly believed this next chapter would be his life
as a husband and a father. That was not something he
would have ever thought was possible for himself before
meeting Lenora. He never saw her coming, he never saw
the change in his moral fibre coming. She was a catalyst
that sparked a new way of thinking, a new way of living.
He was so sure he knew who he was until he met Miss
Taylor, but she turned his image of himself on its head.
She moulded him into a new man.

But that future, that picture, was nothing now. And he
was nothing.

He sat on the ground, a whiskey bottle now in hand
that he pulled from the saddlebags. He sat by the grave of
his lost family. A preacher from his hometown used to tell
them, as children, God had a plan for everyone, and
everything that happened was God's will.

Was it *God's will* to massacre the natives?

Was it *God's will* to make men attack and rape a young, innocent woman and kill her closest friend in the dead of night?

Was it *God's will* to pit brother against brother?

Was it *God's will* to end the life of a mother as she was ready to start anew?

The scripture says Jesus will come again to judge the living and the dead, but if all of this was the will of He and the Almighty Father, who would judge them?

As Harrison sat there, drinking by the grave of his perished love, he looked across the reach of the woods. His eyes fell on a figure.

It was too great a distance to see a face; too much overgrowth from the forest to clearly make out the man in full, but Harrison knew who it was.

Morgan stood right there. Staring.

Staring at the destruction, despair, and death by his hand. Harrison knew he would come no closer. Morgan did not come to offer sympathy or sorrow for his actions. He clearly did not come for a foolish attempt to console his *dear* brother. No, Morgan came for two reasons and only two reasons: to make sure she was truly dead, and to remind Harrison of just who was responsible.

Morgan did not stay in sight for long, just long enough for Harrison to make a final, cold resolve. His brother, his best friend, was dead now too. Neither man realised that the story of a pregnant daughter who lay dead on Old Bill's floor would lead to another woman dead with *her* baby and their worlds torn apart. An eye for an eye.

Chapter 31
Morgan James – US Marshall

It had been eight months since the events at the Laudergill ranch, which was now nothing more than scorched earth. 1871 brought with it many changes for the younger James brother. Morgan was residing with his wife, who was pregnant with their first child, in his hometown, out in the New Mexico Territory, just at the Texas border.

He would never acknowledge it truly, but Morgan was now a shadow of his once-carefree self. The young man, who shrugged at responsibility and carried such a zest for the pleasures that life had to offer, died back in Whitepost. The man he was today was cold, bitter, and vengeful.

The reality was that from the moment Morgan discovered the truth about Lenora, he saw his brother as nothing more than a traitor. Morgan had become so twisted by the ordeal. When he thought of Lenora, he thought of a serpent sent from hell. She caused so much suffering in her wake, so much death. She manipulated and cheated her way through life to achieve her selfish and cruel desires.

When Morgan first contacted the Governor with his discovery of the truth about Lenora Taylor, the Governor convinced him that it was she who was truly responsible for the massacre of the natives and the soldiers they had found. The Governor convinced him that she manipulated both sides to incite violence in order to distract everyone from her killing and plundering. In Morgan's eyes, she was responsible for every wrong he had seen, every cruel deed. The worst thing, however, was that Harrison knew all this. He *knew* what she was and rather than kill her, he fell in love with her? He fell in love with a monster spit from the deepest pits of the underworld. He turned his back on Morgan, his own flesh and blood, to consort with the spawn of Beelzebub.

Every day that passed made Morgan more certain that he did the right thing. His brother betrayed him, betrayed everything they stood for, and in his view, his brother now deserved to die.

Word had reached President Ulysses S. Grant through the ever more influential Hammerton family's connections of the young deputy's valour in defending his Governor against insurmountable odds. The President, in kind, rewarded Morgan with an appointment as US Marshall. The Hammerton family also offered Morgan a reasonable financial reward for 'protecting their interests'.

One particular morning, shortly after receiving this new appointment, he woke to prepare for his first major assignment. He methodically readied himself for the day ahead. He washed up, dressed himself, holstered his weapons and made his way to the kitchen, where his wife had prepared his breakfast.

"Mornin', my love, I'll have all this ready in just a moment. I'm sorry, it's a little late. I was feelin' quite unwell this mornin'. The doctor reckons it's 'cause o' the baby." She lovingly rubbed her pregnant belly.

"Yes, fine." He sat down and read the penny paper.

"How long you think you'll be gone, my love?"

"I don't know."

"It's just… I was wonderin' whether you'd be gone for some time; you'll be back 'fore the baby arrives, though, right? We can decide on a name!" She smiled at him with hope.

"Holly, will you stop pesterin' me while I'm readin'? I cannot read if I am listenin' to *you*. I told you I don't know how long I'll be gone."

Holly's smile dropped into disappointment.

"Okay… sorry."

She finished cooking and served him his meal. They sat together in silence as they ate. This marriage was not one developed from passion or intense romance, but one made from practicality. She was young, pretty, passive, and easily controlled. She was a good, honest Southern woman. She was a practical wife and served a practical purpose for Morgan. His brother was an outlaw, it was Morgan's responsibility now to raise a good family and continue the respectable legacy of his father's name. The only problem was, she was from Whitepost and, therefore, served unintentionally as a constant reminder of Morgan's deep emotional hurt. At times, he seemed to resent her a little, despite her best efforts to be the most perfect wife to him.

When they finished their meal, Morgan left to attend the local barber. He said a brief goodbye to his wife and that was it. When he arrived, he sat down in the same chair as always.

"Morgan, my boy, just a trim and a tidy up – same as usual?"

The barber was a charming, older gentleman. He was probably close to the age Morgan's father would be, were he still alive.

"A touch of pomade as well, if you don't mind; I'm leavin' town today."

The barber retrieved his necessary tools and got to work. As he rotated around Morgan, trimming his beard, he accidentally bumped off Morgan's arm. Morgan grunted in pain.

"Sorry, son, that the bad arm was it? My apologies; I tend to stumble a little now and then with these old bones."

"It's fine." Morgan was annoyed at himself for expressing the pain. He was annoyed at how long it was taking for it to heal. The injury was a result of Harrison shooting him all those months ago. Morgan didn't want anyone thinking he was unfit to assume his duties.

"So where is it you're off to then? They sendin' you 'cross country?"

"Startin' out in Kansas, might end up makin' my way through Missouri or Arkansas."

"That's a ways out! And who is it you said you was looking to catch? The John James gang or somethin'?"

"Jesse James and his gang. They're makin' noise and causin' trouble, so I'm goin' to go out to make sure they're brought to justice."

"And, eh, you heard anythin' 'bout the Marshall?"

Morgan glared at him.

"He ain't the God damn Marshall any more, Beau."

The barber looked uncomfortable, embarrassed as he continued trimming Morgan's hair. He probably knew Morgan would be somewhat *touchy* about this topic, so best to tread carefully.

"Sorry, force of habit, I didn't mean to... uh... *anyway*... have you heard anythin' 'bout him since?"

"No."

"You... you gon' try catch him? What... what'll you do if you find him?"

The barber stopped and was just staring at Morgan now, in anxious anticipation of the answer.

Morgan took a deep breath, then looked right into his eyes to respond.

"If I find him... no, that's not it... *when* I find him, Beau, I'll kill him stone dead without a second, God damn thought. I'll send him straight to hell, where he can rot for the rest of fuckin' eternity with that whore bitch of his. That's what I'll do."

The barber didn't respond; he just awkwardly grimaced, knowing he had put his foot right in it. From then on, there was no more conversation; the barber just quietly continued. When the haircut was finished, Morgan paid and went on his way.

He returned home and readied his horse for the journey. He had yet to choose a deputy for himself, so he was likely to enlist the help of a local sheriff when he arrived in Kansas.

See the reality was, Morgan couldn't really give a single shit about the Jesse James gang, whoever they were. He wanted Harrison. He had to go on this job, but his real plan was to arrive in Kansas, do the bare minimum to assist in apprehending the offenders and then he would start chasing any and every lead he could on Harrison.

He was going to start from Whitepost and travel to every town in the surrounding areas until he picked up a trail. Someone, somewhere, will have seen him. He had to be somewhere, and Morgan would be sure to find him.

Morgan made a pact with God himself that, before his child was born, his brother would die.

Though he would never, ever admit it to himself or anyone alive, the fact was Morgan dressed up his quest for vengeance with morality, principles and his own distorted ethics, but when everything boiled down and the root of his anger was pulled out, it was simple. Morgan was so resentful, so slighted and so deeply hurt that the person he loved and cared for more than anyone in the world chose someone else instead of him.

This resentment ran deep, and Morgan was not going to stop. His brother betrayed him and now…

There was no going back.

Chapter 32
Harrison James – Outlaw

Harrison didn't do much of anything anymore since he left that cabin. His days consisted of drinking, fighting and working as a gun for hire. He made his way down to some town in Mexico; he didn't know what the name was, nor did he care.

People around knew him either as James Walker, an alias he used to keep anyone from his old life catching up to him, or simply '*El jinete solitario*'.

He didn't get to know people; he just drank, ate, slept and worked. He dressed in black, kept himself busy or drunk in order to disassociate from his memories as much as possible. The only piece he carried with him of his lost life was the crescent moon pendant with a '*T*' carved on the back and now an '*L*' carved on the front. He never took it off.

When Lenora's life was turned on its head all those many years ago, the night she was attacked, she was so scorned, so violently angry about what happened to her that she set out on a path of rage and revenge. Harrison, however, felt nothing now. He had experienced so much trauma that could have driven him to the same path, but instead, he buried his heart and his soul in that grave with her. He didn't see the point in anything anymore.

Nothing mattered to him except passing time.

He didn't care when someone paid him to kill a petty rival; he didn't care when a jealous ex-lover wanted her old partner's new flame killed. He didn't care when a group of bandits needed an extra gun to pull off a robbery. Nobody mattered. As far as '*El jinete solitario*' was concerned, just pay him and he'll do the job.

When work dried up, he journeyed to the next town, and the next, and the next. Harrison didn't have a concept of how much time had passed, but to anyone who would have known him in the past, he was entirely unrecognisable now. His hair was long and unwashed. His beard long and unruly. He didn't even speak unless it was absolutely necessary and his posture and demeanour were of a man ruined. In roaming through towns, he seemed more like a ghost than a man. A spirit trapped in an endless loop.

Sometimes, when he was on the road, he'd stop and think of her. He was long past his tears, but not past his pain. Their relationship may not have been the longest in history, but that didn't make it any less significant. It didn't make it any less agonising that she wasn't there.

Harrison truly felt that he would gladly give his life just to spend one more day with her.

It took him a lifetime to encounter a woman who would make him feel the way she did. She was infuriating, sharp, volatile and impulsive, but she was also loving, loyal to those that mattered to her, vulnerable, beautiful and devoted. To Harrison, she was unique – a woman who would not be tamed, would not be controlled and he adored her.

Nobody could replace her.

Sometimes he'd cock his gun and place it against his own head. He never knew why he didn't pull the trigger. Usually, he would pass out before he got that far. Often he would wonder if she would be disgusted that he would just kill himself rather than avenge her.

Harrison couldn't bring himself to find that kind of rage, though. Maybe someone else would have sought out Morgan. Sought to retaliate for the murder of his future wife and child but he just didn't see the point. It wouldn't bring them back. And once it was all done, would he feel whole? Would he feel he had served justice? And then what? Once it was all done with, he would be right back where he was now, so why bother?

The reality was Morgan pulled the trigger, but Harrison felt so much responsibility and guilt around her death that, in his eyes, it wasn't just Morgan who had done this thing – he had also.

He could have trusted his gut and trusted his brother enough to tell him the truth, tell him exactly what was happening and reason with him. Maybe then Morgan would have realised why Harrison chose to stay by her side. Even after that, though, even if things went exactly as they had done and Harrison never said a word to his younger brother, Harrison had an opportunity to kill him in that house and he pulled back twice. Harrison was a faster shot than Morgan. He could have shot him in the head, but instead he shot him in the arm.

When he chased Morgan through the Laudergill house, away from the slaughter in the drawing room, they ended up in a brawl. Morgan had a bullet in his arm and Harrison was winning that fight. He could have killed him then and there and Lenora never would have been shot, but he pulled his punches, because even then, that was still his baby brother, and that was still his best friend.

Because of his misplaced sentiment for someone who had already betrayed him, Morgan got away, hiding at the top gate, knowing they would ride past and then he killed her.

Harrison could see Morgan was angry and hurt. But he never thought for one moment that he would actually follow through and murder her. Harrison, in truth, thought up to that point Morgan would still hold love for him. Harrison thought they were still brothers. And that naïve belief cost him his whole life.

He learned his lesson now, though; Harrison would never trust anyone again for as long as he lived.

Harrison James was a broken man now and there was no doubt in his mind that Morgan would be searching for him, hunting him down to finish what he started. But the thing was, Harrison knew Morgan, better than Morgan probably even knew himself. Morgan was younger and arrogant. He would be under the impression that he has the upper hand because Harrison isn't as spry as the younger

James brother and maybe he isn't as sharp anymore. Maybe grief and despair would make Harrison weak. The thing was, it was the opposite.

The Harrison that Morgan knew had always operated with some form of a morality code, he tried to do what was right – be fair and follow orders. This meant that anything ruthless that Harrison was truly capable of was locked away.

But Harrison was broken now. He had nothing to lose. And whilst he wasn't searching for revenge, if threatened, he was certainly much more dangerous now than ever before.

If the James brothers ever were to cross paths again, the clash would be brutal… and bloody.

Until that happened, however, Harrison would continue going through the motions of his hollow existence. He would drink, he would fight and he would work. Every once in a blue moon, something would crop up that would once again remind him of his final days as a Marshall, his final days with her and his final days of happiness. Whenever these little reminders would appear before him, he would always arrive at the same conclusion.

Nothing good could ever come from taking a job in Whitepost.

Epilogue

George was fearful as he read the letter on Mr Lewis' desk. This family, under which he was now employed, held no compassion or empathy. This letter was a sinister glimpse into their plans and George Clarke had to figure out what he was going to do about it. He anxiously read over the letter once more before he heard Mr Lewis returning to his office.

Arthur,

We found it. The boys have been tireless in their efforts at prospecting and through the Lord's good graces, we have found what we think will be the envy of the territory – maybe even put the Hammerton name on the map across this ever more prosperous nation. More silver than we could have imagined!

I've discussed the plan with the family and Gabe is preparing to venture out to the natives again a fortnight from now with the shipment of weapons once they arrive. He says the elders there had no interest in any dealings with a white man, but after some convincing, he reckons he has sparked the fuse of their young people to defend their land! Ha! The sheer delusion of heathens. They'll be gone soon.

Anyway, please send word when your soldiers are moving in and we will have the offer placed to purchase. The sooner we can get our hands on that land, the better; we can't risk the discovery of the mine by anyone else.

Love and affection from your proud mother.

PS: Rumour across town is that the Laudergill bitch will be destitute on the streets before she knows it and when she is, I believe we should invest in what's left of her cattle ranch; it could prove to be a prosperous business venture and I cannot say I would not take great satisfaction in taking what's left of her wealth. That woman has turned her nose up at us and our family for the last time, I swear to God.

George felt such sorrow, the evil manipulation and sacrifice of so many for their own financial gain. It was so heartless, so ruthlessly cruel and selfish. He needed to get out of Mr Lewis' office, though; he hadn't time to ponder this planned atrocity here for fear of discovery.

He went straight upstairs to his tiny box room on the top floor. Nothing more than a bed and a small set of drawers. He had some personal belongings – not much – but among them were paper and ink.

Many years before George and his family were freed, he worked on a farm in Texas. The masters there were fine enough if you worked hard, but merciless if you put a single foot wrong. While he worked there, a young woman who lived on the property next door used to come by from time to time. She would sometimes walk through the neighbouring fields too. He would never dare even look at these white women; the fear of repercussions was deterrent enough. One day, however, this particular young white woman spoke to George. He was taken aback by a couple of things – her beauty, her immaculate figure – but more importantly than any of that, he was taken aback that she spoke to him as an equal, not as a slave.

That woman was Amelia Montgomery, the woman who would one day end up having to marry a 'suitable' man and become Amelia Laudergill. That was the woman George fell in love with and the surreal thing was, she fell for him too. They had the most scandalous, wild and magnificent hidden love affair, kept entirely secret from the whole world. Every moment they could covertly steal away together was bliss. The prospect of being discovered in this reprehensible entanglement was, of course, terrifying. His masters and the family of this woman would surely wish for his end in the most brutal ways… but she was addictive. Maybe they both became hooked on the rush and adrenaline of possibly being discovered, but getting away with it every time.

After a time, however, Amelia's father grew suspicious that she was *up to no good* and decided it was high time she was married. An arrangement was made and she was moved away to a town called Whitepost, where she was wed. George was devastated; he learned how to read and write with the help of another slave who secretly knew how. He tried to write to her, but he only ever received one letter back, one asking him to stop as it was too painful.

Years passed, then came the war and suddenly, one day, he was a free man. He and his family had less than nothing to their name, so they had to separate and find work wherever they could. George was intelligent; he could read and write, and he found himself to be good with numbers. Before he knew it, somehow, he managed to secure a job within the household of Governor Arthur Lewis. George was much older now and had put away the fond memories of Amelia long ago.

When he read the letter on Mr Lewis' desk that faithful day, however, all the feelings he once had came rushing back. He now felt he needed to write her a new letter. He needed to know that she was all right, and he needed to warn her that these Hammerton's may be planning to cause her harm.

George didn't know it, but Amelia's husband had died a couple of years before. He wrote to warn her of the Governor's plans, but unexpectedly, after a number of letters back and forth, the romance between them bloomed once more. Amelia was intent on forging a plan that would destroy the Hammerton's as retribution for the deaths of her family, she wanted to blackmail them. She would obtain evidence of their crimes, anonymously blackmail them for quite a sum of money, sell her home and leave with George to a secret paradise where they could finally be together. Once she was safely away with George, she would reveal the Hammerton's crimes to the highest authorities in the land and ruin them once and for all.

George was nervous and weary of what might transpire were they to be found out, but Amelia needed him to keep feeding her any information he could find out. He had invaluable access to the Governor's private affairs. There was also a part of George that slowly started to find satisfaction in the thought of destroying this family. This satisfaction soon outgrew the nervousness as he saw this family for what they truly were now. They were the personification of so many rich, deeply racist white families that cared more about pieces of paper than the lives of him and all black people, native people and Mexican people. They were now, in his mind, the face of the overwhelmingly spiteful, hateful and disgusting acts he witnessed and experienced through slavery. They didn't care about anyone but themselves and he wanted to see them pay.

George and Amelia had set their plan in motion; she had engaged a notorious gang to obtain the incriminating letter, and all was underway.

At some point, however, the Governor grew suspicious. He must have noticed a change in George's attitude, or perhaps George accidentally said something that peaked Mr Lewis's curiosity. He would never know. But once the Governor became wary, it was the beginning of the end.

One day, the Governor decided to go and fetch his own mail. George had always – always done this for him, but for some reason, Governor Lewis must have gotten a hunch that he should be the one to do it. By the time George realised this, the Governor would likely already have been on his way back. George knew he was now in real danger. There would almost certainly be a letter from Amelia, and the Governor would almost certainly read it.

George ran up to his room to grab his belongings as fast as possible to get the hell out of there. He would escape his fate and find Amelia in Whitepost, but it was not to be. George heard the Governor arrive back; he was frantic now as he had run out of time.

George had two options. He could try and squeeze through the tiny window in his room, jump down and likely break his legs or he could stand and face Mr Lewis. In truth, no choice at all.

He made his decision.

George sat on his bed for a moment before the Governor reached his room. The door opened and Mr Lewis had a pistol aimed right at his head. George remained where he was. Calm and composed.

"What did you tell her you dirty son of a bitch?"

George opted not to respond.

"I won't ask again, nigger!"

George looked at him with sarcastic surprise.

"Nigger? Your true colours are finally showin' now, *Arthur*."

The Governor stepped right up to him and pressed the gun to George's temple.

"Last chance! Tell me what you told her."

George took a moment before responding. He stood up from the bed, standing ever so slightly taller than the Governor. The gun was still pressed against his head, but George stared right into the Governor's eyes.

"I want you to be haunted by this promise that I make here and now 'fore God. You will kill me today, but I promise you – you will die soon after."

"We'll see 'bout that nigger!"

BANG!

That was the end of George Clarke. However, that murder set in motion events that would see natives slaughtered, innocents killed, bandits shot, good men broken, mothers murdered and the end for Arthur Hammerton Lewis.